Ouida

Held in Bondage

Or, Granville de Vigne. A tale of the day. Vol. 1

.

Ouida

Held in Bondage
Or, Granville de Vigne. A tale of the day. Vol. 1

ISBN/EAN: 9783337072285

Printed in Europe, USA, Canada, Australia, Japan

Cover: Foto ©Andreas Hilbeck / pixelio.de

More available books at **www.hansebooks.com**

"HELD IN BONDAGE;"

OR,

GRANVILLE DE VIGNE.

A Tale of the Day.

By OUIDA

" A young man married is a man that's marred."—SHAKSPEARE.

IN THREE VOLUMES.

VOL. I.

LONDON: TINSLEY, BROTHERS,
18, CATHERINE STREET, STRAND.

1863.

CONTENTS OF VOL. I.

"HELD IN BONDAGE;"

OR,

GRANVILLE DE VIGNE.

CHAPTER I.

THE SENIOR PUPIL OF THE CHANCERY.

IT was pleasant down there in Berkshire, when the water rushed beneath the keel; our oars feathered neatly on the ringing rowlocks; the river foamed and flew as we gripped it; and the alders and willows tossed in the sunshine, while we—private pupils, as our tutor called us,—men, as we called ourselves—used to pull up the Kennet, as though we were some of an University Eight, and lunch at the Ferry-inn off raw chops and half-and-half, making love to its big-boned, red-haired Hebe, and happy as kings in those summer days, in the dead years long past and gone. What a royal time it was!—(who amongst us does not say so?)—when our hearts owned no heavier cares

than a vulgus, and a theorem ; and no skeleton in
the closet, spoiled our trolling, and long bowling;
when old Horace and Euripides, were the only
bores we knew; and Galatæa at the pastry-cook's,
seemed fairer, than do ever titled Helens now;
when gallops on hired shying hacks, were doubly
dear, by prohibition; and filthy bird's-eye, smoked
in clays, sweeter to our senses then, than purest
Havannahs smoked to-day, on the steps of Pratt's,
or the U. S.!   I often think of those days when,
with a handsome tip, from the dear old governor;
and a parting injunction respecting the unspeakable blessings and advantages of flannel, from my
mother; I was sent off to be a private pupil, under
the Rev. Josiah Primrose, D.D., F.R.S., F.R.G.S.,
and all the letters of the alphabet beside, I dare
say, if I could but remember them.

Our modern Gamaliel was an immaculate and
insignificant little man ; who, on the strength of a
Double First, good connections, and M.B. waist-
coats ; offered to train up the sons of noblemen and
gentlemen, in the way they should go, drill Greek,
and instil religious principles into them, for the
trifling consideration of 300l. per annum.   He
lived in a quiet little borough in the south of Berkshire, at a long, low, ivy-clad house, called the
Chancery; which had stupendous pretensions to

the picturesque and the mediæval; and, what was of much more consequence to us, a capital little trout stream at the bottom of its grounds. Here he dwelt with a fat old housekeeper, a very good cook, a quasi-juvenile niece, (who went in for the kitten line, and did it very badly, too,) and four, or, when times were good, six, hot-brained young dogs, worse to keep in order than a team of unbroke thorough-breds. No authority, however, did our Doctor, in familiar parlance, 'Old Joey,' attempt to exercise. We had prayers at eight, which he read in a style of intoning peculiar to himself, more soporific in its effects than a scientific lecture, or an Exeter Hall meeting, and dinner at six; a very good dinner, too; over which the fair Arabella presided : and between those hours we amused ourselves as we chose, with cricket, and smoking, jack and trout, boating and swimming, rides on hacks, such as job-masters let out to young fellows with long purses; and desperate flirtations with all the shop girls in Frestonhills. We *did* do an amount of Greek and Logic, of course, as otherwise the 300*l.* might have been jeopardized; but the Doctor was generally dreaming over his possible chance of the Bampton Lectureship, or his next report for the Geological Society, and was as glad to give us our *congé* as we were to take it.

It was a mild September evening, I remember, when I first went to the Chancery. I had been a little down in the mouth at leaving home, just in the best of the shooting season ; and at saying good-by to my genial-hearted governor, and my own highly-prized bay, ' Ballet-girl ': but a brisk coach drive and a good inn-dinner never yet failed to raise a boy's spirits, and by the time I reached Frestonhills I was ready to face a much more imposing individual than ' Old Joey.' The Doctor received me in his library, with a suspicious appearance of having just tumbled out of a nap ; called me his ' dear young friend ; ' on my first introduction treated me to a text or two, ingeniously dove-tailed with classic quotations ; took me to the drawing-room for presentation to his niece, who smiled graciously on me for the sake of the pines, and melons, and game my mother had sent as a propitiatory offering with her darling ; and, finally, consigned me to the tender mercies of the senior pupil.

The senior pupil was standing with his back to the fire and his elbows on the mantel-piece, smoking a short pipe, in the common study. He was but just eighteen; but even then he had more of the ' grand air ' about him than anyone else I had ever seen. His figure, from its deve-

loped muscle, broad chest, and splendidly-moulded
arm, might have passed him for much older; but
in his face were all the spirit, the eagerness, the fire
of early youth; the glow of ardour that has never
been chilled, the longing of the young gladiator
for the untried arena. His features were clear-
cut, proud, and firm; the lines of the lips delicate
and haughty; his eyes were long, dark, and keen
as a falcon's; his brow was wide, high, and powerful; his head grandly set upon his throat: he
looked altogether, as I told him some time afterwards, very like a thorough-bred racer, who was
longing to do the distance, and who would never
allow punishing by curb, or whip, or snaffle.
Such was the senior pupil, Granville de Vigne.
He was alone, and took his pipe out of his lips
without altering his position.

'Well, sir, what's your name?'

'Chevasney.'

'Not a bad one. A Chevasney of Longholme?'

'Yes. John Chevasney's son.'

'So you are coming to be fleeced by Old Joey?
Deuced pity! Are you good for anything?'

'Only for grilling a devil, 'and riding cross
country.'

He threw back his head, and laughed, a clear
ringing laugh; and gave me his hand, cor-

dially and frankly, for all his hauteur and his seniority.

'You'll do. Sit down, innocent. I am Granville de Vigne. You know *us*, of course. Your father rode with our hounds last January. Very game old gentleman, he seemed ; I should have thought him too sensible to have sent you down here ! You'd have been much better at Eton, or Rugby; there's nothing like a public school for taking the nonsense out of people. *I* liked Eton, at least; but if you know how to hold your own and have your own way, you can make yourself comfortable anywhere. The other fellows are out, gone to a flower-show, I think ; I never go to such places myself, they're too slow. There is only one of the boys worth cultivating, and he's a very little chap, only thirteen, but he's a jolly little monkey; we call him 'Curly' from his dandy gold locks. His father's a peer'—and De Vigne laughed again—' one of the fresh creation ; may Heaven preserve us from it ! This Frestonhills is a detestable place ; you'll be glad enough to get out of it. If it weren't for sport, I should have cut it long ago, but with a hunter and a rod a man can never be dull. Are you a good shot, seat, and oar, young one?'

Those were De Vigne's first words to me, and

I was honoured and delighted with his notice, for I had heard how, at seven years old, he had ridden unnoticed to the finish with Assheton Smith's hounds; how, three years later, he had mounted a mare none of the grooms dare touch, and, breaking his shoulder-bone in the attempt to tame her, had shut his teeth like a little Spartan, that he might not cry out during its setting; how, when he had seen his Newfoundland drowning from cramp in the mere, he had plunged in after his dog, and only been rescued as both were sinking, the boy's arms round the animal's neck:— with many other such tales current in the county of the young heir to 20,000*l.* a year.

I *did* know his family—the royal-sounding ' Us.' They had been the lords of the manor at Vigne ever since tradition could tell; their legends were among the country lore, and their names in the old cradle songs of rough chivalry, and vague romance, handed down among the peasantry from generation to generation. Many coronets had lain at their feet, but they had courteously declined them; to say the truth, they held the strawberry-leaves in supreme contempt, and looked down not unjustly on many of the *roturiers* of the peerage.

De Vigne's father, a Colonel of Dragoons, had fallen fighting in India when his son was six years

old; and how this high-spirited representative of a
haughty House came to be living down in the dull
seclusion of Frestonhills was owing to a circum-
stance very characteristic of De Vigne. At twelve
his mother had sent him to Eton, a match in
pluck, and muscle, and talent, for boys five years
his senior. There he helped to fight the Lord's
men; pounded bargees with a skill worthy of the
P. R.; made himself captain of the boats; enjoyed
mingled popularity and detestation; and from
thence, when he was seventeen, got himself
expelled.

His Dame chanced to have a niece—a niece,
tradition says, with the loveliest complexion and
the most divine auburn hair in the world, and
with whom, when she visited her aunt, all Oppi-
dans and Tugs, who saw the beatific vision, became
straightway enamoured. Whether De Vigne was
in love with her, I can't say; he always averred
not, but I doubt the truth of his statement; at any
rate, he made her in love with him, being already
rather skilled in that line of conquest, and all, I
dare say, went merry as a marriage-bell, till the
Dame found out the mischief, was scandalized and
horrified at it, and confiding the affair to the tutor,
made no end of a row in Eton. She would have
pulled all the authorities about De Vigne's ears if

he had not performed that operation for himself. The tutor, having had a tender leaning to the auburn hair on his own account, was furious; and coming in contact with De Vigne and mademoiselle strolling along by the river-side, took occasion to tell them his mind. Now opposition, much less lecturing, De Vigne in all his life never could brook; and he and his tutor coming to hot words, as men are apt when they quarrel about a woman, De Vigne flung him into the water and gave him such a ducking for his impudence, as Eton master never had before, or since. De Vigne, of course, was expelled for his double crime; and to please his mother, as nothing would make him hear of three years of college life, he consented to live twelve months in the semi-academic solitude of Frestonhills, while his name was entered at the Horse Guards for a commission. So at the Chancery he had domiciled himself, more as a guest than a pupil, for the Doctor was a trifle afraid of his keen eyes and quick wit; since his pupil knew twenty times more of modern literature and valuable available information than himself, and fifty times more of the world and its ways. But Old Joey, like all people, be their tendencies ever so heavenward, had a certain respect for twenty thousand a year. De Vigne

kept two hunters and a hack in Frestonhills. He
smoked Cavendish under the Doctor's own window; he read De Kock and Le Brun in the
drawing-room before the Doctor's very eyes (and
did not Miss Arabella read them too, upon the sly,
though she blushed if you mentioned poor 'Don
Juan!'); he absented himself when he chose, and
went to shoot and hunt and fish with men he
knew in the county; he had his own way, in fact,
as he had been accustomed to have it all his life.
But it was not an obstinate nor a disagreeable
'own way;' true, he turned restive at the least
attempt at coercion, but he was gentle enough to
a coax; and though he could work up into very
fiery passion, he was, generally speaking, sweet
tempered enough, and had almost always, a kind
word, or a generous thought, or a laughing jest,
for us less favoured young ones.

I had a sort of boyish devoted loyalty to him
then, and he deserved it. Many a scrape did a
word or two from him get me out of with the
Doctor; many a time did he send me into the
seventh heaven by the loan of his magnificent four-
year-old; more than once did fivers come from his
hand when I was deep in debt for a boy's fancies,
or had been cheated through thick and thin at the
billiard-table in the Ten Bells, where De Vigne

paid my debts, refreshed himself by kicking the
two sharpers out of the apartment, and threatened
to shoot me if I offered him the money back again.
A warm-hearted reverence I had for him in those
boyish days, and always have had, God bless him!
But I little foresaw how often in the life to come
we should be together in revelry and in-danger, in
thoughtless pleasures and dark sorrows, in the
whirl of fast life and the din and dash of the battle-field, when I first saw the senior pupil
smoking in the study of the old Chancery at
Frestonhills.

One sunny summer's afternoon, while the Doctor
dosed over his ' Treatise on the Wise Tooth of the
Fossil Hum-and-bosh Ichthyosaurus,' and Arabella
watered her geraniums and looked interesting in a
white hat with very blue ribbons, De Vigne, with
his fishing-rod in his hand, looked into the study,
and told Curly and me, who were vainly and
wretchedly puzzling our brains over Terence, that
he was going after jack, and we might go with him
if we chose. Curly and I, in our adoration of
our senior pupil, would have gone after him to
martyrdom, and we sent Terence to the dogs
(literally, for we shied him at Arabella's wheezing
King Charles), rushed for our rods and baskets,
and went down to the banks of the Kennet. De

Vigne had an especial tenderness for old Izaak's gentle art; it was the only thing over which he displayed any patience, and even in this, he might have caught more, if he had not twitched his line so often in anger at the slow-going fish, and sworn against them for not biting, roundly enough to terrify them out of all such intentions, if they had ever possessed any!

How pleasant it was there beside Pope's

" Kennet swift, for silver eels renowned,"

rushing through the sunny meadow lands of Berkshire ; lingering on its way, beneath the chequered shadows of the oaks and elms, that rival their great neighbours, the beech-woods of Bucks ; dashing swiftly, with busy joyous song, under the rough-hewn arch of some picturesque rustic bridge ; flowing clear and cool in the summer sun through the fragrant woodlands and moss-grown orchards, the nestling villages and quiet country towns, and hawthorn hedges dropping their white buds into its changeful gleaming waters! How pleasant it was, fishing for jack among our Kennet meadows, lying under the pale willows and the dark wayfaring tree with its white starry blossoms, while the cattle trooped down to drink, up to their hocks in the flags and lilies and snowflakes fringing the river's edge; and the air came fresh and fragrant over the swathes of new-mown grass and the crimson buds of the little dog-roses! Half its beauty, however, was lost upon us, with our boyish density to all appeals made to our less material senses; except, indeed, upon De Vigne, who stopped to have a glance across country as he stood trolling, spinning the line with much more outlay of strength and vehemence than was needed, or landing every now and then a ten-pound pike, with a violent anathema upon it for having dared to dispute his will so long; while little Curly lazily whipped the water, stretched full length on a fragrant bed of wild thyme. What a pretty child he was, poor little fellow! more like one of Pompadour's pages, or a boy-hero of the Trouvères, with his white skin and his violet eyes, than an every-day slang-talking, lark-loving English lad!

'By George! what a handsome girl,' said De Vigne, taking off his cap and standing at ease for a minute, after landing a great jack. 'I'm not fond of dark women generally, but 'pon my life she is splendid. What a contour! What a figure! Do for the queen of the gipsies, eh? Why the deuce isn't she this side of the river?'

The object of his admiration was on the opposite bank, strolling along by herself, with a certain
dignity of air and stateliness of step which would not
have ill become a duchess, though her station in life
was probably that of a dressmaker's apprentice, or
a small shopkeeper's daughter, at the very highest.
She was as handsome as one of those brunette
peasant beauties in the plains of La Camargue,
with a clear dark skin which had a rich carnation
glow on the cheeks; large black eyes, perfect in
shape and colour; and a form such as would de-
velop with years—for she was now probably not
more than sixteen or seventeen—into full Juno-
esque magnificence.

'By Jove ! she is very handsome; and she
knows it, too,' began De Vigne again. ' I have
never seen her about here before.   I'll go across
and talk to her.'

Go he assuredly would have done, for female
beauty was De Vigne's weakness; but at that
minute a short, square, choleric-looking keeper
came out of the wood at our back, and went up to
little Curly.

'Hallo, you there—you young swell; don't you
know you are trespassing ? '

' No, I don't,' answered Curly, in his pretty soft
voice.

'Don't you know you're on Mr. Tressillian's ground?' sang out the keeper.

'Am I? Well, give my love to him, and say I shall be very happy to give him the pleasure of my company at dinner to-night,' rejoined Curly, imperturbably.

'You imperent young dog—will you march off this 'ere minute!' roared the bellicose guardian of Mr. Tressillian's rights of fishery.

'Wouldn't you like to see me?' laughed Curly, flinging his marchbrown into the stream.

'Curse you, if you don't, I'll come and take your rod away,' sang out the keeper.

'Will you really? That'll be too obliging, you look so sweet and amiable as it is,' said Curly, with a provoking smile on his girlish little face.

'Yes, I *will*; and take you up to the house and get you a month at the mill for trespass, you abominable little devil!' vowed his adversary. laying his great fist on Curly's rod; but the little chap sprang to his feet and struck him a vigorous blow with his childish hand, which fell on the keeper's brawny form, much as a fly's kick might on the Apollo Belvidere. The man seized him round the waist, but Curly struck out right and left, and kicked and struggled with such hearty good will, that the keeper let him go; but, keeping his

hand on the boy's collar, he was about to drag him
up to the lord of the manor, whose house stood
some mile distant, when, at the sound of the
scuffle, De Vigne, intent upon watching his beauty
across the Kennet, swung round to Curly's rescue:
the boy being rather a pet of his, and De Vigne
never seeing a fight between might and right
without striking in with a blow for the weak
one.

'Take your hands off that young gentleman!
Take your hands off, do you hear? or I will give
you in charge for assault.'

' Will yer, Master Stilts,' growled the keeper,
purple with dire wrath. ' Ill give *you* in charge,
you mean. You're poaching—ay, poaching, for
all yer grand airs; and I'll be hanged if I don't
take you and the little uns, all of yer, up to the
house, and see if a committal don't take the rise
out of yer, my game-cocks! '

Wherewith the keeper, whom anger must have
totally blinded ere he attempted such an indignity
with our senior pupil, whose manorial rights
stretched over woods and waters twenty times the
extent of Boughton Tressillian's, let go his hold
upon Curly, and turned upon De Vigne, to collar
him instead.

De Vigne's eyes flashed, and the blood mounted

hot over his temples, as he straightened his left arm, and received him by a plant in the middle of his chest, with a dexterity that would have done no discredit to Tom Sayers. Down went the man under the tremendous punishing, only to pick himself up again, and charge at De Vigne with all the fury which. in such attacks, defeats its own ends, and makes a man strike wildly and at random. De Vigne however had not had mills at Eton, and rounds with bargees at Little Surley, without becoming a boxer, such as would have delighted a Ring at Moulsey. He threw himself into a scientific attitude ; and, contenting himself with the defensive for the first couple of rounds, without being touched himself, caught the keeper on the left temple, with a force which sent him down like a felled ox. There the man lay, like a log, on the thyme and ground-ivy and woodbine, till I fancy his conqueror had certain uncomfortable suspicions that he might have killed him. So he lifted him up, gave him a good shake; and finding him all right, though he was bleeding profusely, was frightfully vengeful, and full of most unrighteous oaths, though not apparently willing to encounter such another round, De Vigne pushed him on before him, and took him up to Mr. Tressillian's to keep his word, and give him in charge.

Weive Hurst, Boughton Tressillian's manor-
house, was a fine, rambling, antique old place, its
façade looking all the greyer and the older in
contrast to the green lawn, with its larches, foun-
tains, and flower-beds which stretched in front.
The powdered servant who opened the door looked
not a little startled at our unusual style of morning visit; but gave way before De Vigne, and
showed us into the library, where Mr. Tressillian
sat—a stately, kindly, silver-haired old man. De
Vigne sank into the easy-chair wheeled for him,
told his tale frankly and briefly, demonstrated,
as clearly as if he had been a lawyer, our right to
fish on the highway side of the river (an often-
disputed point for anglers), and the consequent
illegality of the keeper's assault. Boughton Tressillian was open to conviction, though he *was* a
county magnate and a magistrate, admitted that
he had no right over that part of the Kennet,
agreed with De Vigne that his keeper was in
the wrong, promised to give the man a good
lecture, and apologized to his visitor for the interference and the affront.

'If you will stay and dine with me, Mr. De
Vigne, and your young friends also, it will give
me very great pleasure;' said the cordial and courteous old man.

'I thank you. We should have been most happy,' returned our senior pupil; 'but as it is, I am afraid we shall be late for Dr. Primrose.'

'For Dr. Primrose!' exclaimed Tressillian, involuntarily. 'You are not—'

'I am a pupil at the Chancery,' laughed De Vigne.

Our host actually started; De Vigne certainly did look very little like a pupil of any man's; but he smiled in return.

'Indeed! Then I hope you will often give me the pleasure of your society. There is a billiard-table in wet weather, and good fishing and shooting in the fine. It will be a great kindness, I assure you, to come and enliven us at Weive Hurst a little.'

'The kindness will be to us,' returned De Vigne, cordially. 'Good day to you, Mr. Tressillian; accept my best thanks for your—'

A shower of roses, lilies, and laburnums, pelted at him with a merry laugh, stopped his harangue. The culprit was a little girl of about two years old, standing just outside the low windows of the library—a pretty child, with golden hair waving to her waist, and no end of mischief in her dark blue eyes. Unlike most children, she was not at all

c 2

frightened at her own misdemeanours, but stood
her ground, till Boughton Tressillian stretched out
his arm to catch her. Then, she turned round, and
took wing as rapidly as a bird off a bough, her
clear childish laughter ringing on the summer air;
while De Vigne gave chase to the only child in
his life he ever deigned to notice, justly thinking
children great nuisances, and led her prisoner to
the library, holding the blue sash by which he had
caught her.

' Here is my second captive, Mr. Tressillian—
what shall we do to her?'

Boughton Tressillian smiled.

' Alma, how could you be so naughty? Tell
this gentleman you are a spoilt child, and ask him
to forgive you.'

She looked up under her long black lashes half
shyly, half wickedly.

' *Signor, perdonatemi!*' she said, with a mischievous laugh, in broken Italian, though how a
little Berkshire girl came to talk Neapolitan
instead of English I could not imagine.

' Alma, you are very naughty to-day,' said
Tressillian, half impatiently. ' Why do you not
speak English? Ask his forgiveness properly.'

' I will pardon her without it,' laughed De
Vigne. ' There, Alma, will you not love me now?'

She pushed her sunny hair off her eyes and looked at him—a strangely earnest and wistful look, too, for so young a child. ' *Si! Alma vi ama!*' she answered him with joyous vivacity, pressing upon him with eager generosity some geraniums the head-gardener had given her, and which but a moment ago she had fastened into her white dress with extreme admiration and triumph.

' Bravo!' said Curly, as five minutes afterwards we passed out from the great hall door. ' You *are* a brick, De Vigne, and no mistake. How splendidly you pitched into that rascally keeper!

De Vigne laughed.

' It was a good bit of fun. Always stand up for your rights, my boy; if you don't, who will? I never was done yet in my life, and never intend to be.'

With which wise resolution the senior pupil struck a fusee and lit his pipe; reaching home just in time to dress, and hand Arabella in to dinner, who paid him at all times desperate court, hoping, doubtless, to make such an impression on him with her long ringlets, and bravura songs, as might trap him in his early youth into such ' serious ' action as would make her mistress of Vigne and its long rent-roll. That Granville

saw no more of her than he could help in common
courtesy, and paid her not so much attention as
he did to her King Charles, was no check to the
young lady's wild imaginings. At eight-and-twenty,
women grown desperate don't stick to probabili-
ties, but fly their hawks at any or at all quarries,
so that 'peradventure they may catch one!'

Weive Hurst proved a great gain to us   Tressillian was as good as his word, and we were at all
times cordially welcomed there, when the Doctor
gave us permission, to shoot and fish and ride
about his grounds. He grew extremely fond of
De Vigne, who, haughty as he could be at times,
and impatient as he was at any of the Doctor's
weak attempts at coercion, had a very winning
manner with old people; and played billiards,
heard his tales of the Regency, and broke in his
colts for him, till he fairly won his way into Tressillian's heart. It was for De Vigne that the
butler was always bid to bring the Steinberg and
the 1815 port; De Vigne, to whom he gave a mare
worth five hundred sovs., the most beautiful piece
of horse-flesh ever mounted; De Vigne, who might
have knocked down every head of game in the
preserves if he had chosen; De Vigne, to whom
little Alma Tressillian, the old man's only grandchild, and the future heiress, of course, of Weive

Hurst, presented with the darling of her heart—a donkey, minus head or tail or panniers.

But De Vigne did not avail himself of the sport at Weive Hurst so much as he might have done had he no other game in hand. His affair with Tressillian's keeper had prevented his going to make impromptu acquaintance with the handsome girl across the Kennet; but she had not slipped from his mind, and had made sufficient impression upon him for him to try the next day to see her again in Frestonhills, and find out who she was and where she lived, two questions he soon settled, by some means or other, greatly to his own satisfaction. The girl's name was Lucy Davis; whence she came nobody knew or perhaps inquired; but she was one of the hands at a milliner's in Frestonhills, prized by her employers for her extreme talent and skill, though equally detested, I believe, for her tyrannous and tempestuous temper. The girl was handsome enough for an Empress; and had wonderful style in her when she was dressed in her Sunday silks and cashmeres, for dress was her passion, and all her earnings were spent in imitating the toilettes she assisted in getting up to adorn the rectors' and lawyers' wives of Frestonhills. 'The Davis' was handsome enough to send a much older man mad

after her; and De Vigne, after meeting her once
or twice in the deep shady lanes of our green
Berkshire, accompanied her in her strolls, and—
fell in love with her, as De Vigne had a knack of
doing with every handsome woman who came
near him. *We* all adored the stately, black-
eyed, black-browed Davis, but she never deigned
any notice of our boyish worship; and when
De Vigne came into the field, we gave up all
hope, and fled the scene in desperation. The
Doctor, of course, knew nothing of the affair,
though almost every one else in Frestonhills did,
especially the young bankers and solicitors and
grammar-school assistant-masters, who swore at
that 'cursed fellow at the Chancery' for monopolizing the Davis—especially as the 'cursed fellow'
treated them considerably *de haut en bas.* De
Vigne was really in love, for the time being; one
of those hot, vehement, short-lived attachments
natural to his age and character; based on eye-
love alone, for the girl had nothing else
lovable about her, and had one of the worst
tempers possible; which she did not always spare
even to him, and which, when his first glamour
had a little cooled, made De Vigne rather glad
that his departure from Frestonhills was drawing
near, some four months after he had seen her

across the Kennet, and would give him an opportunity to break off his liaison which he otherwise
might have found it difficult to make.

The evening of the day which had brought the
letter which announced him as gazetted to the
—th P. W. O. Hussars; little Curly and I, having
been sent with a message to a neighbouring rector
from the Doctor, were riding by turns on Miss
Arabella's white pony, talking over the coming
holidays' 'vacation,' as Old Joey called them,
and of the long sunny future that stretched before
us in dim golden haze,—so near and yet so far from
our young longing eyes—when De Vigne's terrier
rolled out of a hedge, and jumped upon us.

'Holloa!' cried Curly, 'where's your master,
eh boy? There he is, by Jove! Arthur, talking
to the Davis. What prime fun! I wish I dare
chaff him!'

Curly, being on the pony's back, could see
over the hedge; I could not, so I swung myself upon an elm-bough, and saw at some little
distance De Vigne and Lucy Davis in very earnest conversation, or rather, as it seemed to me,
altercation; for De Vigne was switching the
long meadow grass impatiently with his cane,
looking pale and annoyed, while the girl Davis
stood before him, seemingly in one of those

violent furies which reputation attributed to her,
by turns adjuring, abusing, and threatening
him.

Curly and I stayed some minutes looking at
them, for the scene piqued our interest, making us
think of Eugène Sue, and Dumas, and all the love
scenes we had devoured, when the Doctor sup-
posed us plodding at the *Pons Asinorum* or the
De Officiis : but we could make nothing out of
it, except that De Vigne and the Davis were
quarrelling; and an intuitive perception, that the
senior pupil would not admire our playing the spy
on him, made me leave my elm branch, and Curly
start off the pony homewards.

That night De Vigne was silent and gloomy in
the drawing-room; gave us but a brief 'Good
night,' and shut his bedroom door with a bang;
the next morning, however, he seemed all right
again, as he breakfasted for the last time in the
old Chancery.

'What a lucky fellow you are, De Vigne!'
sighed Curly, enviously, as he stood in the hall,
waiting for the fly to take him to the station.

He laughed:

'Oh, I don't know! We shall see if we all say
so this time twenty years! If I could foresee the
future, I wouldn't: I love the glorious uncer-

tainty; it is the only *sauce piquante* one has, and I can't say I fear fate very much!'

And well he might not at eighteen! Master, when he came of age, of a splendid fortune, his own guide, his own arbiter, able to see life in all its most deliciously attractive forms, truly it seemed that he, if any one, might trust to the *sauce piquante* of uncertain fate? *Qui lira, verra.*

Off he went by the express with his portmanteaus, lettered, as we enviously read, 'Granville de Vigne, Esq., —th P. W. O. Hussars;' off with *Punch* and an Havannah to amuse him on the way, to much more than Exeter Barracks,—on the way to Manhood; with all its chances and its changes, its wild revels and its dark regrets, its sparkling champagne-cup, and its bitter aconite lying at the dregs! Off he went, and we, left behind in the dull solitude of academic Freston-hills, watched the smoke curling from the engine as it disappeared round the bend of a cutting, and wondered in vague schoolboy fashion what sort of thing De Vigne would make of Life.

CHAPTER II.

" A SOUTHERLY WIND AND A CLOUDY SKY PROCLAIM IT A HUNTING MORNING."

'CONFOUND it, I can't cram, and I won't cram, so there's an end of it!' sang out a Cantab one fine October morning, flinging Plato's Republic to the far end of the room; where it knocked down a grind-cup, smashed a punch-bowl, and cracked the glass, that glazed the charms, of the last pet of the ballet.

The sun streamed through the oriel windows of my rooms in dear old Trinity. The roaring fire crackled, blazed, and chatted away to a slate-coloured Skye that lay full-length before it. The table was spread with coffee, audit, devils, omelets, hare-pies, and all the other articles of the buttery. The sunshine within, shone on pipes and pictures, tobacco-boxes and little bronzes, books, cards, cigar-cases, statuettes, portraits of Derby winners, and likenesses of fair Anonymas—all in confusion, tumbled pell-mell together among sofas and easy-chairs, rifles, cricket-bats, boxing-gloves, and skates. The sunshine without, shone on the backs, where outriggers and four-oars were pulling up and down the cold classic muddy waters of the Cam, more celebrated, but far less clear and lovely, I must say, than our old dancing, rapid, joyous Kennet. Everything looked essentially jolly, and jolly did I and my two companions feel, smoking before a huge fire, in the easiest of attitudes and couches, a very trifle seedy from a prolonged Wine the night previous.

One of them was a handsome young fellow of twenty, a great deal too handsome for the peace of the master's daughters, and of the fair *patissières* and *fleuristes* of Petty Cury and King's Parade; the self-same, save some additional feet of height and some fondly-cherished whiskers, as our little Curly of Frestonhills. The other was a man of six-and-twenty, his figure superbly developed in strength and power without losing one atom in symmetry, showing how his nerve and muscle would tell pulling up stream, or in a fast fifty minutes across country, or, if occasion turned up, in that 'noble art of self-defence,' now growing as popular in England, as in days of yore at Elis.

'Cram?' he said, looking up as Curly spoke.
'Why should you? What's the good of it? Youth
is made for something warmer than academic
routine; and knowledge of the world will stand a
man in better stead, than the quarrels of com-
mentators, and the dry demonstrations of mathe-
maticians.'

'Of course. Not a doubt about it,' said Curly,
stretching himself. 'I find soda-water and brandy
the best guano for the cultivation of *my* intellect,
I can tell you, De Vigne.'

'Do you think it will get you a double first?'

'Heaven forefend!' cried Curly, with extreme
piety. 'I've no ambition for lawn sleeves, though
they *do* bring with them as neat a little income as
any Vessel of Grace, who lives on clover, and for-
swears the pomps and vanities of this wicked world,
can possibly desire.'

' *You*'ll live in clover, my boy, trust you for
that,' said De Vigne. 'But you won't pretend
that you only take it because you're "called" to
it, and that you would infinitely prefer, if left to
yourself, a hovel and dry bread! Don't cram,
Curly; your great saps are like the geese they
fatten for foie gras; they overfeed one part of the
system till all the rest is weak, diseased, and
worthless. But the geese have the best of it, for

their livers *do* make something worth eating, while
the reading-man's brains are rarely productive of
anything worth writing.'

'Ah!' re-echoed Curly, with an envious sigh
of assent. 'I wonder whose knowledge is worth
the most; my old Coach's, a living miracle of
classic research, who couldn't, to save his life,
tell you who was Premier, translate " *Comment
vous portez-vous?* " or know a Creswick from a
Rubens, or yours; who have everything at your
fingers' ends that one can want to hear about, from
the last clause in the budget, to the best make in
rifles?'

De Vigne laughed. 'Well, a man can't tumble
about in the world, if he has any brains at all,
without learning something; but, my dear fellow,
that's all "superficial," they'll tell you; and it is
atrociously bad taste to study leading articles
instead of Greek unities! *Chacun à son goût,*
you know. That young fellow above your head
is a mild, spectacled youth, Arthur says, who gives
scientific teas, where you give roistering wines,
wins Craven scholarships where you get gated, and
falls in love with the fair structure of the Œdipus
Tyrannus, where you go mad about the unfor-
tunately more perishable form of that pretty little
girl at the cigar-shop over the way! You think

him a muff, and he, I dare say, looks on you as
an *âme damnée*, both in the French and English
sense of the words. You both fill up niches in
your own little world; you needn't jostle one
another. If all horses ran for one Cup only, the
turf would soon come to grief. Why ain't you
like me? I go on my own way, and never trouble
my head about other people!'

'Why am I not like you?' repeated Curly,
with a prolonged whistle. 'Why isn't water as
good as rum punch, or my bed-maker as pretty
as little Rosalie? Don't I wish I *were* you, instead
of a beggarly younger son, tied by the leg in
Granta, bothered with chapel, and all sorts of
horrors, and rusticated if I try to see the smallest
atom of life. By George! De Vigne, what a jolly
time you must have had of it since you left the
Chancery!'

'Oh, I don't know,' said De Vigne, looking
into the fire with a smile. 'I've gone the pace, I
dare say, as fast as most men, and there are few
things I have not tried; but I am not *blasé* yet,
thank Heaven! When other things begin to bore
me, I turn back to sport—that never palls; there's
too much excitement in it. Wine one cannot
drink too much of—I can't, at the least—without
getting tired of it; women—well, for all the poets

write about the joys of constancy, there is no pleasure so great as change *there*; but with a good
speat in the river, or clever dogs among the
turnips, or a fine fox along a cramped country, a
man need never be dull. The ping of a bullet, the
shine of a trout's back, never lose their pleasure.
One can't say as much for the brightest Rhenish
that ever cooled one's throats, nor the brightest
glances that ever lured one into folly; though
Heaven forbid that I should ever say a word
against either!'

'You'd be a very ungrateful fellow if you did,'
said I, ' seeing that you generally monopolize the
very best of both!'

He laughed again. ' Well, I've seen life—I
told you young fellows at Frestonhills, I trusted to
my *sauce piquante*; and I must say it has used
me very well hitherto, and I dare say always will
as long as I keep away from the Jews. While a
man has plenty of tin, all the world offers him the
choicest dinner; though, when he has overdrawn
at Coutts's, his friends wouldn't give him dry
bread to keep him out of the union! Be able to
dine *en prince* at home, and you'll be invited out
every night of your life; be hungry *au troisième*,
and you must not lick the crumbs from under
your sworn allies' tables, those jolly good fellows,

who have surfeited themselves at yours many a
time ! Oh yes, I enjoy life ; a man always can
as long as he can pay for it ! '

With which axiom De Vigne rose from his
rocking-chair, laid down his pipe, and stretched
himself.

' It looks fine out yonder. Our club think of
challenging your University Eight for love, good
will, and—a gold cup. We never do anything
for *nothing* in England ; if we play, we must play
for money or ornaments : *I* should like to do
the thing for the sake of the fun, but that isn't a
general British feeling at all. Money is to us, all
that glory was to the Romans, and is to the
French. Genius is valued by the money it makes ;
artists are prized by the price of their pictures.
If the nation is grateful, once in a hundred years,
it votes—a pension; and if we want to have a good-
humoured contest, we must wait till there are
subscriptions enough to buy a reward to tempt us !
Come along, Arthur, let's have a pull to keep us
in practice ? '

We accordingly had a pull up that time-
honoured stream, where Trinity has so often won
challenge cups, and luckless King's got bumped,
thanks to its quasi-Etonians' idleness. Where
grave philosophers have watched the setting

sun die out of the sky, as the glories of their own youth have died away unvalued, till lost for ever. Where ascetic reading-men have mooned along its banks blind to all the loveliness of the water-lily below, or the clouds above, as they took their constitutional and pondered their prize essay. Where thousands of young fellows have dropped down under its trees, dreaming over Don Juan or the Lotus-eaters ; or pulled along, straining muscle and nerve against the Head-Boat ; or sauntered beside it in sweet midsummer eves, with some fair face upraised to theirs, long forgotten, out of mind now, but which then had power to make them oblivious of proctors and rustication! We pulled along with hearty good-will, aided by an oar with which, could we have had it to help us in the University race, we must have beaten Oxford out-and-out. For the Brocas, and Little Surley, could have told you tales of that long, lofty, slash-ing, stroke ; and if, monsieur or madame, you are a 'sentimental psychologist,' and sneer it down as 'animal,' let me tell you it is the hand which is strong in sport, and in righteous strife, that will be warmer in help, and firmer in friendship, and more generous in deed, than the puny weakling's who cannot hold his own.

'By George!' said De Vigne, resting at last

upon his oar, 'is there anything that gives one
a greater zest in life than bodily exertion ? '

A sentiment, however, in which indolent
Curly declined to coincide. ' Give me,' said he,
'a lot of cushions, a hookah, and a novel; and
your "bodily exertion" may go to the deuce
for me!'

De Vigne laughed; he was not over merciful
on the present-day assumption in beardless boys
of effeminacy, nil admirari-ism and blasé indifference. He was far too frank himself for
affectation, and too spirited for ennui; at the
present, at least, his *sauce piquante* had not lost
its flavour.

He *had* seen life; he had hunted with the
Pytchley, stalked royals in the Highlands, flirted
with maids of honour, supped in the Bréda Quartier,
had dinners fit for princes at the Star and Garter,
and pleasant hours in *cabinets particuliers* at Vé-
fours and the Maison Dorée. He and his yacht,
when he had got leave, had gone everywhere that
a yacht could go; the Ionian Isles knew no figure-
head better than his Aphrodite's of the R.V.Y.S.;
it had carried him up to salmon fishing in Norway, and across the Atlantic to hunt buffaloes and
cariboos; to Granada, to look into soft Spanish
faces by the dim moonlight in the Alhambra; and

to Venice, to fling bouquets upwards to the balconies, and whisper to Venetian masks which showed him the glance of long almond eyes, in the riotous Carnival time. He had a brief campaign in Scinde, where he was wounded in the hip, and tenderly nursed by a charming Civil Service widow; where his daring drew down upon him the admiring rebuke of his commanding officer, but won him his troop, which promotion brought him back to England and enabled him to exchange into the ——th Lancers, technically the Dashers, the *nom de guerre* of that daring and brilliant corps. And now, De Vigne, who had never lost sight of me since the Frestonhills days, but, on the contrary, had often asked me to go and shoot over Vigne, when he assembled a crowd of guests in that magnificent mansion; having a couple of months' leave, had run down to Newmarket, for the October Meeting; and had come at my entreaty to spend a week in Granta, where, I need not tell you, we fêted him, and did him the honours of the place in style.

Crash! crash! went the relentless chapel-bell the next morning, waking us out of dreamless slumber that had endured not much more than an hour, owing to a late night of it with a man at

John's over punch and vingt-et-un; and we had to tumble out of bed and rush into chapel, twisting on our coats, and swearing at our destinies, as we went. The Viewaway (the cleverest pack in the easterly counties, though not, I admit, up to the Burton, or Tedworth, or Melton mark) met that day, for the first run of the season, at Euston Hollows, five miles from Cambridge; and Curly, who overcame his laziness on such occasions, staggered into his stall, the pink dexterously covered with his surplice, his bright hair for once in disorder, and his blue eyes most unmistakably sleepy. 'Who'd be a hapless undergrad? That fellow De Vigne's dreaming away in comfort, while we're dragged out by the heels, for a lot of confounded humbug and form,' lamented Curly to me as we entered; while the readers hurried the prayers over, in that sing-song recitative in favour with college-men—a cross between the drone of a gnat, and the whine of a Suffolk peasant. We dozed comfortably, sitting down, and getting up, at the right times, by sheer force of habit; or read Dumas, or Balzac, under cover of our prayer-books. The freshmen alone, tried to look alive and attentive; those better seasoned knew it was but a ritual, much such an empty, but time-honoured, one, as the gathering of Fellows at the Signing of the

Leases, at King's; or any other moss-grown formula of Mater; and attempted no such thing; but rushed out of chapel again, the worse instead of the better for the ill-timed devotions, which forced us, in our thoughtless youth, into irreverence and hypocrisy: a formula as absurd, as soulless, and as sad to see, as the praying windmills of the Hindoos, at which those 'heads of the Church,' who uphold morning-chapel as the sole safeguard of Granta, smile in pitying derision!

When I got back to my rooms I found breakfast waiting, and De Vigne standing on the hearth-rug. Audit and hare-pie had not much temptation for us that morning; we were soon in the saddle, and off to Euston Hollows. After a brisk gallop to cover, we found ourselves riding up the approach to the M.F.H.'s house, where the meet took place in an open sweep of grassland belted with trees, just facing the hall, where were gathered all the men of the Viewaway, mounted on powerful hunters, and looking all over like goers. There was every type of the *genus* sporting man; stout, square farmers, with honest bull-dog physique, characteristic of John Bull plebeian; wild young Cantabs, mounted showily from livery-stables, with the fair, fearless, delicate features characteristic of John Bull patrician; steady old whippers-in, very suspicious of brandy; wrinkled feeders, with stentorian voices that the wildest puppy had learned to know and dread; the courteous, cordial, aristocratic M.F.H., with the men of *his* class, the county gentry; rough, ill-looking cads, awkward at all things save crossing country; no end of pedestrians, nearly run over themselves, and falling into everybody's way; and last, but in our eyes, not least, the ladies who had come to see the hounds throw off.

De Vigne exchanged his reeking hack for his own hunter, a splendid thorough-bred, with as much light action, he said, as a danseuse, and as much strength and power as a bargeman. Then we rode up to talk to the M.F.H 's wife, who was mounted on a beautiful little mare, and intended to follow her husband and his hounds over the Cambridge fences.

'Who is that lady yonder?' asked De Vigne, after he had chatted some moments with her.

'The one on the horse with a white star on his forehead? Lady Blanche Fairelesyeux. Don't you know her? She is a widow, very pretty and very rich.'

'Yes, yes, I know Lady Blanche,' laughed De Vigne. 'She married old Faire two years ago, and persuaded him to drink himself to death most opportunely. No, I meant that very handsome woman there, talking to your husband at this moment, mounted on a chesnut with a very wild eye.'

'Oh, that is Miss Trefusis!'

'And can you tell me no more than her mere name?'

'Not much. She is some relation—what I do not know exactly—of that detestable old woman Lady Fantyre, whose "recollections" of court people are sometimes as gross anachronisms as the Comte de St. Germain's. They are staying with Mrs. St. Croix, and she brought them here; but I do not like Miss Trefusis very much myself, and Mr. L'Estrange does not wish me to cultivate her acquaintance.'

'Then I must not ask you to introduce me?' said De Vigne, disappointedly.

'Oh yes, if you wish. I know her well enough for that; and she dines here to-night with the St. Croix. But there is a wide difference, you know, between making passing acquaintances, and ripening them into friends. Come, Captain de Vigne, I am sure you will ride the hounds off the scent, or do something dreadful, if I do not let you talk to your new beauty,' laughed the young mistress of Euston Hollows, turning her mare's head towards the showy chesnut, whose rider had won so much of De Vigne's admiration.

She was as dashing and magnificent in her way as her horse in his with a tall and voluptuously-perfect figure, which her tight dark riding-jacket showed in all the beauty of its rounded outlines, while her little hat, with a single white feather, scarcely shadowed, and did not conceal, her clear profile, magnificent eyes, and lips by which Velasquez or Titian would have sworn. Splendid she was, and she had spared no pains to make the tableau; and though to a keen eye, her brilliant colour, which was *not* rouge, and her pencilled eyebrows, which *were* tinted, gave her a trifle of the actress or the lorette style, there was no wonder that De Vigne, impressible as a Southern by women's beauty—and at that time as long as it was beauty, not caring much of what stamp or of what order— was not easy till Flora L'Estrange had introduced him to her. So we rush upon our doom! So we, in thoughtless play, twist the first gleaming and silky threads of the fatal cord which will cling about our necks, fastened beyond hope of release, as long as our lives shall last!

The Trefusis (as she was called in the smoking-rooms), surrounded as she was by the best men of the Viewaway, ruling them by force of

that superb form and face, bowed very graciously to De Vigne, and smiled upon him. He
had caught her eyes once or twice before he
had asked Mrs. L'Estrange who she was; and
now, displacing the others with that calm, un-
conscious air of superiority, the more irritating
to his rivals that it was invariably successful,
he leaned his hand on the pommel of her saddle,
and talked away to her the chit-chat of the hour.
The Trefusis intended to follow the hounds, as
well as L'Estrange's wife and Lady Blanche Fairelesyeux; so De Vigne and she rode off together
as the hounds, symmetrical in form, and all in
good condition, though they *were* a provincial
establishment, trotted away, with waving sterns
and eager eyes, to draw the Euston Hollow's
covert.

The cheery 'Halloo!' rang over coppice and
brushwood and plantation; the white sterns of
the hounds flourished among the dark-brown
bushes of the cover; stentorian lungs shouted out
the 'Stole away!—hark for-r-r-r-rard!' and as
the finest fox in the county broke away, De Vigne
struck his spurs into his hunter's flanks, and rattled
down the cover, all his thoughts centered on the
clever little pack that streamed along before him;
while the whole field burst over the low pastures

and oak fences and ox-rails, across which the fox
was leading us. I dashed along the first three
meadows, which were only divided by low hedges,
with all the excitement and breathlessness of a
first start; but as we crossed the fourth at an easy
gallop, cooling the horses before the formidable leap
which we knew the Cam, or rather a narrow sedgy
tributary of it, would give us at the bottom, I took
time, and looked around. Before any of us, De
Vigne was going along, as straight as an arrow's
flight, working his bay up for the approaching
trial ; never looking back, going into the sport
before him as if he never had had, and never
could have had, any other interest in life. The
Trefusis, riding as few women could, sitting well
down in her saddle, like any of the Pytchley or
Belvoir men, was some yards behind him, 'riding
jealous,' I could see ; rather a hopeless task for a
young lady with a man known in the hunting-
field as he was. The M.F.H. was, of course,
handling his hunter in masterly style, his little
wife keeping gallantly up with him, though she
and her mare looked as likely to be smashed by
the first staken-bound fence as a Sèvres figure or
a Parian statuette. Curly, who, thanks to his
half-broken hunter, had split four strong oak bars,
and been once pitched neck and crop into Cam-

bridge mud, was coming along with his pink sadly stained; while Lady Blanche and four of the men were within a few paces of him, and the rest of the field were scattered far and wide: quaint bits of scarlet, green, and black, dotting the short brown turf of the pasture lands.

Splash! went the fox into the sedgy waters of this branch of classic Cam, and scrambled up upon the opposite bank. For a second the hounds lost the scent; then, they threw up their heads with a joyous challenge, breasted the stream, dashed on after him, and sped along beyond the pollards on the opposite side far ahead of us, streaming out like the white tail of a comet. De Vigne put his bay at the leap, but before he could lift him over, the Trefusis cleared it, with unblanched cheek and unshaken nerve. She looked back with a laugh, not of gay girlish merriment, such as Flora L'Estrange would have given, but a laugh with a certain gratified malice in it: and he gave a muttered oath at being 'cut down' by a woman, as he landed his bay beside her.

I cleared it, so did the M.F.H., and, by some species of sporting miracle, so did his wife and her little mare. One of the yeomen found a watery bed among the tadpoles, clay, and rushes—it might be a watery grave, for anything I know to the contrary — and poor dear Curly was tumbled straight off his young one, and lay there, a helpless mass of human and equine flesh, while Lady Blanche lifted her roan over him, with a gay, unsympathizing 'Keep still, or Mazeppa will damage you!'

The run had lasted but ten minutes and a half as yet, and the hounds, giving tongue in joyous concert, led the way for those who could follow them, over blackthorn hedges, staken-bound fences, and heavy ploughed lands, while the fox was heading for Sifton Wood, where, once lodged, we should never unearth him again. On we went at a killing pace; De Vigne leading the first flight, by two lengths, up to a cramped and awkward leap; a high, stiff, straggling hedge, with a double ditch, almost as wide as a Leicestershire bullfinch. Absorbed as I was in working up my hunter for the leap, I looked to see if the Trefusis funked it. Not she!—and she cleared it, too, lifting her chesnut high in the air, over the ugly blackthorn boughs; but on the slippery marshy ground the horse fell, heavily and awkwardly, flinging her forward; so at least they told me afterwards. The courtly M.F.H. stopped to offer her assistance, but she waved him on; De Vigne had forgotten all his chivalry, and led straight ahead without looking back; while picking up her hunter, the Trefusis remounted, nothing daunted by her fall. Lady Blanche's Mazeppa refused the leap; and with a little petulant French oath, she rode further down, to try and find a gap; while my luckless under-bred one flung me over his head, rolling on his back in rushes, nettles, mud, and duckweed, and before either he or I could recover ourselves and shake off the slough, the fox was killed, and the whoop of triumph came ringing far over plantations and pastures, on the clear October air.

With not a few unholy oaths, less choice than Lady Blanche's, I rode through the gap lower down, and made my way to the finish. The brush was awarded to De Vigne by the old huntsman, who might have given it to the Trefusis, for she was only a yard or two behind him; but Squib had no tenderness for the sex; indeed, he looked on them as having no earthly business in the field, and gave it with a gruff word of compliment to Granville, who of course handed it to Miss Trefusis, but claimed the right of sending it up to town, to be mounted on ivory for her. That dashing Amazon herself, sat on her trembling and foam-covered chesnut, with the dignity and royal beauty of Cynisca, returning in her cha-

riot from the Olympic games, and De Vigne seemed
to think nothing more attractive than this haughty,
triumphant, imperial woman, who had skill and
pluckworthy a Pytchley Nestor. *I* preferred little
Flora's girlish pity for the 'poor dear fox,' and
her pathetic lamentation to her husband that she
'dearly loved the riding, but she would rather
never see the finish.' However, as De Vigne
said the morning before, *chacun à son gout* ; if we
all liked the same style of woman where *should*
we be ? We rival and jostle and hate each other
enough as it is, about that centre of all mischief,
the Beau Sexe, Heaven knows !

We had another run that day, but it was a very
slow affair. We killed the fox, but he made
scarcely any running at all, and we might have
scored it almost as a blank day; but for our first
glorious twenty minutes, one of the fastest things
I ever knew, from Euston Hollows up to Sifton
Wood. Lady Blanche went back in ill-humour :
missing that ditch had put the pretty widow in
dudgeon for all the day ; but the Trefusis!—it's
my firm conviction that Mazeppa's gallop could
not have tired that woman. She rode, as De
Vigne observed admiringly to me, with as firm a
seat and as strong a hand as any rough-rider.
Excellence in his own art pleased him, I suppose,

for he watched her more and more; and rode back
to Euston Hollows, with her through the gloam-
ing, some nine miles from where the last fox was
killed, looking down on her beauty with bold,
tender glances.

CHAPTER III.

IN THE ACADEMIC SHADES OF GRANTA.

L'ESTRANGE had bid us send our things over to his house, and make our toilettes there, after the day's sport; and when we went down into the drawing-room, we found the Trefusis sitting on an amber satin couch, queening it over the county men, a few college fellows or professors, and the borough Members. There were Mrs. St. Croix and her two daughters, showy, flighty, hawked-about women, and the Gwyn-Erlens, fresh, nice-looking girls; and Lady Blanche, recovered from her ill-humour, and ready to shoot down any game worth or not worth the hitting; and the Countess of Turquoise, who thought very few people knew what fun was, she told me, and instanced the dreary social torture called dining out; and Mrs. Fitzrubric, a bishop's wife, staying in the neigh-bourhood, who considered the practice of giving buns at school feasts sensual, but showed herself no disrelish for champagne and mock turtle.   And

there was that 'detestable old woman,' according
to Flora, the Lady Fantyre, widow of an Irish
peer,—a little, shrivelled, witty, nasty-thinking,
and amusing-talking old lady, with a thin, sharp
face, a hooked nose, very keen, bright, cunning,
quizzical eyes, a very candid wig, and unmistak-
able rouge. She chattered away, in a shrill treble,
of intimate acquaintance with court celebrities,
some of whom certainly she could never have
known, for the best of reasons, that they were
dead before she was born; and, having seen a
vast deal of life, not all of the nicest, and picked up
a good deal of information, she passed current in
nine cases out of ten, with her apocryphal stories
and well-worn title, which covered a multitude of
sins, as coronets do and charity doesn't. But she
was 'not visited' where her departed lord's rank
might have entitled her to be, partly because she
had a rather too marked skill at cards; but chiefly,
I have no doubt, because she had no balance
at any bank save Homburg and Baden, and was
obliged to live by her wits, those wits being represented by the four honours and the odd trick. If
poor old Fantyre had had a half-million or so at
Barclay's, I dare say the charitable world would
have let her buy oblivion for all the naughty secrets hidden in her old wigged head.

'Diana turned to Venus, and no mistake,' whispered Curly to me, as we looked at the Trefusis, her beauty heightened by her toilette, which was as tasteful as a Parisienne's, and would have chimed in with M. Chevreul's artistic notions. De Vigne, the moment he entered, crossed over to her, and, seating himself, began to talk. Whether the lustrous gaze of his eyes, which knew how to express their admiration, got their admiration returned ; or whether she had wit enough to appreciate his conversation, where the true gold of sense, and talent, rang out in distinction to the second-hand platitudes, or *Punch-*cribbed mots, of the generality of people, I will not pretend to decide. At any rate, by some spell or other, he distanced his rivals by many lengths.

They naturally spoke of the run of that morning, and the Trefusis, flirting her fan with stately movement, and turning her full glittering eyes upon him, asked very softly, ' What do you think you did this morning that pleased me ? '

De Vigne expressed his happiness that any act of his should do so.

' It was when we took that ditch by Sifton Wood, and my stupid chesnut fell with me. You rode on, and never looked back ; your thoughts were with the hounds, not with me ! '

'You are more forgiving to my discourtesy than I can be to myself,' smiled De Vigne. 'What you are so generous as to pardon I cannot recall without shame.'

'Then you are very silly,' she interrupted him. 'A man in a time of excitement or danger should have something better to think about than a woman.'

'It is difficult, with Miss Trefusis before us, to think there *can* be anything better than a woman,' whispered De Vigne.

She looked at him and smiled, too; with something of malice in it as when she had cleared the Cam before him—a smile that at once repulsed, and fascinated; annoyed, and piqued him. Just then dinner was announced as served. L'Estrange took away my bewitching Countess of Turquoise; Curly led in Julia St. Croix, with whom he seemed wonderfully struck, Heaven knows why, except that young fellows will go down before any battered or war-worn arrows at times; and De Vigne gave his arm to the Trefusis, to whom he talked during all the courses with a devotion which must have interfered with his proper appreciation of the really masterly productions of the Euston Hollows *chef*, and the very excellent hock and claret of L'Estrange's cellar. Whether

he had much response I cannot say—for I was
absorbed in looking at Lady Turquoise from far too
respectful a distance to please me: but I should
fancy not, for the Trefusis was never, that I heard,
much famed for conversation; still someway or
other she fascinated him with her basilisk-beauty,
and when Flora gave the move she looked into
his eyes rather warmly for an acquaintance not
twelve hours old as yet. We were some little
time before we followed them, for De Vigne and
the Members got on the Reform Bill, and did not
get off it again in a hurry; and though Lady
Turquoise was bewitching, and the Trefusis' eyes
magnificent, and the St. Croix very effective as
they sang duets in studied poses, Château Mar-
gaux and unfettered talk proved more attractive
to us. When we returned to the drawing-room,
however, De Vigne took up his station beside the
Trefusis again, paying her marked attention, while
Flora L'Estrange sang charming little French
chansons, and Julia St. Croix tortured us with
bravuras, and the cruel Countess of Turquoise
flirted with the county Member. What an into-
lerably empty-headed coxcomb, he seemed to *me*,
I remember!

   'What a fine creature that Trefusis is!' said
De Vigne, as he drove us back to Cambridge in a

dog-cart. 'On my life, she is a magnificent woman! Arthur, she reminds me of somebody or other—I can't tell whom—somebody, I dare say, I saw in Spain or in Italy, or in India, perhaps.'

'Shall I tell you?' said Curly.

'Yes, pray do; but you've never been about with me, old boy, how should you know?'

'I was with you at the Chancery, and I haven't forgotten Lucy Davis.'

'The Davis!' exclaimed De Vigne, the light of old days breaking in upon him, half faded, half familiar. 'By Jove! she is something like that girl; I declare I had forgotten that schoolboy episode, Curly. So she *is* like her,—if Lucy had been a lady instead of a dressmaker. The deuce! I hadn't bad taste then, boy as I was! How many things of that kind one forgets—'

'Lucy didn't look like a woman who'd allow herself to be forgotten. She'd make you remember her by fair means or foul,' said Curly.

'What! do you recollect her so well, young one?' laughed De Vigne. 'I must say, she seems to have made more impression upon you, than she has done on me. There was the very devil in that girl, poor thing, young as she was! She was bold, bad, hardened to the core. But this Tre-

fusis, Curly!—she does bring that girl to my
mind, certainly, and there is in her something
there was in Lucy Davis—a something intangible
which repels, while her exterior beauty allures
one. Perhaps it is in both alike—a cold heart
within.'

' If we were only allured where there are warm
hearts, we should keep in a blessed state of indifference,' said I, thinking savagely of Lady Turquoise and that confounded county Member.

' Hallo, Arthur! what has turned you cynic?'
laughed De Vigne. 'Only this very morning
were you sentimentalizing over the " Lady of
Shalott," and wanting to inflict it on me !'

' Yes, and you stopped me with the abominable
quotation, " Ass! am I *onion*-eyed ?" I say, De
Vigne, I wish you'd tell us how that affair with
Lucy Davis ended ? Curly and I saw you quarrelling the day before you left.'

' I never quarrelled!' said De Vigne, contemptuously. ' I never do with anybody; if they
don't say what I like, I tell them my mind at once,
and there's an end of it. But I never quarrel !
I met Lucy that evening as I was going into
Frestonhills, and when I told her I was about to
leave, she demanded—what do you think?—
nothing less than a promise of marriage! Only

fancy—from *me* to *her!* She even said I had
made her one! I've been guilty of many mad
things, but never of one quite so insane as that.
I told her flatly it was a lie—so it was, and it put
me in a passion, to be saddled with such an
atrocious falsehood: I never can stand quiet,
and see people trying to chisel me, you know. I
offered to do anything she liked for her; to pro-
vide for her as liberally as she chose. But not
a word would she hear from me; she was mad,
I suppose, because she could not startle or chicane
me into admitting the promise of marriage, having
possibly in her eye the heavy damages an enlight-
ened court would grant to her "innocent years"
and her "wrongs!" At any rate, she would not
hear a word I said, but she poured her invectives
into my ear, letting out that she had never loved
me, but had intended to make me a stepping-stone,
to the money, and rank, she was always pining
after; that, having failed, she hated me, and that
before she died, would be revenged.

'By George! what an amusing idea. She'd be
puzzled to do it, I fancy.'

'Rather,' laughed De Vigne, reigning up his
mare; 'but women say anything in a passion.
Lucy Davis had gone straight out of my mind, till
you said that handsome Trefusis made you think

of her. I am glad the St. Croix and L'Estranges
are coming to lunch with you, Curly; I want to
see more of my imperial beauty; and I must
be back at Vigne by Saturday. Sabretasche, and
Pigott, and Severn, and no end of men are coming
down for the pheasants; I wish you were too,
old fellows! Good night; *Au revoir!*' And De
Vigne set us down before Trinity, and drove on to
the Bull; smoking, and thinking, very likely, of
his superb Trefusis.

Oh, those jolly Cambridge days! The splendid
manner in which we bumped Corpus and Kathe-
rine Hall, and carried off the Cup, to the envy of
all the University; the style in which we thrashed
the Exeter Eight, with ignominy unspeakable,
before the eyes of Henley; the row and scuffle of
Town and Gown rows, dear to the British passion
for hard hits, where Curly knocked a cobbler down
and then gave him in charge for an assault; the
skill with which that mischievous young Honourable caught his whip round the shovel-hat of a
dean, raising that venerated article of dress in mid-
air, and only escaping rustication by dashing on
with his tandem-team too quickly for identifica-
tion: were they not all written, in their day,
among the records of Trinity men's larks?

We used to vow we were confoundedly tired of

Granta, and so I dare say we might feel at the time; but how pleasant they were, those light-hearted college days!—the honours of the Eight-oar; the thrashing of the Marylebone Eleven; the rattle cross country, for the Cesarewitch, or the Cambridge Sweepstakes; the flirtations of pretty shop-girls in Petty Cury, or Trumpington Street; the raving politics of the Union, occasional prelude to triumphs, forensic and senatorial; the noisy wines, where scanty humour woke more merriment than wittiest *mots* do twenty years after; and Cambridge port passed with a flavour, that no olives or anchovies can give to Comet claret now. How pleasant they were, those jolly college days! As I think of them, many kindly faces and joyous voices rise before me! Where are they all? Some lying with the colours on their breast beside the Euxine Sea, and along the line of the Pacific; some struck down by the assassin's knife in the temples at Cawnpore; some sleeping beneath the sighing of the Delhi palms, or of the sad Atlantic waves; some wasting classic eloquence on country hinds, in moss-grown village churches; some fighting the great fight, between science and death, in the crowded hospital-wards of London; some wearing honour, and honesty, and truth from their hearts, in the breathless, up-hill press of the great

world ;—all of them, living or dead, scattered far
away over the earth, since those old days, in the
shadow of the academic walls !

The time to lionize Cambridge, as everybody
knows, is May and June, when the backs are all
in their glory; when the graceful spires of King's
rise up against blue skies ; when the white towers
of John's stand bosomed in green leafy shades;
when the Trinity limes fill the air with fragrance,
and the sun peers through the great shadowy elm-
boughs, of Neville's Court; and the brown
Cam flows under its bridges, with water-lilies
and forget-me-nots on its breast, gliding, as though
conscious that it was in classic shades, through
vistas of waving boughs, and past gray, stately
college walls; bringing into the grave haunts of
Learning, the glad and vernal freshness of the
Spring. May is the time for Cambridge; still,
even in October, we managed to give the
L'Estranges, and the St. Croix, a very good recep-
tion. Women are always royally received by
Cantabs, and our guests were calculated to excite
the envy of all the University. We did the lions
with very little architectural appreciation ; but the
science of eyes and smiles, is a pleasanter one than
the science of styles and orders; and we were
quite as contented, and I have no doubt much

better amused, than if, Ruskin *à la main*, we had
been competent to pull to pieces the beauty of
King's, and prate of 'severity' and 'purity.'
Happy in our barbarianism, we crossed the Bridge
of Sighs with a laugh at old Fantyre's jokes;
strolled down the Fellowship Walk, telling Julia
St. Croix, who had not two ideas in her head,
that Bacon's Gate would, to a surety, fall down on
her; went in at Humility, through Virtue, and out
at Honour, flirting desperately under those grave
archways; and hurried irreverently through the
libraries, where reading-men, cramming in niches,
looked up, forgetting their studies at the rustle of
Lady Blanche's silk flounces, and Thorwaldsen's
'Byron' seemed to glance with Juanesque admiration at the superb eye of the Trefusis, as she
lifted them to that statue; which does, indeed, as
the poet himself averred, make a shocking nigger
of him.

'How strange it seems to me,' said De Vigne,
as, entering King's Chapel, we brushed against
one of the senior Fellows, who had dozed away in
college chambers all the prime of his life—' how
incomprehensible, that men can pass a whole
existence, in the sort of chrysalis state of which
one sees so much in Universities. That muff is
a Kingsman; he obtained his fellowship by right,

his degree without distinction. He lives on, fud-
dling his brains—which he has never worked since
he got his Eton captaincy—with port, and playing
solemn rubbers, and eating heavy dinners, till a
living falls as fat as his avarice desires. He has
no thoughts, no ambition, no sphere beyond the
academic pale.'

' And no love, I dare say, save audit, and no mistress save turtle-soup,' laughed Flora L'Estrange.

'Perhaps he had once, one whom the selfish
creeds of the Fellowship system parted from him
long ago,' said Curly, with a tender glance at that
very practical-minded flirt, Julia St. Croix.

' That's right, Curly,' said De Vigne, amusedly,
' make a romance of it. Fellows of colleges, with
snuff and whist, and dry routine, are such appro-
priate subjects for sentiment ! But after all, Miss
Trefusis, that man is not a greater marvel to me
than one of those classical scholars, who is nothing
but a classical scholar, such as one meets here and
in Oxford, binding down his ambitions to the
elucidation of a dead tongue, exhausting his
energies in the evolving of decayed philosophies,
spending, as Pelham says, " one long school-day
of lexicons and grammars," his memory the charnel-
house for the bones of a lifeless language, his brain
enacting the mechanical *rôle* of a dictionary or an

encyclopædia, living all his life without human aspirations or human sympathies, and in his death leaving no void among men, not missed even by a dog.'

' It would not suit you?' asked the Trefusis, smiling.

' No, no,' chuckled the old Fantyre to herself, ' he'll have his pleasure, I take it, cost him what it may.'

' *I!*' echoed De Vigne, ' chained down to the limits of a commentator's studies ; or a Hellenist's labours ! Heaven forbid ! I love excitement, action, change ; a mill-wheel monotony would be the death of me. I would rather have storms to encounter, than no movement to keep me alive.'

' Are you so changeable, then?'

' Well, yes !—I fancy I am. At least, I never met anything that could chain me long as yet.'

He laughed as he spoke, leaning against one of the stalls, the sun streaming through the rich stained glass full upon his face, and his dark lustrous eyes, gleaming with amusement, at a thousand reminiscences evoked by her speech. The Trefusis looked at him with a curious smile, perhaps of longing to chain the restless and wayward spirit, perhaps of pique at his careless words, perhaps of resolve to conquer and to win him ; it

might have been hate, but—it certainly was not
love! Still Flora L'Estrange whispered to her
husband :

'Miss Trefusis will marry De Vigne if she
can ?'

L'Estrange laughed, and looked at Granville
and his companion, as they were (in appearance)
discussing the subjects of the storied windows of
Holy Henry's chapel, but talking, I fancy, of other
topics than sacred art or history.

'Quite right, my pet, but I hope she *won't*. I
would as soon see him marry a tigress!'

Tired of lionizing, we soon returned to Curly's
rooms, where the best luncheon which could be had
out of Cambridge shops, and Trinity buttery, with
London wine, and game from his governor's preserves, was ready for us. Curly never did anything without doing it well, and his rooms were,
I think, the most luxurious in all Granta, with his
grand piano, his bronzes, and his landscapes, mixed
up with tobacco-pots, boxing-gloves, pipes, and
portraits of ballet pets, and heroes of the Turf and
the P. R. The luncheon was as merry as it was
lavish—what college meal, with fast, pretty women
at the board, ever was not?—and while the Badminton and Champagne-cup went round, and the
gyps waited as solemnly and dreadfully as gyps

ever do, on like occasions, a cross-fire of wit and
fun and nonsense, shot across the table, and mingled
with the perfume of Curly's hothouse bouquets,
enough to bring the stones of time-honoured
Trinity about our irreverent heads. De Vigne, in
very high spirits, laughed and talked with all the
brilliance for which society had distinguished him;
Flora and Lady Blanche were always full of mischievous repartee; Curly and Julia St. Croix
flirted so desperately, that if it had not been for
the publicity of the scene, I believe the boy would
have gone straight away into a proposal. Lady
Fantyre, especially, when the claret cup had gone
round freely, was so amusing that we forgot she
was old, and the Trefusis, if she did not contribute
equally to the conversation, sat beside De Vigne,
darting glances at him from her large Spanish
eyes, and looking handsome enough to be inspiration to anybody.

'So you leave Cambridge to-morrow?' she said,
as they were waiting for the St. Croix carriage
to take them home again.

'Yes. If *you* were going to remain I should
stay too; but Mrs. St. Croix tells me you leave
on Monday,' said De Vigne, in a low tone, with
an admiring glance, to which few women would
have been insensible.

She looked at him with that cold, malicious smile, which, had I been he, would have made me very careful of that woman.

' It is easy to say that, when, as I *am* going on Monday, I cannot put you to the test! '

De Vigne's eyes flashed; he threw back his head, coldly and haughtily.

' I never trouble myself to say what I do not mean, Miss Trefusis.'

She laughed; she had found she had power to pique him !

' Then will you come and see me in town after Christmas ?'

What he answered I know not, but I dare say it was in the affirmative; he would hardly have refused anything to such a glance as she gave him. He lingered beside their carriage, and when it rolled away, stood in the Trinity gateway with a smile on his lips, twisting in his fingers a white azalea she had given him. But, two hours after, the flower was thrown into the college grate, and the bedmaker swept it out with the cinders ! So he was not very far gone as yet. The next morning, after we had ' done chapel,' De Vigne, who had sent on his groom, hunters, and luggage the day before, walked down to the station, and we with him.

'I wish you two fellows were coming to Vigne with me,' he said, as we went along. 'You don't know what a bore it is having a place like that! So much is expected of one. You belong to the county, and the county makes you feel the relationship pretty keenly, too. You must fill the house in .the Recesses. You must hear horrible long speeches from your tenantry, wishing you health and happiness, while you're wishing them at the devil. You must have confounded interviews with your steward, who looks frightfully glum at the pot of money that has been dropped over the Goodwood, and hints at the advisability of cutting down the very clump of oaks that makes the beauty of the drawing-room view. Then, worst of all, you're expected to hunt your own county, even though it be as unfit as the Wash or the Black Forest, while you're longing to be with the Burton or Tedworth, following Tom Smith, or Tom Edge, or Pytchley men, who don't funk at every bullfinch!'

'Do you hunt the Vigne pack, then, always?' asked Curly.

'I? No. I never said I *did* all those things. I only said they are expected of me, and it's tiresome to say no.'

'Then you must make love to the Trefusis, if

you dont't like "No," for her eyes say, "Do do
it," as clearly as eyes can speak.'

He laughed. 'Yes. I must admit she doesn't
look a very impregnable citadel.'

'Not if you make it worth her while to surrender?'

'None of them surrender for nothing,' said De
Vigne, smiling. 'With some, it's cashmeres;
with others, yellow-boys; with some, it's position;
with others, a wedding-ring. I can't see much
difference myself, though I'd give cashmeres in
plenty, and should be remarkably sorry to be
chiselled into settlements.'

'I should fancy so,' said Curly; 'only think of
the annihilation of larks, liberty, fun, claret, latch-
keys, oyster suppers, guinguettes, and Cafés Ré-
gence, expressed in those two doomed words, "a
married man!" To my mind, marrying's as bad
as hanging, and equally puts a finish to all life
worth supporting!'

'Did you tell Julia your views, Curly?' asked
De Vigne, quietly.

'Pooh! stuff! What's Julia to do with me?
the girl at the Cherryhinton public, is a vast lot
better-looking,' muttered Curly, with an embar-
rassment that made me doubt if the limes of
Trinity had not heard different opinions enunciated

with regard to the Holy Bond.—*N.B.* Julia St. Croix that day three months, tied herself to that same snuffy, portly, wine-embalmed Fellow, she had laughed at with us, in King's Chapel. To be sure he had then become rector of Snooze-cum-Rest; and when Ruth goes to woo Boaz, we may always be pretty certain she knows he is master of the harvest, and has the golden wheat-ears in her eye, sweet innocent little dear though she look.

'The Cherryhinton public! I see—that's why skittles and beer have become suddenly delightful,' laughed De Vigne.

'Why not?' asked Curly, meekly. 'Skittles are no sin, and malt and hops are man's natural aliment; and as for barmaids! why, if one's denied houris and nectar, one must take to Jane and bitter beer, *n'est-ce pas?*'

'Don't know,' said De Vigne. 'I prefer Quartier Bréda and Champagne. As Balzac says, "*Une femme, belle comme Galatée ou Hélène, ne pourrait me plaire tant soit peu qu'elle soit crottée!*"'

'You forgot that once—you didn't repudiate Lucy Davis?

'Lucy was half a lady, in dress at least,' laughed De Vigne, 'and she got up uncommonly well, too; however, that was in my schoolboy days. After vulguses and problems a kitchen-maid is

pardonable; and as for the young woman who
presides over the post-office, or the oyster patties,
she is perfectly irresistible! The *laissez-aller* of
the Paphian Temple, as the fine writers say, is so
delightful after the stiff stoicism of the Porch!'

'Well, thank Heaven, the Paphian Temple is
built everywhere,' said Curly, 'and you find it
under the taps of XXX, as well as in the gilt walls
of a Bréda boudoir; or the poor wretches who
haven't the Bréda gold key, would get locked into
very outer darkness indeed! Here's the train just
starting. By Jove, that's lucky! All right, old
fellow. Here's Puck; tumble in, old boy.'

And the 'old boy' being 'tumbled in' (he was
a wiry blue terrier), De Vigne seated himself, and
was rolled off en route to Vigne with a pretty
brunette opposite him, who seemed imbued with
extreme admiration of the terrier or—his master.
Girls always begin by calling his children 'little
loves' to a widower, though the brats be as ugly
as sin; and by admiring his dog to a bachelor,
though frightened to death it should snap at them!

Curly and I saw the train off and walked back
to Granta, to console ourselves, first with billiards
and beer at Brown's, then with some hard practice
on the river.

Eheu! fugaces! . . . . . . I belong to the Blue

Jersey B.C., the first in England; but somehow I don't feel the zest now that I used to feel, with 'Time, Five!' 'Well pulled Five!' in my ear from our Stroke (poor fellow! he went down with jungle-fever, and is lying in the banyan shadows, in Ceylon sand) and the shrill imperous shrieking, as the speed and bottom of Oxford told against us, of that wicked little dog Hervey, our Coxswain (*he's* a bishop now, and hush-hushes you, and strokes his apron, if you whisper the smallest crumb of fun over his capital comet wine). Dear old Cambridge! I wouldn't give a straw for a Cambridge man who didn't grow prolix as he talked, or wrote of her, and didn't empty a bumper of Guinness's or Moët—as his taste may lie—in her honour. A man may read, or he may not read, at college. I prefer the boy who knows how to feather his oar, to one who only knows Latin quantities and Greek unities; but at any rate, whether he get first classes or not, he will find his level, measure his weight, and learn—unless he be obtuse indeed—that through college life, as through all other life, the best watchwords are —Pluck, and Honour!

I learnt that much at least, and it is no mean lesson, though I must admit that, after having had my cross taken away, been gated times innumerable, having done all the books of Virgil by way

of penance (paying little Crib, my wine-merchant's
son, to write them out for me), and been shown
up before the proctor on no less than six separate
occasions, I got rusticated in my fourth term, and
finally took my name off the books. The governor
laughed, preferred the Pewter I had to show, and
my share in winning the Challenge Cup, to any
Bell's or Craven's scholarships, and paid my debts
without a murmur. Too good to be true, you will
say, *ami lecteur?*   No ; there *are* fathers who can
remember they have been young ; though they are
unspeakably rare—as rare as ladies who can let you
forget it !

Now came the question, what should I do?
'Nothing,' the correct thing, according to the
governor. 'Stand for the county,' my mother
suggested. 'Go as attaché to my cousin, the
envoy to St. Petersburg,' my relatives opined,
who had triumphed, with much unholy glory, over
my rustication, as is the custom of relatives from
time immemorial. As it chanced, I had no fancy
for either utter *dolce*, the bray of St. Stephen's or
the snows of Russia, so I put down my name for
a commission. We had plenty of interest to push
it, and the 'Gazette' soon announced, '—th P. O.
Lancers, Arthur Vane Tierney Chevasney, to be
Cornet, *vice* James Yelverton, promoted ;' and the

—th, always known in the service as the Dashers,
was De Vigne's regiment, my old Frestonhills hero.
The Dashers were then quartered at Kensington
and Hounslow, and the first person I saw as I drove
through Knightsbridge was De Vigne's groom,
Harris, riding a powerful thorough-bred, swathed in
body-clothing, whom I recognized as the bay of the
Euston Hollows run. As soon as my interview
with the Adjutant and the Colonel were over, I
found out De Vigne's rooms speedily. He had
the drawing-room floor of a house in Kensington
Gore, well furnished, and further crowded with
crowds of things of his own, from Persian carpets
bought in his travels, to the last new rifle sent
home only the day before. I made my way up
unannounced, and stood a minute or two in the
open doorway. They were pleasant rooms, just
as a man likes to have them, with all the things
he wants about him, ready to his hand; no madame
to make him miserable by putting his pipes away
out of sight, and no housekeeper to drive him
distracted by sorting his papers, and introducing
order among his pet lumber. A setter, a retriever,
and a couple of Skyes, were on the hearth-rug
(veritable tiger-skin); breakfast, in dainty Sèvres,
and silver, stood on one table, sending up an
aroma of coffee, omelettes, and devils; the morn-

ing papers lay on the floor, a smoking-cap was
hung on a Parian Venus; a parrot, who apparently considered himself master of the place, was
perched irreverently on a bronze Milton, and
pipes, whips, pistols, and cards, were thrown down
on a Louis Quinze couch, that Louise de Kéroualle
or Sophie Arnould might have graced.   From the
inner room came the rapid clash of small-swords,
while "*Touche, touche, touche! riposte! hola!*" was
shouted, in a silvery voice, from a man who, lying
back in a rocking-chair in the bay-window of the
front room, was looking on at a bout with the foils
that was taking place beyond the folding-doors.
The two men who were fencing were De Vigne
and a smaller, slighter fellow; the one calm, cool,
steady, and never at a disadvantage, the other,
skilful indeed, but too hot, eager, and rapid : for in
fencing, whether with the foils or the tongue, the
grand secret is to be cool, since, in proportion to
your tranquillity, grows your opponent's exaspera-
tion!` The man in the bay-window was too deeply
interested to observe me, so I waited patiently
till De Vigne had sent his adversary's foil flying
from his hand.

He turned with one of his sunny smiles : ' Ah !
dear old fellow, how are you ? Charmed to see you.
This is the best move you ever made, Arthur.   Mr.

Chevasney, Colonel Sabretasche, M. de Cheffontaine, a trio of my best friends. We only want
Curly to make the *partie carrée* perfect. Sit
down, old boy; we have just breakfasted, I am
sorry to say, but here are the things, and all the
sardines, and you shall soon have some hot choco-
late, and côtelettes.'

While he talked he forced me into an arm-
chair, and disregarding all my protests that I had
already breakfasted twice—once at Longholme
and once at a station—rang for his man. De
Cheffontaine flung himself on a sofa, and began
with a *mot* on his own defeat; the fellow in the
bay-window got lazily out of his rocking-chair
and strolled over to us. De Vigne took his meer-
schaum, and we were soon talking away as hard as
we could go, of the belles of that season, the pets
of the ballet, Richmond, the Spring Meetings, the
best sales in the Yard, the last matches at Lord's,
the chances of Heliotrope's being scratched, the
certainty that Vane Stevens's roan filly would
lose the trotting-match, with other like topics of
the Town and the Hour. Sabretasche was, I
found, a Brevet Lieutenant-Colonel, and Major of
the Dashers, and a most agreeable man he seemed,
lying back in his chair, making us laugh at witti-
cisms which he spoke, quietly and indolently, in a

soft, low, mellow voice. Had I been a woman
that beautiful face would have done for me irretrievably, as, according to report, it had done for
a good many. Beautiful it was; with its pallid,
aristocratic features, its large mournful eyes, its
silky moustaches, and rich wavy hair. Reckless
devil-may-care, the man looked, the recklessness of
one who heeds nothing in heaven or earth; a little
hardened by the world and its rubs, rendered
cynical, perhaps, by injustice and wrong; but in
the eyes there lay a kindness, and in the mouth a
sadness which betokened better things. He might
have been thirty, five-and-thirty, forty. One could
no more tell his age than his character, though,
looking at him, one could fancy it true what the
world said of him—that no man ever found 'so
faithful a friend, and no woman so faithless a
lover, as in Vivian Sabretasche.

'Chevasney, who do you think is one of the
reigning beauties up here?' asked De Vigne,
pushing me some cubas.

'How should I know? The Cherryhinton bar-
maid?'

'Don't be a fool.'

'The Trefusis, then?'

'Of course. She is still living with that abominable old Irish woman. They're in Bruton Street;

—a pleasant house, only everybody wonders
where the Peeress finds the needful. They give
uncommonly agreeable receptions. Don't they,
Sabretasche?'

'Oh, very!' answered the Colonel, with an
enigmatical smile, 'especially to you, I've no
doubt; and the only tax levied on one for the
entertainment is to pay a few compliments to
mademoiselle, and a few guinea points to my lady.
I can't say all the guests are the best ton; there
are too many ladies designated by the definite
article, and too many gentlemen with cordons in
their button-holes; but they know how to amuse
one another, and the women, if not exclusive, are
at least remarkably pretty. The Trefusis is more
than pretty, especially smoking a cigarette. Shall
you allow her cigars when you're married to her,
De Vigne?'

'Not *when* I am.'

'There's an unjust fellow! How like a man
that is!' cried Sabretasche. 'What's charming
in any other woman becomes horrid in his wife.
You remind me of Jessie Villars: when her husband smokes, she vows the scent will kill her;
when Wyndham meets her on the terrace, taking
his good-night pipe, she lisps there's nothing so
delightful as the scent of Latakia! Come, Mr.

Chevasney, I don't mind prying into my friends'
affairs before their faces. Have not De Vigne
and the Trefusis had some nice little flirtation
before now ? '

' To be sure,' I answered. ' It began to be
rather a desperate affair ; the Trinity backs could
tell you many a tale, I dare say. He came down
for Diana, and forsook her for Venus.'

' But you can't say, old fellow, I ever deserted
the Quiver for the Ceinture,' cried De Vigne.
' The Viewaway was never eclipsed by the Trefusis ! '

' I don't know that. Have you taken up the
affair where you left it ? '

' I never reveal secrets that ladies share,' said
De Vigne, with a demure air, ' but I'll be very
generous, Arthur. I'll take you to call on
her.'

' *Bien obligé.* What do you think of this
beauty, M. de Cheffontaine ? ' I asked of the
lively little Baron.

' Oh ! ' laughed he, ' all your English women are
superb, divine, when they are not prudes ! '

' And that is a fault you cannot pardon ? ' asked
Sabretasche, with his low silvery laugh.

' Nor you ! but one cannot reproach the Trefusis with it ! '

Sabretasche laughed again, and quoted

'Non, jamais tourterelle
N'aima plus tendrement.
Comme elle était fidèle
A—son dernier amant !'

De Vigne did not appear best pleased ; he lifted
his head to look out of the window into the park,
and as he looked his annoyance seemed to increase.
I followed his glance, and saw the Trefusis on a
very showy bay, of not first-rate action, taking
her morning canter.

' Ah, talk of an angel, you know !—there she
is,'. said Sabretasche. ' Wise woman to show
often *en amazone*; it suits her better than anything. She has met little Jimmy Levison, and
taken him on with her. Poor Jimmy ! between
her smiles and old Fantyre's honours he won't
come off the better for those Bruton-street *soirées*.
Why, De Vigne, you look quite wrathful ! You
wouldn't be jealous of little Jimmy, would
you ?'

I don't suppose De Vigne was jealous of little
Jimmy; but I dare say he was not flattered to see
the same wiles given to trap that very young
pigeon, which were bestowed to lure a fiery hawk
like himself.

' It amuses me to see all those women taking

their morning rides,' Sabretasche continued.
' They love their darling horses so! and they do
so delight in the morning air; and the green trees
look so pleasant after the dusty *pavé!* and they
never hint that they know the Knightsbridge men
will be looking out for them, and that Charlie will
be accidentally lounging by the rails, and Johnnie
be found reading the " Morning Post" under
the large avenue. The Trefusis will tell us that
she cannot exist without her morning trot on
" dear Diamond," but, *sans doute,* she remembered
that De Vigne would be pretty sure to be break-
fasting by this window, not to mention that she
had whispered to little Jimmy her wish to see his
new grey hack. I always look *under* women's
words as I look under their veils; they mean
them to embellish, but I don't choose they should
hide.'

' How do you act, Colonel,' laughed De Vigne,
' when you come to a Shetland veil tied down
very tight?'

'I never yet met one that hadn't some holes!'
said Sabretasche. ' No women are long a puzzle;
they are too inconsistent, and betray their artifices by overdoing them. She is out of sight now,
De Vigne. Would you like your horse ordered?'

De Vigne laughed.

'Thank you, no. Do you go to the new opera to-night, Sabretasche?'

' Yes; though I should go with infinitely more pleasure, if I could get the glories of Gluck, and Mozart, instead of the sing-song ballads of Verdi and Balfe.'

' Music is the god of his idolatry!' said De Vigne, turning to me. ' It is positively a passion! Your heaven will be composed of sweet sounds, eh, Sabretasche?'

'As yours of houris and of thorough-breds?'

' Perhaps! I should combine Mahomet's and the Indian's ideas into one—almond eyes and a good hunting-ground! Look here, Arthur, at this "Challenge." That man yonder did it. Isn't he a clever fellow—too good to lie still in a rocking chair, and talk about women?'

I looked at the ' Challenge '—a little marble statuette from Landseer's picture; and product of the Colonel's chisel. It was really a wonderful little thing; every minutia, even each fine point of the delicate antlers, being most beautifully and perfectly finished.

' How immensely jolly to have such talent!' said I, involuntarily expressing my honest admiration. ' What a resource it must be—what a refuge when other things pall!'

He smiled at my enthusiasm, and raised his eyebrows.

' *Cui bono?* ' he said softly, as he rose and pushed back his chair.

The man interested me; and when he and the Baron were gone, I asked De Vigne what he knew of him, as we stood waiting for his tilbury, to go and call in Bruton Street.

' Of Vivian Sabretasche ? I know much of him socially, little of himself; and of his history—if history he have—nothing. He is excessively kind to me ; honourable and generous in all his dealings ; a gentleman always. More of him I know not, nor, were we acquainted ten years, should I at the end, I dare say, know more.'

' Why ? '

' Why ? For this reason—that nobody does. Hollingsworth and he were cornets together; yet Hollingsworth is as much a stranger to the real man as you or I. There are some fellows, you know, who don't wear their hearts on their sleeves ; he is one, I am another. Men are like snowballs: to begin with, it's a piece of snow, soft and pure and malleable, and easily enough melted ; but the snowball soon gets kicked about and mixed up with other snow, and knocked against stones and angles, and hurried, and shoved, and pushed along

till, in sheer self-defence, it hardens itself into a
solid, impenetrable, immovable block of ice!'

'Nonsense? *You* are not that.'

' Not yet, thank God!'

I should say he was not! The passionate blood
of six-and-twenty, was more likely to be at boiling-
point, than at zero.

CHAPTER IV.

A SUBTLE POISON DRUNK IN THE CHAMPAGNE AT AN OPERA SUPPER.

VERY good style was the Bruton Street house, and
very good style the Trefusis, with the rose light
falling on her from the window, where she was
surrounded by plants, and birds in cages and on
stands, with a little fellow of the Guards, and a
courtly French exile, lounging away their morning
there. She was dressed in the extreme of fashion
—almost too well, if ladies will admit such a
thing to be possible. She always reminded
me of some first-rate actresses at the Fran-
çais or the Bouffes playing the *rôles* of high-bred
women, looking and speaking like ladies of the
best society; and yet whom, do what one will, and
be they as graceful as they may, one cannot divest
of a certain aroma, due rather to the proximity
of the proscenium and foot-lights, than to any
fault of breeding in themselves; yet a something
which we know we should not discover in the

true Marquises and Baronnes of the Fau-
bourg.

She looked up with a smile of conscious power,
gave her hand tenderly to De Vigne, with a full
sweep of her superb eyes under their thick fringes;
bent her head to me, and put her Pomeranian dog
on his knee. Old Lady Fantyre was there playing propriety, if Propriety could ever be persuaded
to let herself be represented by that hook-nosed,
disreputable, detestable, amusing old woman, who
sat working away at the tapestry-frame, with her
gold spectacles on, occasionally lifting up her little
keen brown eyes and mingling in the conversation,
telling the old tales of '*ma jeunesse*,' of the Bath
and the Wells, of Ombre and Quadrille, Sheridan and Selwyn, Talleyrand and Burke, 'old Q.'
and Lady Coventry.

'I remember you at Cambridge, Mr. Chevasney,
and our merry luncheon too,' said the Trefusis,
as if Cambridge belonged to some dim era of her
childhood, which it was astonishing she could
recall at all.

'What! my dear,' burst in Lady Fantyre, 'you
don't mean to say you remember all your acquaintances, do you? If so, ye'll have enough to do.'

'Certainly not. But when they are as agreeable as Mr. Chevasney—'

' Of course—of course. *Les présents ont toujours raison,*' continued the Viscountess, in her lively treble, 'as true, by the way, that is, as its twin maxim, *Les absents ont toujours tort ;* it would be hard, indeed, if we might not tell tales of our friends when they couldn't hear us! But I know *we* used to give cuts by the dozen. I remember walking down the Birdcage Walk with Selwyn, (poor dear Selwyn, there isn't his like in this day; I remember him so well, though I was but a little chit then !) and a man, a very personable man, too —but Lord! my dear, not one of us—came up and reminded George he had known him in Bath. What do you think Selwyn did, my dear? Why, stared him in the face, of course, and said, " Well, sir, in Bath I may possibly know you again." '

'That beats Brummel, when a lady apologized for keeping him so long standing by her carriage : " My dear lady, there is no one to see it! " ' said De Vigne, laughing.

' Abominable !' cried the Trefusis. ' If I had been that woman, I would have told him I had made sure of that, or I would not have hazarded my reputation by speaking to him !'

' Brummel would have been very willing to have been seen with *you,*' said De Vigne, fixing his eyes on her, and he knew pretty well how to make his eyes talk.

'There's not one of you men now-a-days like Selwyn,' began the old *raconteuse* again, while the Trefusis bent her stately head to her boy Guardsman, and De Vigue balanced his cane thoughtfully on the Pomeranian's nose. 'You talk of your great wit Lord John Bonmot, why, he hasn't as much wit in his whole body as there was in poor dear George's little finger! Ah! there isn't one half the *verve* among you new people there was in my young time. Where is the man among you, who can make laughter run down the table as my friend Sheridan could? Which of you can move heads, and hearts, like Billy Pitt? Where among those idle lads in the Temple, who smoke Cavendish, and drink Bass, till they *think* nothing better than tobacco and beer, shall I see another Tom Erskine? Which among those brainless scribblers who print poems, that make one want a Tennyson's Dictionary only to understand the foolish adjectives in 'em, can write like that boy Byron, with his handsome face and his wry foot? Lord! and what a fuss there was with him when he was first made a lion! And then to turn his coffin from the Abbey! Such comic verses as he made on my parrot too, he and young Hobhouse!'

And old Fantyre, having fairly talked herself
out of breath, at last halted ; and De Vigne, annoyed first of all with little Jimmy in the morning, and secondly with the attention the Trefusis
gave her Cornet, neglected her for the Viscountess, with much parade thereof.

'I fear you are right, madam,' he said, laughing.
'Ours is an age of general action rather than
individual greatness.   We have a good catalogue
of ships, but no Ulysses, no Atrides, no Agamem-
non—'

'Ah! I don't remember them; they weren't in
our set!' responded Lady Fantyre, naively.

'Or perhaps,' continued De Vigne, stroking his
moustaches with laudable gravity, 'it is rather
that education is diffused so much more widely
that the particular owners of it are not so much
noticed.   Arago may be as great a man as Galileo,
but it is natural that a world which teaches the
laws of gravitation in its twopenny schools,
scarcely regards him with the same wonder
as if they disbelieved in the earth's movement, and were ready to burn him for his
audacity.'

'Ours is an age of science and of money,'
suggested the Frenchman, 'whose chief aim is to
economize labour and time; an age in which

everything is turned to full account, from dead seaweed, to living brains.'

'Yes,' said De Vigne, 'we are eminently practical; we extract the veratrin from crocuses, and value Brunel more than Bulwer! We throw our millions into a scheme for cutting through an isthmus, but we should not spare our minutes to listen to the music of the spheres though Pythagoras were resuscitated to teach us them. So best! Many more of us find it, of much greater importance to get quickly to India, than to wait for all the learning of the schools; and Adam Smith, though infinitely more prosaic, is a much more useful philosopher than Bolingbroke.'

'Captain de Vigne, why don't you stand for your county?' asked the Trefusis, playing with her breloques, and looking truly magnificent in her rose-velvet setting.

'Because I'm before my time,' laughed De Vigne. 'If I could have a select Cabinet of *esprits forts* I should be delighted to join them, and help them to seminate liberty and tolerance; but really to settle Maynooth grants, to quarrel on "rags or no rags," to settle whether we shall confine ourselves to "corks squared for rounding" or admit rounded corks into the country, to hear one noble lord blackguard his noble friend opposite, and one

hon. member split hairs with another hon. member
—it would be beyond me, it would indeed! I
would as soon go every night to an old ladies' tea-
fight, where bonnets were rancorously discussed
and characters mercilessly blackened over Sou-
chong and muffins!'

'Come!' said the Trefusis, 'you find such fault
with your generation, you should set to work and
regenerate it? Hunting with the Viewaway, and
lounging about drawing-rooms, won't do much
towards improving your species?'

'Why should I? As Sabretasche says, "*Cui
bono?*"' answered De Vigne, annoyed at her sar-
castic and *nonchalant* tone.

'Then you have certainly no business to sit at
home at ease and laugh at other men over your
claret and Cubas! Why may not other geniuses
have equal right to that easy put off of yours,
"*Cui bono?*"'

'They have not equal right, if they have once assumed to be geniuses. Let a man assert himself to
be *something*, be it a great man or a scoundrel, and
the world expects him to prove his assertion. But
an innocent man like myself, who troubles nobody;
and never sets up for a mute inglorious Milton,
declining to sing, only because his audience isn't
good enough for him; has a right to be left to his

claret and Cubas, and not to be worried, because it happens he is not, what he never pretended to be.'

The Trefusis looked at him maliciously; there was the very devil in that woman's eye.

'And are you content to be lost in the bouquet of the wine, and buried in the smoke of the tobacco? Are you satisfied with spending your noble existence in an allegorical chaise-lounge, picking out the motes and never remembering the beam?'

The tone was provoking in the extreme; it put up De Vigne's blood, as the first touch of the snaffle does a young thorough-bred. He stroked his long moustaches.

'That depends upon circumstances. When I have had my full swing of devilries, extravagances, dissipations, pleasures, Trefusises, and other charming flowers which beset the path of youth, I may, perhaps, turn to something better!'

It was an abominably rude speech; and though De Vigne spoke in the soft, courteous tone he used to all women, whether peeress or peasant, eighty or eighteen, it had its full effect on the Trefusis. She flushed deeply, then turned pale, and I should not have cared to provoke the malignant glance those superb eyes shot upon him. She

took no notice, however, and, turning to her
Guardsman, thanked him for a bouquet which
he had sent to her, and pointed it out to him,
set on a console near.

De Vigne drove the tilbury from the door
supremely gloomy and silent :

'I say, Arthur,' he said at last, 'Victor Hugo
says, somewhere, that we are women's playthings,
and women are the devil's. I fancy Satan will
get the worse of the bargain, don't you ?'

'The deuce I do!—that's to say, if the war's in
words ; though I must say you polished off the
Trefusis neatly enough just now. Did you see
the look she gave you ?'

'Yes,' said De Vigne, shortly. 'However—anything's better than a milk-and-water woman. I
should grow sick of a girl who always agreed with
me. They look so pretty when their blood's up!
Where shall we go now ? Suppose we turn into
the Yard, and take a look at those steel greys
Sabretasche mentioned ? I want a new pair to
run tandem. And then we can take a turn or
two round the Ring, and I'll show you the women
worth cultivating, young one.'

We followed out his programme, bargained for
the greys at two hundred and fifty—and immensely
cheap, too, for they were three-parts thorough-

bred, with beautiful action—drove half-a-dozen
times round the Ring, where fifty pair of bright
eyes gleamed softly on De Vigne, from the Marchioness of Hautton in her stately barouche, to
little Coralie of Her Majesty's ballet in her single
horse brougham; and then went to mess, where,
the Dashers (being as crack a corps as the Tenth,
the Eleventh, or the Blues,) had a peculiar pattern
for their plate, a *Cordon bleu* for their cook, and
a good claret connoisseur in their Colonel. The
claret was better than Cambridge port, the dinner
was rather superior to Hall, and the men furnished
wit choicer than Monckton's Joe Miller jokes, and
Phil Hervey's Simon the Cellarer, at our Wines.
I liked this dash of my new life at any rate,
and I regretted leaving the table when Sabretasche
invited me to go with him, to the Opera, for I
didn't care two pins for music; I did not dare,
however, to refuse the first favour from such an
exclusive man, and, besides, having just seen little
Coralie in the Ring, I consoled myself with the
thought of the ballet. De Vigne was going too,
for reasons best known to himself; and went to
his stall, while I followed the Colonel to his box,
in the middle of the second act.

Sabretasche spoke not at all while Grisi was on
the stage, and I put my lorgnon up and took a

glance round the house. I always think Her Majesty's, on a grand night, with all the boxes filled with the handsomest and best-dressed women in town, one of the prettiest sights going; and I did the grand tier deliberately, going from loge to loge, so that it was some little time before I got on the second; and in one of its centre boxes, with the scarlet folds of an opera cloak floating round her, and scarlet camellias against her white lace dress, and in her rich dark hair, sat the Trefusis, with little bright-eyed, hooked-nosed, bewigged, and black Mechlin'd, old Fantyre as a foil.

Presently the Trefusis raised her bouquet to her lips quite carelessly, to take its perfume, I presume! I happened to look down at De Vigne: his lorgnon was fixed on her too. He smiled, left his stall, and in a minute or two I saw him displacing young Lascelles of the Blues and bending down over the Trefusis.

'What do you think of that affair, Chevasney?' said the Colonel to me, as the curtain came down.

'I don't know how it stands. Enlighten me, will you?'

Sabretasche shook his head.

'I know no more than yourself. De Vigne, like all wise men, is silent upon his own business, and I never attempt to pry into it. I see the

thing on its surface, and it seems to me that the
lady is serious, whatever he be.'

'Serious?   Oh, hang it ! he can't be serious.'

' *Tant pis pour lui* if he be,' said the Colonel,
smiling.   'But, my dear boy, you do not know
women as yet ; how should you, in two-and-
twenty years, have read that enigmatical book,
which is harder to guess at than Sanscrit or Black
letter?   You can never fathom the deep game
that a clever one like the Trefusis, if I mistake
her not, can play when she chooses.'

I, the most knowing hand in Granta—I, who if
I did pique myself on any one thing, piqued myself on my skill and knowledge in managing the
beau sexe—*I*, to be told I did not know women !
I pocketed the affront, however, as best I might,
for I felt a growing respect for the Colonel, with
his myriad talents, his brilliant reputation, and
mysterious reserve ; and told him I did not believe
De Vigne cared an atom more for the Trefusis
than for twenty others before her.

'I hope so,' he answered ; 'but that chess they
are playing yonder ends too often in checkmate.
However, we will not prophesy so bad a fate for
our friend ; for worse he could not have than to fall
into those soft hands.   By the way, though, her
hands are *not* soft, they are not the hands of a lady.'

'You have a bad opinion of the Trefusis, Colonel?'

'Not of the Trefusis in particular.'

'Of her sex, then?'

'I may have cause,' he answered briefly. 'How full the house is, and how few of those people come for music! How few of them would care if it were dance trash of D'Albert's, instead of Donizetti's symphonies, if the dance-music chanced to be most in fashion. Make it the rage, and three-quarters of the music lovers here would run after a barrel-organ ground on that stage, as they are now doing after Mario. Half England, if the Court, the Peerage, and Belgravia voted the sun a bore, and a rushlight *comme il faut*, would instantly shut their shutters and burn rushlights while the fashion lasted! And then people care for the world's opinion!'

'Because they can't get on without it.'

'True enough!—they despise it, but they must bow to it before they can use it and turn it to their own ends; those must, at least, who live by sufferance on it, and through it. Thank God, I want nothing from it, and can defy it at my leisure; or rather forget and neglect it; defying is too much trouble. A man who *defies* is certain to raise a hue and cry at his heels, whose bray and clamour is as senseless as it is deafening, and no more able to declare what it has come out after than Dogberry. Ah, you are studying that girl in the fifth from the centre. That is little Eulalie Papillon. Does she not look a pretty, innocent dove? Yet she will cost those three fellows with her more than a racing stud, and she is as avaricious as Harpagon! I should like to make a computation of how many of these people come for music. That old man there, who droops his head and takes snuff during the entr'actes; those fellows on the ground-tier taking shorthand notes for the daily journals; one or two dilettante ladies who really know something of fugues and symphonies: those are all, I verily believe. Little Eulalie comes to show herself, and carry Bevan off to her *petit souper*, for fear any fairer Lais should pounce on him; those *decolletées* and diamondized old ladies come because it is one of the Yards where their young fillies tell best, and may chance to get a bid. Lady Ormolu there, that one with marabouts in her hair, comes because her lord is a Georges Dandin, and she has no chance of meeting Villiers, who is her present lover, anywhere else. Mrs. Lacquers is here because there was a rumour that her husband's Bank would not stand, and he, who

is a Bible Society president and vessel of grace,
but who still keeps one eye open on terrestrial
affairs, has told her to exhibit here to-night, and
be as lively as possible, with plenty of rubies about
her, so that he may get off to Boulogne. Dear
man ! he remembers "*Aide-toi et Dieu t'aidera*." '

'Have you a private Belphégor in your pocket,
sir ? ' said I, dropping my lorgnon, 'to help you
unroof the houses and unlock your acquaintances'
brains ? '

'My Belphégor is Experience,' laughed Sabretasche. 'And now hush, if you please, Chevasney ; there is Grisi again, and as *I* come for
music, though nobody else may, I like to be
quiet.'

It was curious to note the change that came
over his melancholy expressive countenance, as he
listened to the prima donna, and I saw the gaze of
many women fixed upon him, as, with his eyes
half-closed, and his thoughts far away, he leaned
against the side of his box. They said he was
dangerous to women, and one could hardly wonder if he were. A gallant soldier in the field ; a
charming companion in club or mess-room ; accom-
plished in music, painting, sculpture, as in the
hardier arts of rifle and rod ; speaking most conti-
nental languages with equal facility ; his manners

exquisitely tender and gentle, his voice soft as the
Italian he best loved to speak, his face and form
of unusual beauty; and, to back him, all that
subtler art which is only acquired in the Eleusinia
of the boudoir, no marvel if women, his pet playthings, did go down before Vivian Sabretasche.
He had been born in Italy, where his father, having
spent what money he had at the green tables,
lived to retrench — retrenchment being always
synonymous in English minds with the Continent,
though whether a palace, even if a little tumble-
down, ortolans, lachryma-christi, and nightly
reunions, *do* tend to tighten purse-strings and
benefit cheque - books, is an open question.
Luckily for Sabretasche, his uncle, a rich old *roué*,
of the Alvanley and Pierrepoint time, went off the
stage without an heir, and he came in for all the
property, a princely balance at Barclay's, a town
house, and a moor up in Inverness-shire. On his
accession, he left the Neapolitan Hussars, entered
the Queen's, and took the position to which his
old name and new wealth entitled him. It was
always the popular idea that Sabretasche had
some history or other, though *why* he should have
nobody could probably have told you; but everybody loved him, from the charger that followed
him like a dog and ate out of his hand, to the

H 2

young cornets who, in their debts and their difficulties, always found a lenient judge and a kind
friend in gay, liberal, highly-gifted, and ultra-
fashionable Vivian Sabretasche.

When he had drunk his fill of music, and I had
clapped little Coralie to my heart's content ; an
ovation that young lady little needed, having a
hired *claque* of her own in omnibus-boxes, not to
mention some twenty men who threw her bouquets
with genuine bracelets and *bravissime*; Sabretasche and I, passing through the crush-room, or
rather the draughty, catarrh-conferring passages
which answer to that portion of Her Majesty's now-
a-days, came close to De Vigne with the Trefusis
on his arm, while little Lascelles escorted Lady
Fantyre, nowise enraptured apparently at the
charge of that shrewd old dame, with her sandal-
wood perfume, and her old lace, of a price, and dirt,
untold.   Lady Fantyre's carriage was not yet up,
and we stood and chatted together, the Trefusis
smiling very graciously on us, but reserving all
her most telling glances for De Vigne, on whose
arm she hung with a sort of proprietorship, for
which I cursed her with most unchristian earnestness.

' Come home to supper with us,' whispered the
Trefusis, as their carriage was at last announced.

De Vigne accepted the invitation with a flash of his eyes, which showed one well enough the Trefusis was beginning to play the deuce with him; and old Fantyre extended it to Sabretasche and to me. The Colonel smiled, bowed his acquiescence, and told his man to drive us to Bruton Street, as De Vigne sprang into the Fantyre brougham.

'I was engaged to what I liked much better, lansquenet at Hollingsworth's; but I want to see how the game lies in Bruton Street. I fancy that woman's moves will be worth watching,' said Sabretasche, throwing himself back on his cushions. 'By the way, *who* is she—do you know?'

'The devil I don't! Somebody up at Cambridge said she was old Fantyre's companion; others whispered her daughter, others her niece, others, what the old woman said herself, that she is the child of her brother—a John, or James, or something monosyllabic, Trefusis.

'No very exalted lineage that,' returned Sabretasche; 'for if report be true—and I believe it is—the Fantyre at sixteen was an orange-girl, crying, "Who'll buy 'em, two a penny!" up Pall Mall; that Fantyre, the most eccentric of eccentric Irishmen (and all Hibernians have a touch of madness!) beheld her from his window in Arthur's, fell in

love with her foot and leg, walked out, offered to
her in the street, was accepted of course, and
married her at seventy-five. What fools there
are in the world, Chevasney! She pushed her
way cleverly enough, though as to knowing all
the exclusives she talks about, she no more knew
them than my dog did. She heard of them, of
course; saw some of the later ones at Ranelagh
and the Wells; very likely won francs at piquet
from poor Brummel, when he was in decadence at
Caen, to put him in mind of the palmy days when
he fleeced Coombe of ponies; possibly entertained
Talleyrand when he was glad of an English
asylum; and, of course, would get together Moore,
and Jeffreys, and Tom Erskine, and all the young
fellows; for a pretty woman and a shrewd woman
can always make men forget she sprang from the
gutter. But as to the others—pooh! she was no
more intimate with them than I; old Fantyre
himself was in far too *mal odeur*, and left his widow
to live by her wits rather than to figure as a leader
of ton. Here we are: it will all be very *comme il
faut*. I bet you, Chevasney, Lady Fantyre is
afraid of my eye-glass!'

It was all *comme il faut*. De Vigne was sitting
beside the Trefusis, his glowing, passionate eyes
fixed on hers; while in her face was merely the

look of calm, conscious beauty, gratified at triumph
and exigeant of homage ; a beauty the embodiment
of tyranny; a beauty which would exult in denying
the passion it excited ; a beauty only a tool in the
hands of its possessor, to pioneer a path for her
ambitions, and draw within her reach the prizes
that she coveted.

De Vigne did not look best pleased to see us.
I dare say he would have preferred a *tête-à-tête*
supper with old Lady Fantyre dozing after her
champagne!   Such, however, was denied to him ;
perhaps they knew how to manage him better
than to make his game too easy.   Do any of us
care for the tame pheasants knocked over at our
feet in a battue, as we do for an outlying royal that
has led us many hours' weary toil, through burn
and bracken, over rock and furze ?   We knock
down the pheasants to swell our bag, and leave
them where they fall, to be picked up after us;
but difficulty and excitement warm our blood and
fire our pride, and we think no toil or trouble too
great to hear the ping of the bullet, and see the
deer grallocked at last !

We had a very pleasant supper.   Opera-
suppers are always pleasant to my mind; there
is a freedom about them that gives a certain
pointe à la sauce, which it would be better for

ladies to put down among their items for entertainment, a good deal oftener than they do. There
was plenty of champagne, and, under its genial
influences the Fantyre tongue was loosened, and
Sabretasche amused himself with the old lady's
shrewd wit and not over-particular stories;—a
queer contrast enough himself to the little
snuffy, rouged, and wigged Irish peeress, with his
delicate beauty of feature, and singular refinement
of tone; while De Vigne, fired by the Parthian
glances which had been so freely bestowed on
him, and the proximity of that superb Trefusis, his
idol—at least for the present—talked with the
wit of which, when he chose, no man on earth
could give out more brilliant corruscations. The
Trefusis never said very much; hers was chiefly
silent warfare.

'What did you think of the ballet, Colonel?'
asked old Fantyre, peering up into his face. At
seventy-six women are still much kinder to a
handsome man than to a plain one.

'I thought very little of it,' answered Sabretasche. 'Coralie has no grace; boys make a fuss
with her because she happens to be pretty, but as
for her dancing—faugh! scores of Castilian girls
I have seen doing the fandango, under the village
chesnut-trees, would beat her hollow.'

' Glorious dance that fandango is!' said De Vigne. 'I have danced the fandango; no more able to help myself when the girl and the castanets began, than the holy cardinals, who, when they came to Madrid to excommunicate the cachucha, ended by joining in it! Like the rest of us, I suppose, they found forbidding a thing to other people, very easy and pleasant, but going without it themselves rather more difficult.'

' *You* never go without a thing you like, do you?' asked the Trefusis.

' Certainly not. Why should I?'

' I don't know; only—boys who have revelled in Bath buns, sometimes rue it, when they realize Chromate of lead.'

' Oh!' as for that,' laughed De Vigne, ' the moralists make out that a sort of Chromate of lead follows, as natural sequence, any Bath buns one may fancy to eat. I don't see it myself.'

' Your best Bath buns are women, De Vigne?' said Lady Fantyre, with her silent chuckle, ' and you'll be uncommonly lucky, my dear, if you don't find some Chromate of lead, as you call it, after one or two of *them.*'

' He will, indeed,' smiled Sabretasche. ' Ladies are the exact antipodes of olives: the one begins in salt, and leaves us blessed with a delicious rose

aroma; the other, with all due deference, is nectar
to commence with, but how soon, through our
fault entirely, of course, they turn into very gall!'

Lady Fantyre chuckled again; she was a wise
old woman, in her way, and enjoyed nothing more
than a hit at her own sex. To be sure, she was
leaving the field very fast, and perhaps grudged
the new combatants her cast-off weapons.

' True enough, Colonel; yet, if one may believe
naughty stories, the flavour's been one uncommonly
to your taste?.'

Sabretasche shrugged his shoulders.

' My dear lady, can one put aside the Falernian
because there will be some *amari aliquid* at the
bottom of the glass? Nobody loved the sex
better than Mahomet, yet he learned enough
from his favourite almond eyes to create his heaven
without women!'

' What a heathen you are, Sabretasche!' cried
De Vigne. ' If I were Miss Trefusis, I wouldn't
speak to you!'

' My dear fellow, I could support it!' said
Sabretasche, naively, with such delicious Brum-
melian impudence that I believe Lady Fantyre
could have kissed him—a favour for which the
Colonel would have been anything but grateful.

The Trefusis's eyes glared; De Vigne, sitting

next her, did not catch their expression, or I
think, though he might be getting mad about her,
he would not have taken the trouble he did, to
look so tenderly at her, and whisper, 'If he could
bear it, *I* could not.'

'Yes, you could,' said the Trefusis, through her
pearly teeth. 'You would make me the occasion
for an epigram on female caprice, and go and pay
the same compliments to Lady Hautton or Coralie
the danseuse. I never knew the man who could
not support, with most philosophic indifference,
the cruelty of one woman if he had another to
turn to!—provided indeed she had not left him for
some one else, when, perhaps, his pride *might* be
a little piqued.'

De Vigne smiled; he was pleased to see her
annoyed.

'Well! we are philosophic in self-defence,
probably; but you are mistaken in thinking so
lightly of the wounds you give: and I am sorry
you should be so, for you will be more likely to
refuse to what you fancy a mere scratch, the heal-
ing touch that you might, perhaps, be persuaded
to accord if you were more fully aware of the
harm you had done.'

Sabretasche interrupted him.

'Talking of wounds, De Vigne? My dear

fellow, who gets them now? (This vanille cream
is excellent, Lady Fantyre. Vanille is a very
favourite flavour of mine.) The surest way of
wounding, if such a thing be possible when the
softest little *ingénue* wears a chain-armour of
practical egotism, is to keep invulnerable yourself. Miss Trefusis teaches us that.'

'Curse the fellow!' muttered De Vigne.

He liked Sabretasche cordially, but he could
have kicked him at that moment with an intense
degree of pleasure !

'You know the world, Colonel,' smiled old
Fantyre. 'I like men who do: they amuse one.
When one's been behind the scenes oneself, those
poor silly fools who sit in front of the stage, and
believe in Talma's strut and Siddons's tears, in
the rouge and the paint, and the tinsel and the
trap-doors, do tire one so! You talk of your
ingénues; I'm sure they're the most stupid lot
possible !'

'Except when they're *ingénues de Saint Lô,*'
laughed De Vigne.

'Which most of them are,' said the Fantyre.
'Take my word for it, my dear, if you find a
woman extra simple, sweet, and prudish, you will
be no match for her! Sherry's a very pleasant,
light, innocent sort of wine, but strychnine's

sometimes given in it, you know, for all that; and if a girl cast her eyes down more timidly than usual, you may be pretty sure those eyes have looked on queerer scenes than you fancy.'

'To be sure,' said De Vigne. 'I would a good deal sooner have to deal with an Athénais de Mortemar, than with a Françoise d'Aubigné. I should be on my guard against the wicked little Montespan, but I should be no match for Sainte Maintenon. " *C'est trop contre un mari*" (or *un amant*) " *d'être coquette et dévote : une femme devrait opter.*" '

"Then when you marry, you will take your wife out of a *guinguette* rather than a convent?' asked the old lady, with a comical smile.

The Trefusis shot a keen, rapid, hard glance at him, as he laughed, 'Come, come, Lady Fantyre, is there no medium?'

'Between prudes and Aspasias?' said her shrill little treble. 'No, sir—not that I ever saw—and even, *les extrémes se touchent*, you know.'

'Hush! hush!' cried Sabretasche, 'you will corrupt me, Lady Fantyre—positively you will— you will make me think shockingly of all my kind, soft-voiced, soft-skinned friends!'

'Somebody has made you think as badly of women as you can,' said the sharp old woman.

'Not I! What do you think of that Moselle, De Vigne?'

He thought it good, but not so good as the Trefusis, who acted out the song, 'Drink to me with thine eyes,' in a manner eminently calculated to intoxicate him more, than all the wine ever pressed from Rhenish vineyards. And when she took a little dainty cigarette between her lips, and leant back on her favourite rose couch, laughing at the Fantyre scandals, and flashing on De Vigne her brightest glances; even Sabretasche and I, who were set against her by that most dogged thing, a prejudice, could not deny that a finer woman had never worried a man's peace of mind out of him, or sent him headlong into follies which shut out all chance of a fairer future or a wiser path.

'Come in and smoke a pipe, Arthur,' said De Vigne, when we had at length left the Fantyre *petit souper*, and Sabretasche had gone to his lans-quenet at Hollingsworth's. ' 'Tisn't worth while going anywhere else to-night; it's three now. I have some splendid Glenlivet (how naturally one offers a Cantab something to drink! as naturally as to a cabman, I declare), and I shall like a chat with you. Hallo! where's my number. Confound it! why do they build town-houses all alike,

that one can't know one's own by a particular
mark, as the mother in the novels always knows
her stolen child? Symmetry? Oh! that's like
Sabretasche. One wants symmetry in a racer, I
allow, but in one's lodging-house I could put up
without it, rather than pull up Vivandière on
her haunches twice for nothing. Where's my
latch-key? Right on, up the stairs; I'll follow
you. By George! who's that smoking in my
rooms? It can't be Harris, because I gave him
leave to go to Cremorne, and not come home till
morning, in time to fill my bath. It *is* tobacco,
Arthur. What a devilish impertinence!'

He pushed open the door. On De Vigne's pet
sofa, with a French novel in his hand, and a meer-
schaum in his lips, lay lazy, girlish-looking, light-
hearted 'Little Curly.'

'Curly!' cried De Vigne. 'By Jove, how
delighted I am! Curly! Where, in Heaven's
name, did you spring from, my boy?'

'I sprang from nowhere,' responded Curly,
taking his pipe out of his mouth. 'I've given up
gymnastics, they're too fatiguing. I drove down
from Claridge's, in a cab that privately informed
me it had just taken six cases of scarlet fever, and
three of small-pox, to the hospitals; I found you
were out—of course I knew you would be—and

with the philosophy which always characterizes my
slightest movements, took Le Brun, found out a
pipe (how well you brown yours, by the way), and
made myself jolly.'

'Quite right,' responded De Vigne, who was a
perfect Arab for hospitality. 'Delighted to see
you. We're quite a Frestonhills reunion. What
a pity the Doctor is not here, and dear Arabella!
But I say, Curly, have you got quit of Granta,
like this direputable fellow, or are you only run
up on leave, or how is it?'

'Don't you remember my degree was given me
this year because I am a Peer's son?' asked Curly,
reprovingly. ' See what it is to be a Goth, without a classical education! You *should* have gone
to Granta, De Vigne, you'd have been Stroke of
the Cambridge Eight, not a doubt of it. There's
muscle gone to waste! It's very jolly, you see,
being an Honourable, though I never knew it;
one gets credit for brains whether one has them
or not. What an inestimable blessing to some of
the pillars of the aristocracy, isn't it? I suppose
the House of Lords was instituted on that principle; and its members are no more required to
know why they pass their bills, than we, their sons
and heirs, are required to know why we pass our
examinations, eh?'

'And what are you going to do with yourself now?' put in De Vigne. 'For the present you'll keep on that sofa, and make yourself whisky-toddy; but *après?*'

'*Après?* Well, the governor wanted me to go in for diplomacy, but I wasn't up to it—lies are not my specialty, they're too much trouble; so I demonstrated to him that it was clearly my mission to drink brandy, distract women, run into debt, curse parade, turn out on show days, move from Windsor to Knightsbridge and back, and otherwise enjoy life, and swear at ennui with you fellows in the Queen's. His mind was not open to it at first, but I soon improved his limited vision, and my name's now down at the Horse Guards, where, after a little neat jobbery, I dare say the thing'll soon be done.'

'Your governor manageable?' said I.

Curly yawned, and opened his blue eyes a little wider.

'Of course; I should cut him if he wasn't. You see he's a snob (I wanted him to put on his carriage-panel—

"Who'd have thought it?
Cotton bought it!"

but he declined), and my mother's a Dorset; gave her title for his yellows. Now my brother Gus,

poor devil! is the regular *parvenu* breed: short,
thick, red whiskers, snub nose, and all the rest of
it; while I, as you see, gentlemen,' said Curly,
glancing at himself with calm, complacent vanity,
'am a remarkably good-looking fellow, eminently
presentable and creditable to my progenitors: a
second Spurina, and a regular Dorset. Therefore,
the governor hates Gus (sneaky I consider it,
as it is through his remarkable likeness to him
that Gus is fit to frighten his looking-glass), but
adores *me*, and lets me twist him round this little
finger of mine, *voyez-vous?*'

'And how's Julia?' asked De Vigne.

Curly looked as savage as *he* could look.

'Julia? Confound her! how should I know?
She's been and hooked some old boy or other, I
believe, poor devil!'

'Who's the poor devil?' laughed De Vigne;
'the man for being caught, or you for being
deserted? Take comfort, Curly; there never was
a man jilted yet who didn't return thanks for it
twelve months after. When I was twenty, and
went over to Canada for six weeks' buffalo-hunt-
ing, I fell mad in love with a great Toronto
beauty, a sheriff's widow. Such ankles she had,
and didn't she show them on the Ontario! It
was really one of the most serious affairs I ever

had, and she flirted me into a downright proposal. The most wide-awake man, is a donkey when he is young. But who should come on the scene just then but a rich old fur-merchant, with no end of dollars, and a tremendous house at New York; and my little widow, thinking I was very young, and knowing nothing whatever of Vigne and its belongings, quietly threw me over, forswore all the pretty things we'd said to one another in sledging and skating, and went to live among the Broadway belles. I swore and suffered horribly; she turned the pampas into swamps, and absolutely made me utterly indifferent to bison. I lived on pipes and soda-water for a week, and recovered. But when I ran over to America last winter to see Egerton of the Rifles, I met in Quebec a dreadful woman, ten stone at the least, in a bright green dress, with blue things in her hair, and rubies for her jewels, her skin as yellow as gold, and as wrinkled as the Fantyre's; and *I* might have married that woman, with her shocking broad English, and her atrocious " Do tell! " What fervent thanks I returned for the fur-merchant's creation and my own preservation! So will you, Curly, when, ten years hence, you happen to drop in at the Snoozeinrest Rectory, and find Julia as stiff as her brown-paper tracts, and as vinegar as

I 2

the moral lessons she gives her parishioners, re-
stricting her pastor and master to three glasses,
and making your existence miserable at dessert
by the entrance of four or five brats with shrill
voices and monkey propensities, who make you
look at them and their mother with a thrill of the
deepest rapture, rejoicing that, thank Heaven, you
are not a family man ! '

De Vigne spoke the truth.   Why the deuce
did not he remember that his passion for the
Trefusis might be quite as utterly misplaced as
his fancy for the Toronto widow, or the Cantab's
flirtation with Miss Julia ?   But, ah me ! if the
truth were always in our minds, or the future
always plain before us, should we make the fifty
false steps that the wisest man amongst us is certain to rue before half his sands are run ?   If they
knew that before night was down the sea-foam
would be whirling high, and the curlews screaming
in human fear, and the gay little boat lying keel
upwards on the salt ocean surf, would the plea-
sure-party set out so fearlessly in the morning
sunshine, with champagne flowing and bright eyes
glancing, and joyous laughter ringing over the
golden sands and up to the fleecy heavens ?

CHAPTER V.

WHAT WAS UNDER THE CARDS.

THAT night, after we were gone, old Fantyre sat with her feet on the fender of her dressing-room, sans wig, teeth, rouge, cosmetique, velvet, or lace; and an uncommonly hideous old woman she must have looked in that guise, I am certain, though, thank Heaven! I cannot speak to the fact from ocular observation. The Trefusis sat there, too, looking all the handsomer for dishabille, in a cerise-hued *peignoir* and fur slippers, and her thick long raven hair unbraided, and hanging to her waist.

'My dear,' began the Fantyre, 'do you think you hold the trumps in that game you're playing?'

'Certainly I do. Why?'

'Beause I'm not so sure. You're playing fast and loose with De Vigne, and that don't always succeed. Brummel said to me, "If we pique a woman, she is ours." That's true enough with us, because we're such fools; nine times out of ten a

woman don't care a rush for a man who's dying
at her feet; while she's crazy about some ugly
brute, who takes no more notice of her, than he
does of his dirty boots. Women love to go to
heel, and they'll crawl after a man who double-
thongs them, in preference to one who lets them
rule him. Besides, *we*'re jealous; we hate one
another like poison from our cradles; and if a man
neglects us we fancy he likes somebody else, and,
of course, that's quite enough to make us want to
trap him away from her, whoever she be! But
with men sometimes it's a dangerous game.
They're the most impatient creatures in creation,
and if one trout won't rise to the fly, they go off
and whip another stream. All fish are alike pretty
well to 'em, so that they fill their basket. Men's
aim is Pleasure, and if you don't give it to 'em
they will go somewhere else for it.'

'True enough,' said the Trefusis; ' but, at the
same time, to a good many men Difficulty is
everything. Men of hot passion and strong will
delight in pursuit, and soon grow tired of victory.
They enjoy knocking the bird over; that done, it
loses all interest for them. De Vigne is such a
man : rouse his pride, you win him—yield easily,
and you miss him.'

'Maybe, my dear—maybe! You know him

better than I do, and must manage him as you choose. I dare say he does like climbing over spikes and chevaux-de-frise to get what he fancies; he's the stamp of creature that's never happy out of excitement or danger, and Montaigne thinks like you : " *Elles nous battent mieux en fuyant, comme les Scythes.*" How racy his old French is! I wish I had known that man! I say, those two friends of his, shouldn't be with him too much, for they don't like us: that boy Chevasney—'

' Boy, indeed!' echoed the Trefusis.

' But De Vigne is fond of him?'

' I believe so; but De Vigne is never influenced by anybody.'

' I hope he may not be, except by you, and that won't be to his advantage, poor fellow! He's a very handsome pigeon, my dear—a very handsome one, indeed!' chuckled the old lady. ' But the other one is more dangerous than Chevasney; I mean that beautiful creature—what's his name? —Vivian Sabretasche. He don't think much about us, I dare say; but he don't like us. He sees through us, my dear, and, ten to one, he'll put De Vigne on his guard.'

' De Vigne listens to nobody who comes between him and his passion of the moment; and how is it possible that Sabretasche should see through us, as you term it?'

'Not all our hand, my dear, but one or two cards. That calm nonchalant way of his conceals a wonderful deal of keen observation—too keen for us. Vivian Sabretasche is very witty and very careless, and the world tells very light stories of him; but he's a man that not Satan himself could deceive.'

'Well, nobody wants to deceive him.'

'Don't you want to marry his friend?'

'Enough of that, Lady Fantyre! I will neither be lectured nor schooled. You agreed to help me, but you agreed, too, to let me succeed in my own way. I tell you, I know how to manage him, and that before this year is out, in spite of Chevasney, Sabretasche, or anybody—yes, in spite of *himself*—I shall be Granville de Vigne's wife!'

'I wish you may, my dear,' said the Fantyre, with another chuckle. 'Well, don't talk to me any more, child. Get Le Brun, will you, and read me to sleep.'

CHAPTER VI.

A DOUBLED-DOWN PAGE IN THE COLONEL'S BOOK
OF LIFE.

WHAT a pace one lives at through the season! And, when one is fresh to it, before one knows that its pleasant, frothy, syllabub surface is only a cover to intrigues, petty spites, jealousies, partisanships, manœuvres; alike in St. Stephen's as at Almack's; among uncompromising patriots as among poor foreigners farming private banks round about St. James's Street; among portly aristocratic mothers, trotting out their innocent daughters to the market, as among the gauze-winged, tinselled, hard-worked deities of the coulisses;—how agreeable it is! Illusion in one's first season lasts, I think, about the space of one month. With its blissful bandeau over our eyes, we really do admire the belles of the Ring and the Ride; we go to balls to dance, and to dinners for society. We swallow larks for ortolans, and Cremorne gooseberry for Clicquot's. We believe in the innocent demoiselles,

who look so naive, and such sweet English rose-
buds at morning fêtes, and do not dream those
glossy braids cover empty, but world-shrewd little
heads, ever plotting how to eclipse dearest Cecilia
or win old Hauton's coronet; we accept their
mamma's invitations, and think how kindly they
are given, not knowing that we are only asked
because we bring Shako of the Guards with us,
who is our bosom chum, and has fifteen thousand
a year, and that, Shako fairly hooked, we, being
younger sons, shall be gently dropped. We go
to the Lords and Commons, and believe A. when
he says he has the deepest admiration for his
noble friend B., whom he hates like poison; and
we reverence D. when he pleads for the liberty
of 'the people,' whom over his claret he classi-
fies as 'beastly snobs.' We regard the coulisses
with delight, as a temple whose Eleusinia it is
high honour to penetrate, and fall veritably in
love with all those fair nymphs fluttering their
spirit veils as Willis's, or clanking their spurs as
Mazurka maidens.

That delightful state of faith lasts about a
month, then we discard the bandeau, and use
an eye-glass instead; learn to confine ourselves
to 'Not bad-looking' before the handsomest
woman in the Park; find out that dinners are

a gathering to consume hock and turbot, but
not by any means bound to furnish society; pro-
nounce balls a bore, and grow critical of Moëts.
We are careful of the English rosebuds, knowing
that, kept out of view, those innocent petals have
thorns, which they know well how to thrust out
and dexterously impale us on them. We take
mamma's invitations at their worth, and watch
the dragons' teeth opening for that luckless Shako,
with grim terror of a similar fate; we laugh over
rum-punch with a chum of ours, a whip in the
Commons, who lets us into a thing or two con-
cerning the grandiose jobbery of Downing Street;
and find out that coulisses atmosphere, however
agreeable, is no exclusive boon; that its sesame
is a bracelet to the first dancer, who, though she
may take a Duke's brougham, is not insensible
to even a Cornet's tribute, if it come from Hunt
and Roskill, and we give less love and more
Cremorne lobster-salad to the Willis and Mazurka
maidens!

Such, at least, was my case; and when I was
fairly in the saddle and off at a pace, like a
Doncaster favourite's, through my first season,
enjoyed it considerably, even when the bandeau
was off my eyes, which, thanks to De Vigne and
Sabretasche, took place very speedily.

Of De Vigne I did not see so much as if no
Trefusis had been in being, for he was constantly
after her, going with her to morning concerts, or
Richmond luncheons; riding with her in the
Park; lending her a horse, too, for that showy
bay of hers had come out of Bruton Mews, and
no livery-stable mount is fit for any mortal, much
less for a female; attending her everywhere, but
not as yet 'compromising' himself, as, according
to the peculiar code of honour in such cases, we
may give a girl a bracelet with impunity to ourselves; but are lost if we hazard a diamond
circlet for her 'third finger;' That comes rather
hard on those poor women, by the way; for
Lovelace may talk, and look, and make love, in
every possible style; yet, if he stop short of the
'essential question,' Lovelace may go scot free!
We remark what a devil of a girl it is to
flirt; and her sworn allies, who have expressed
sympathy to her in crossed notes of the fondest
pathos, agree among themselves 'How conceited
poor Laura is to fancy Lovelace *could* be serious!
Why, dear, all that means nothing; only Laura,
poor thing! has had so little attention, she
doesn't know what it is. If she had had a man
mad about her, as you and I have had, love—ah!
do you remember poor Frank Cavendish at the

race ball?' Whereon the sworn allies scent their *vinaigrettes*, indulging pleasurable recollections; and Lovelace burns Laura's lock of hair which he asked for, under the limes in the moonlight; thinks ' How deucedly near I was! must be more careful next time,' and wonders what sort of girls he shall find at Brighton.

De Vigne, however, as long as he would not come well up to hand, received no flirting kindnesses from the Trefusis—not even so much as a note to thank him for his concert-tickets, or a flower from the very bouquet he had sent her. Perhaps she knew by clairvoyance, that her Cambridge azalea had gone ignominiously into the grate; for she tried on that style no more, but was coy and reserved, as if Hannah More had been her *chaperone* instead of old Sarah, Lady Fantyre. This worried, excited, and roused De Vigne, and I saw, without needing much penetration, that he was drinking deeper and deeper of a stimulant which he never refused when it was fairly to his lips, and which brings worse follies and wilder deeds, and more resistless madness to men than lie in the worst insanities of *del. trem.*, or the dreams of a thousand grains of opium ! Sabretasche and I used to swear at the power of the Trefusis, and lament De Vigne's infatuation together; but we could do nothing to weaken either : opposition to a man in love is like oil to fire !

Sabretasche was remarkably kind to me ; he introduced me in his set, one of the most intellectual in town ; he admitted me to his charming dinners ; and he let me into his studio, the most luxurious miniature art-palace possible, where, when employed on his marble or on his canvas, no one was ever allowed to disturb him. Sabretasche knew to perfection the great art, ' How to live,' and he had every facility for enjoying life : riches, refined taste, art, intellect; men who sought him, women who courted him, a facile wit, a sweet temper; yet, somehow or other, you could trace in him a certain shadow, often dissipated, it is true, in the sunshine of his gay words, and the music of his laugh; but certain to creep over him again—an intangible shade of disappointment. Perhaps he had exhausted life too early; perhaps his excessive refinement was jarred by the very pleasures he sought; perhaps the classic mould of his mind was not, after all, satisfied with the sedatives he gave it :—however,—as for speculating on Sabretasche, all town pretty well did that, more or less, but nobody in town was ever any the wiser for it. One morning I was going to breakfast with him; his nominal breakfast-hour was noon; though I believe he often rose very much earlier, took a cup of coffee, and chipped, or read, or painted in his studio. I took my way across the Gardens to Sabretasche's house, which was at the upper end of Park Lane, taking that *détour* for motives of my own. Gwendolina Brandling, Curly's eldest sister, an exquisite nymph of eighteen, with *crépé* hair, had confided to me the previous day, over strawberry-ice, at a fête at Twickenham, that she was in the habit of accompanying her little sisters in their morning walk with their governess, to 'put her in mind of the country,' and the Hon. Gwen being a fresh, honest-hearted, and exceedingly nice-looking girl, I took my way through the Gardens about eleven, looking out for Curly's sister among the pretty nursemaids, ugly children, and abominable ankle-breaking, dress-tearing perambulators which filled the walks. There was no Hon. Gwen at present; and I threw myself down under one of the trees, put my eye-glass in my eye, and took out that day's 'Punch' to while away the time till Gwen and her attendants might come in sight.

Suddenly a voice fell on my ear, speaking coarsely and jocosely in Italian, 'Come, signor, why waste time about it? You know that your secret

is worth more than I ask. You know you would
give half your riches to make sure it would never
be known by anybody, to efface it altogether—eh,
excellenza? Come! I ask a very low price; not
worth jangling about; no more to you than a few
scudi to me. Why waste time? You know I
can bring proofs over in twenty-four hours, and
then the show-up—'

'Take it, and begone with you!'

Ye gods!—that last voice, cold, contemptuous,
full of disgust and wrath, I recognized as Sabretasche's! Involuntarily I turned to look; and saw
the most fastidious and the proudest man in town,
in company with a shabbily, showily-dressed fellow,
with rings on his fingers and a vulgar, insolent
face, which wore at that minute an abominably
insulting smile, as the Colonel shoved a roll of
bank-notes into his hand, loathing and impatience
quivering over his own features. The man laughed
—a laugh as impudent as his smile :

' Thank you, signor, a thousand thanks. I won't
trouble you again till—I'm again in difficulties.'

Sabretasche gave him no answer, but turning
his back upon the man, folded his arms upon his
chest, and walked away across the Gardens, with
his head bent down, while the fellow counted the
notes with glistening, triumphant eyes, crushed

them up as if he loved their crisp new rustle,
stroked his beard, whistled an air from 'Figaro,'
and strolled on towards the gate; leaving me in a
state of profound amazement at the vulgar acquaintance the Colonel had selected, and the
secret, by which this underbred foreigner seemed
able to hold in check, so profound a man of the
world as Sabretasche.

Just at that minute, Gwen and her duenna
appeared in the distance; and I went to meet
them, and talked of Grisi and Mario, of Balfe's
new song, and Sims Reeve's last concert, with the
hundred topics current in the season, while the
little ones ran about, and the French governess
chatted and laughed, and Gwen smiled and looked
like a sunbeam, and told me about her ponies and
dogs and flowers down in Hampshire. Poor Gwen!
She is Madame la Duchesse de La Vieillecour now,
not over happy, I fear, despite the diamonds I saw
flashing on her brow and neck last night at the
Tuileries. In the gorgeous glories of her Champs
Elysées hotel, in the light beauty of her summer
villa at Enghien, in the gloomy state and magnificence of her château in the Côte d'Or, whose mas-
sive iron gates close like a death-knell, does she ever
think, I wonder, of those spring mornings in the
Gardens when *she* was in her spring-time too?

It was just twelve when I reached the Colonel's
house.   I was shown straight to his own room;
and there he lay on one of the couches, calm, cool,
imperturbable as ever, not a trace visible of his
past excitement and irritation, very unlike a man
with a secret hanging over his head and darkening
his life!   He stretched out his hand with a kind
smile :

'Well, Arthur.   Good morning to you.   You
are just in time for the match; Du Loo has not
been here five minutes.'

Du Loo was a heavy, good-humoured, stupid
fellow in the Blues, who prided himself on his fine
teeth and his boxing, and who was going, at half-
past twelve, to have a little play with Fighting
Chatney, one of the Fancy, who let himself out to
beat gentlemen, in order that gentlemen might
learn to beat.

On the carpet at Sabretasche's feet lay a great
retriever, the one thing in the whole world for which
he cared, chiefly, I believe, because, when a stray
pup, it had trusted itself to his kindness.

'Poor old Cid!' said he, pausing in his breakfast to set the dog down some larded guinea-fowl.
'I spoil him for sport, you say?   Perhaps; but I
don't want him for sport, and I make his life
comfortable.   I see in him one thing in this Via

Dolorosa; that is perfectly content and happy; and it is a treat to see it. Cid and I are fast friends; and we love one another, don't we, old boy?'

The Cid looked up at him with two honest, tender brown eyes, and wagged his tail: Sabretasche had talked to him till, I believe, the dog understood him, quite as well as I did.

'There are lots of women, Colonel,' said Du Loo, 'who'd bid high for the words you throw away on that dog!'

'Possibly. But are any of them as faithful, and honest, and worthy, as my Cid? The Cid would like broken bones and a barn with me, as well as French cookery and velvet cushions. I'm sorry I couldn't say as much for my fair ladies, Du Loo.'

'The devil! no,' yawned the Guardsman. 'Catch a woman giving up her opera-box, and her milliner. Why, the other night I saw Nelly Lacquers, the British Beggars' Bank man's wife, got up no end at the Silverton drum, laughing and talking, waltzing, and carrying pearls worth two thousand; and, by George! if there isn't a warrant out against her husband this morning for swindling! Mustn't she be a horrid, heartless, little bit of flippery?'

'It doesn't follow,' said Sabretasche. 'Most likely he sent her there to disarm suspicion, while

he shipped off his specie to France or America, and
got his passport to Calais. I never judge people;
seemingly bad actions may have good motives,
good ones may spring from base and selfish ends.
" Judge not, lest ye be judged." When will the
world take that gentle injunction to heart ? Never !
It loves to quote " An eye for an eye," and " Depart
from me, ye accursed ; " but it is oblivious of the
" Mote and the beam," and of " He that is without
sin among you, let him cast a stone at her ! " If
a man break his own leg, he thinks it a " sad accident," a " great affliction ; " if he see his friend
break his, he has no hesitation in pronouncing it
" a judgment." '

Du Loo stared at him.

' What the deuce, Colonel ! *you* turning ser-
monizer ? '

' No, my dear fellow, I have enough conscience
left not to preach before practising ; though truly
if that were the rule in the land, few pulpits would
be filled ! But I *have* one virtue—tolerance; therefore I may preach that. There is your friend,
Fighting Chatney. Now for your seventh heaven,
Du Loo ! '

' And yours too ? '

' Mine? No! there is a degree of absurdity in two
mortals setting solemnly to work to pommel one

another; there is something unpoetic, and coarse,
and savage, about blood and bruises; and, besides,
—it is so much exertion! However, go at it; it
is for Arthur's delectation, and I can go into my
studio if I'm tired.'

Du Loo and his pet of the Fancy retired to the
far end of the room, and there set-to, delivering
from the left shoulder, and drinking as much beer
between their rounds as a couple of draymen. As
the match had been arranged for my express pleasure, of course I watched it with the deepest interest, though Sabretasche's remarks for once gave
the noble art a certain degree of ludicrousness, mingled with the admiration with which I had been
accustomed to regard such 'little mills.' Du Loo
finally floored the bruiser, to his own extreme
glorification, while the Pet very generously growled
out to him that he might be as great a man as the
Tipton Slasher, if he would but train himself properly. Du Loo left, and Sabretasche asked me to
stay ten minutes, to let him finish a picture which
he had been amusing himself by taking of me, in
crayons ;—a portrait, by the way, which is a far
better one than any I have ever had done by R.A.s,
and which my mother still cherishes devotedly at
Longholme.

'What a strange fellow Du Loo is,' said the

Colonel, 'or, rather, what a common one ! The
man's greatest delight is a Moulsey mill, and his
ambitions are locked up in the brutalities of the
Ring. Of any higher world he is utterly ignorant.
Talk to him of art and genius, you might as well
discourse to him in Hebrew ! Take him out under
the summer stars, he would look bored, yawn, and
ask for his cigar. Positively, Arthur, he makes
one feel one's link to the animals mortifying close.
In truth, the distance between the zoophytes and
man, is not wider than the gulf between a Goethe
and a prize-fighter, is it ? It is proportion of brain
which makes the master superior to his dog;
should it not make as distinct a mark, between
the clod of the valley, and the cultured scholar ?
But why am I talking all this nonsense to
you ? You have more amusing occupation than
to listen to my fancies. Turn a little nearer
the light. That is it ! Have you seen De Vigne
to-day ? '

'No; he was gone to Albert Smith's with the
Trefusis and Fantyre, confound them ! Do you
think she will win, Colonel ? '

'My dear boy, how can I tell. I think she
will if she can. " *Donne gentile devote d'amore* "
generally manage to marry a man if they have full
play with him. If De Vigne only saw her in

morning calls, when his head was cool, and others were with him, possibly he might keep out of it; but she waltzes with him—she waltzes remarkably well, too—she shoots Parthian glances-at him in the *tête-à-tête* of conservatories, after the mess champagne; moreover, ten to one, in some of those soft moments, he will say more than, being a man of honour, he can unsay.'

' And be cursed for life!'

' Possibly. Love does that for a good many, and in the fantasy of early passion many men have surrendered their entire lives to one who has made them—a blank! Troublesome eyes yours are, Arthur; I can't make out their colour. What present will you give Mrs. de Vigne on her wedding-day?'

' Confound her, none!' I shouted. 'He's a vast deal too good for fifty such as she—a cold, calculating, ambitious, loveless intriguer—'

' One would think you were in love with her yourself, Chevasney! Let me catch that terrific expression, it would do for a Jupiter Tonans.'

' And she is so wretchedly clever!' I groaned.

' In artifice! yes; by education! no. Her knowledge is utterly superficial. I cannot imagine where she has lived. She speaks shockingly

ungrammatical French, with a most atrocious
English accent;' she neither plays nor sings. Yet
she waltzes, rides, and dresses splendidly, and has
a shrewd, sharp sarcasm, which passes muster as
wit among her admirers. In fact, she is a para-
dox ; and I shall regret nothing more, than to see
De Vigne misled through his senses by her magnificent beauty, stooping to tie himself for life
to a woman with whom he will have nothing in
common, who will have neither feeling to satisfy
his heart, nor mind to satisfy his intellect, and
with whom I would bet great odds a week after
the honeymoon he will be disgusted.'

'Can't you persuade him?' I began. He
stopped me with an expressve gesture; he had
much of the Italian gesticulation.

'Persuade? *Bon garçon!* if you want to
force a man into any marriage, persuade him
against it! No one should touch love affairs.
Third persons are certain to *barbotter* the whole
thing. The more undesirable the connection, and
the more you interfere, the more surely will the
"subject" grow obstinate as a mule under your
treatment. Call a person names to anybody over
whom she has cast a glamour, and if he have anything of the gentleman, or the lover, in him, out of
sheer *amour propre*, and a sort of wrong-headed,

right-hearted chivalry, he will swear to you she is an angel.'

' And believe it, perhaps.'

' Most likely, until she is his wife!   There is a peculiar magic in that gold circlet, badge of servitude for life, which changes the sweetest, gentlest, tenderest betrothed into the stiffest of domestic tyrants.   Don't you know that, when she's engaged to him, she is so pretty and pleasant with his men friends, passes over the naughty stories she hears of him from "well-intentioned" advisers, and pats the new mare that is to be entered for the Chester Cup?   But twelve months after, his chums have the cold shoulder and the worst wine; and she gives him fifty curtain orations on his disgraceful conduct, while he wonders if the peevish woman who comes down an hour too late for breakfast, can by any possibility be identical with the smiling young lady who poured his coffee out for him, with such dainty fingers, and pleasant words, when he stayed down at her papa's for the shooting.'

I laughed.   'Don't ever get married yourself, Colonel, for the sake of Heaven, women, and consistency!'

He smiled, too, as he answered :

' "A young man married is a man that's

marred." ' That's a golden rule, Arthur ; take it
to heart. Anne Hathaway, I have not a doubt,
suggested it; experience is the sole abestos,
only unluckily one seldom gets it before one's
hands are burnt irrevocably. Shakspeare took to
wife the ignorant, rosy-cheeked, Warwickshire
peasant girl, at *eighteen!* Poor fellow! I picture
him, with all his untried powers, struggling like
new-born Hercules for strength and utterance,
and the great germ of poetry within him, ting-
ing all the common realities of life with its rose
hue; genius giving him power to see with God-
like vision, the " fairies nestling in the cowslip
chalices," and the golden gleam of Cleopatra's sails ;
to feel the " spiced Indian air " by night, and the
wild working of kings' ambitious lust; to know
by intuition, alike the voices of nature unheard
by common ears, and the fierce schemes and
passions of a world from which social position
shut him out! I picture him in his hot imagi-
native youth, finding his first love in the yeoman's
daughter at Shottery, strolling with her by the
Avon, making her an " odorous chaplet of sweet
summer buds," and dressing her up in the fond
array of a boy's poetic imaginings! Then—when
he had married her, he, with the passionate ideals
of Juliets and Violas, Ophelias and Hermiones

in his brain and heart, must have awoke to find
that the voices so sweet to him, were dumb to her.
The "cinque spotted cowslip-bells" brought only
thoughts of wine to her. When he was watching
"certain stars shoot madly from their spheres,"
she most likely was grumbling at him for mooning
there after curfew-bell. When he was learning
Nature's lore in "the fresh cup of the crimson
rose," she was dinning in his ear that Hammet
and Judith wanted worsted socks. When he was
listening in fancy to the "sea-maid's song," and
weaving thoughts to which a world still stands re-
verentially to listen, she was buzzing behind him,
and bidding him go card the wool, and weeping
that, in her girlhood, she had not chosen some
rich glover or ale-taster, instead of idle, useless,
wayward Willie Shakspeare! Poor fellow! I can
picture him in his vehement youth and his re-
gretful manhood. He did not write, I would
swear, without fellow-feeling, and yearning, over
souls similarly shipwrecked, that wise saw "A
young man married, is a man that's marred!" My
dear Arthur, I beg your pardon! I am keeping
you a most unconscionable time, but really your
eyes are very troublesome. I say, some men are
coming here for lansquenet to-night, will you
come too? and do bring De Vigne if you can.

One sees nothing of him now, and there are few
so well worth seeing. *Au revoir, mon cher.* I
have an immense deal of work before me. I am
going to the Yard to bid for Steel Patterson's
cream filly; then to the Twelfth's mess luncheon;
next I have an appointment to meet the Go-
dolphin—all town's talking of that fair lady, so I
reveal no secret; and *après*, I must dress to dine
in Eaton Square, and I much question if any of
them are worth the exertion they will cost me,
except, indeed, the cream filly!'

Wherewith the Colonel dismissed me. As I
saw him that night when De Vigne and I went
there for the promised lansquenet, courteous, ur-
bane, gay, nonchalant, witty, I saw no trace of any
mysterious secret, nor any lingering touch of the
haughty anger and impatient disgust which he had
shown to his singular companion of the morning. But then—no more did I see, what all the
world said they saw, that Vivian Sabretasche was
a heartless libertine, an unprincipled gambler,
an egotist, a sceptic, a sinner of the deepest dye,
to be condemned immeasurably in boudoir scandals and bishops' dinners, and only to be courted,
and visited, and have his crimes passed over, because he was rich, and was the fashion.

CHAPTER VII.

THE LITTLE QUEEN OF THE FAIRIES.

' ARTHUR, who do you think has gone to the dogs through that rascally British Beggars' Bank?' said De Vigne one afternoon, unharnessing himself after one of the greatest bores in life—a field-day in Hyde Park—and talking from his bedroom to me, as I sat drinking sherry and seltzer, before going into my rooms in the barracks.

' How should I know, out of half-a-million!'

' Do you remember old Tressillian, of Weive Hurst?'

' Of course. The devil; you don't mean him?'

' I am sorry to say I do; he has lost every penny. To think of that scoundrel, Sir John Lacquers, flinging Bible texts at your head, thrusting his charities into your face, going to church every Sunday as regularly as a verger, and to morning prayers on a week-day, building his almshouses, and attending his ragged schools! And now he's cut off to Boulogne, with a neat surplus,

I'll be bound, hidden up somewhere; and widows, and children, and ruined gentlemen will reap the harvest he has sown. Bah! it makes one sick of humanity!'

'And is Tressillian one of his victims?'

'I believe you! I saw his name on the list some days ago, and on Monday I met him with the child that used to be at Weive Hurst— daughter; no, grand-daughter—wasn't she?'

'Little Alma. Yes. We used to say she'd be a pretty woman. Well, go on?'

'I was very pleased to see him. You know I always liked him exceedingly. I asked him where he was living: he said, with a smile, "In lodgings, in Surrey Street; you know I can't afford Maurigy's now:" and I called on him there yesterday: such a detestable lodging-house, Arthur! Brummagem furniture and Irish maids! He is just the same simple, courtly old man as ever. I'm not a susceptible fellow; but, I give you my honour, it cut me to the heart to see that gallant old gentleman beggared through that psalm-singing, pharisaical swindler; and bearing his reverses like the plucky French *noblesse* that my father used to shelter at Vigne after the '89.'

'And has he nothing now?'

'Nothing. His entire principal was placed in

Lacquers's hands; Weive Hurst is gone to pay
his creditors, and one can do nothing to aid him :
he is so deucedly—no! so *rightly* proud.   Come
with me to-day and see him ; we shall drive there
in ten minutes, and we must be doubly attentive
to him now.   There will be just time between this
and mess, if you ring, and tell them to bring the
tilbury round.'

The tilbury soon came round, and the new steel
greys, tandem, set us down in Surrey Street.

One of the Irish maids who had so excited De
Vigne's disgust showed us up-stairs.   Tressillian
was not at home, but was expected in every
minute ; and we sat down to wait for him.   Through
the windows, on those dismal leads which admit to
the denizens of Surrey Street a view of the murky
Thames and steam transports of the Cockneys, the
little girl was standing, who, as soon as she caught
sight of De Vigne, ran into the room and welcomed him with exceeding warmth and an accession
of colour that might have flattered him much had
she been a few years older.

She was about nine or ten, an awkward and
angular age ; but she had neither angles nor
awkwardness, and was as pretty as they ever are
in their growing time, with hair of glistening gold,
bright in shade as in sunshine, and deep blue eyes,

brilliant and dark under her black silken lashes, which promised, in due time, to do a good deal of damage. In her little dainty Paris-mode dress of soft white muslin and floating azure ribbons, the child looked ill-fitted for the gloomy atmosphere of Surrey Street. Poor little thing! a few weeks before she had been the heiress of Weive Hurst, now, thanks to that goodly creature Sir John Lacquers, her future promised to be a struggle almost for daily bread.

'I am glad you are come!' she exclaimed, running up to De Vigne. 'Grandpapa will be pleased to see you, and you will do him good. When he is alone he grows so sad, and I can do nothing to help him. I am no companion for him, and if I try to amuse him—if I sing to him, or talk, or draw—I think it only makes him worse: he remembers Weive Hurst still more!'

'Do you not miss Weive Hurst, Alma?' asked De Vigne.

The child's eyes filled with tears, and the blood rushed over her face.

'*Miss* Weive Hurst! Oh, you do not guess how much, or you would not ask me! My beautiful, darling home, with its trees, and its flowers, and its sunshine! *Miss* Weive Hurst! In this cold, dark, smoky place, where I never see

the sun, or hear the birds, or. feel the summer
wind!'

And the little lady stopped in her vehement
oration, and sobbed as if her heart would break.

'What an excitable little thing!' said De
Vigne, raising his eyebrows; then he bent gently
towards her, as courteously as if she had been
a Duchess. 'I beg your pardon, Alma; I am
sorry if I have vexed you. I could not know
how much you loved your home; and, perhaps—
who knows?—you will go back to it again some
day.'

She raised her head eagerly.

'Ah! if I could hope that!'

'Well, we *will* hope it!' smiled De Vigne.
'Some of those flowers which love you so much,
will tell the fairies that sleep in their buds, to
come and fetch you back, because they want to see
their little Queen.'

She looked at him half in surprise.

'Ah! you believe in fairies, then? I love you
for that.'

'Thank you. Do you, then?'

'Of course,' said Alma, with the reproving tone
of a believer in sacred creed, to a heathenish sceptic.
'Shakspeare did, you know. He writes of Ariel
and Puck, Peas-blossom and Cobweb, who "pluck

the wings from painted butterflies," and "kill
cankers in the musk rose-buds." Milton, too,
believed in Fairy Mab, and the Goblin, whose
"shadowy flail had threshed the corn that ten
day-labourers could not end." Flowers would not
be half flowers to *me* without their fairies, and,
besides!' continued Alma, with the decision of a
person who clinches an argument, 'I have seen
them, too!'

'Indeed! But so have I.'

'Where?' asked Alma, breathless as a dilettante to whom one breathes tidings of a lost
Correggio.

'There!' said De Vigne, lifting her up in his
iron grasp before the high mirror on the mantel-
piece.

She laughed, but turned upon him with injured
indignation.

'What a shame! You do not believe in them
—not the least more than grandpapa. I will not
love you now—no, never again!'

'My dear child,' laughed De Vigne, 'even your
sex don't love and unlove, *quite* in such a hurry.
Don't you care for your grandpapa, then, because
he has never seen fairies?'

'Care for grandpapa! Oh, yes!' she cried
passionately, 'as much as I hate—*hate!*—those

cruel men who have robbed him of his money.
I would try not to care for Weive Hurst if he
were happy, but he will never be happy without it any more than I.'

'Do you remember me, Alma?" I asked, to
change her thoughts.

She shook her head.

' Do you remember him?'

She looked very tenderly and admiringly on
De Vigne.

' Oh yes! When I read "Sintram," I thought
of him as Sir Folko.'

De Vigne laughed.

' You bit of a child, what do you understand of
"Sintram?"'

' I understand Sir Folko, and I wish I had been
Gertrude.'

' Then you wish you had been my wife, mademoiselle?'

Alma considered gravely for a moment, looking
steadily in De Vigne's face.

' Yes; I think I should like to have you to
take care of me, as he took care of Gertrude.'

We went off into shouts of laughter, which
Alma could not understand. She could not see
that she had said anything laughable.

' I thought you were never going to love me

again, Alma? A wife ought to love her husband,'
said De Vigne.

Alma made a *moue mutine* and turned away,
her blue ribbons and her gold hair fluttering
impatient defiance. Just then her grandfather
came in, the stately, old master of Weive
Hurst.

'How do you do?' cried De Vigne. 'I am
having an offer made me, Mr. Tressillian, though
it is not leap year. I hope you will give your
consent?'

'I will never marry anybody who does not
believe in fairies!' interrupted Alma, running back
again to her leads.

'If she make a like proposal five or six years
hence to any man, she'll hardly have it neglected,'
said I, when Tressillian had recalled who I was,
and shaken hands with me.

Tressillian smiled sadly. 'Her love will be a
curse to her, poor child, for she will love too well;
as for her being neglected, she will not have the
gilding necessary to make youth protected, beauty
appreciated, or talent go down, if she should chance
to have the two latter as she grows older.'

'Which she is pretty sure to have, unless she
alters dreadfully.'

Boughton Tressillian sighed. 'Yes, she is

pretty enough, and she is clever. I believe she
already knows much more than young ladies
who have just "finished." She would learn even
better still if she were not so wildly imagina-
tive. *Poverina!* she is ill-fitted to grapple with
the world. Whether I spend my few years
between four bare walls or not, matters little;
but hers— Well, De Vigne, what news to-
day. Is the Ministry going to keep in or
not?'

De Vigne stayed some half-hour chatting with
him, telling him all the amusing *on dits* of the Clubs,
and all the fresh political tittle-tattle of the morning, while Tressillian, after that single expression
of regret for Alma, alluded no more to his own
affairs, and discussed current topics with the intelligence and interest of a man of intellect; enter-
taining us with the same cheerful ease as he had
done at Weive Hurst, meeting his reverses with
a philosophy of the highest, yet of the simplest,
order. De Vigne was more courtly, more delicate,
more respectful to the ruined gentleman, than he
was to many a leader of high ton, for, haughty
and imperious on occasion as he was, there was
a touch of true chivalry in his character. Go
down in the world, De Vigne stretched out his
hand to you, be you what you might; rise high,

and he cut you, or snubbed you, as he might see fit. De Vigne was not like the world, messieurs !

'How I should enjoy straightening my left arm for the benefit of that cursed hypocrite of the British Beggars Bank,' began De Vigne, tooling the tilbury back again through the Strand ; and, so far forgetting himself in his irritation as to venture to use the whip to his wheeler, who revenged the insult by a *pas d'extase*, which produced frightful commotion among the omnibusses, whose conductors swore in inelegant language at 'the confounded break-neck nob!' 'The morality of the age is too ridiculous! For the banker's clerk, who, with a sick wife and starving children, yields to one of the fiercest temptations that can beset a man, and takes one drop out of the sea of gold around him, it thinks penal servitude too kind a boon! To the Banker himself, who has reduced forty thousand people to want, the world is lenient, because he stuck his name on missionary lists, and came to public meetings with the Bible on his lips: and, after a little time has slipped away, men will see him installed in a Roman palace, or a Paris hotel, and will flock to his *soirées* by the dozens!'

'Of course ; don't you think that if Mephis-

tophcles set up here in Belgravia, and gave the
best dinners in London; he would get us all
to dine with him?'

'To be sure. Men measure you by what you
give them. If you're a poor devil with only small
beer in your cellar you are ostracized, though you
be the best and wisest man in Athens; if you've
good claret, they will come and drink it with
you, and only discuss your sins behind your back;
and if by any chance you have pipefuls of
Johannisberg and Tokay, you will have all the
cardinal virtues voted to you, without your giving
testimony to your even recognizing the cardinal
virtues at all! Hallo! gently, gently, Psyche!
what a hard mouth she has. Confound her! she
will set Cupid off again, and I shall figure in the
police reports as taken up for furious driving. I
say, what can Tressillian do?'

' Do?'

' Yes. What can he do that I can find him?
he is a gentleman and a scholar, but his age shuts
him out from any post such as he could ever
accept. He has no money—he must do something. I shall talk to Sabretasche; he has no
end of interest everywhere if he would only exert
it. I think he would if I asked him, so that we
might get some pleasant gentlemanlike sinecure

for the old man, where he would not have much
to remind him painfully of his reverses.   I'll see!
By the way, Chevasney, you'll try and get leave
to come down with me for the 1st.   It's a horrid
bore, but I can't get mine till then.   I wanted
it a month earlier.'

'To go to Brighton?'   I knew the last
week in July would see the Fantyre and Trefusis transplanted from Bruton Street to Kemp
Town.

He laughed.   'Well, Brighton's very pleasant
in its season, and town is utterly detestable in
August, when everybody not tied by the leg as
we are is yachting in the Levant, or fishing in
Norway, or bagging black game, or doing something worth doing.   However, we must make up
for it among the turnips and stubble; I think
my preserves are the best in the county.   You
must come down, Arthur, I can't do without
you, it's a crying cruelty to coop military men
up in the shooting season; besides, you are a
great pet of my mother's.'

'Doesn't she ever come to town!'

'Oh, yes; but her health is delicate.   She has
no daughters to bring out, and I think she prefers
the country in the spring and summer.   Here one
loses Summer altogether.   We don't know such a

word; it is merged into the Season, and the
flowers grow on ladies' bonnets instead of meadow
lands. Well! I like it best. I prefer society to
solitude. St. Simon Stylites had very fine medi-
tations, I dare say, and a magnificent bird's-eye
view of the country; but I must say Rabela-
sian Philosophies would seem more like life to
me, and I fancy I see more of human nature in
the Pré Catalan than the Prairies.'

' Yet you go mad after nature sometimes, you
odd fellow ? '

' Of course. There is a grandeur about the
wide stretch of sea in a sunny dawn, or the sweep
of hills and birch woods on a Highland moor,
beside which the fret and flippery of human life
are miserably insignificant. No man, who has
any manhood in him at all, but feels the better
for the fresh rush of a mountain wind. But for
all that, I am neither poet nor philosopher enough,
to live with nature always, and forswear the
coarser elements of life; lansquenet, racing, Co-
ralies, champagne, and all one's other habitual
agréments. Hang it, Arthur, why do you set
me defining; can't you let me *enjoy?* Ten years
hence I will theorize on life as much as you
please, just now I prefer taking it as it comes.
There! we did the distance in no time. Re-

mind me to speak to the messmen about that
would-be '15 port. It is the most daring sloes-
and-damsons that was ever palmed off on anybody. Thank Heaven, nobody can deceive me
in wine.'

'Nor in anything else?'

'I hope not. If they can, I have not knocked
about the world to much purpose, eh?'

If De Vigne set his mind on doing anything,
whether it was taking a cropper, or winning a
woman, hooking a salmon, or canvassing a county,
he never rested till it was done; therefore, having
taken Boughton Tressillian's cause steadily to
heart, he set all the levers going which were
available, to find something suitable to the old
man's broken fortunes and refined tastes. He
never let Sabretasche alone till the Colonel,
who knew everybody, used his interest too, a
thing he detested doing, because, as he said, it
'gives you so much trouble, and lays you under
Obligation; a debt nobody ever allows you to
forget that you owe them.' To please De Vigne,
however, he exerted himself; and between them
they procured a consulate for Tressillian, at a
large pleasant town on the Mediterranean shore,
which had of late years become almost an English
settlement, 'whose climate was exquisite, scenery

perfect, combined with admirable English and Italian society,' according to the elegant language of the guide-books, who told no lies about it for a wonder.

Anybody who wanted to see the side of De Vigne's character that made those who really knew him love him with the love of Jonathan for David, should have seen him offering his consul-ship to Tressillian, with the most delicate tact and feeling, so that the ruined gentleman could feel no obligation which could touch his pride, and could receive it only as a thoughtful forestalling of his wishes. That Tressillian felt it deeply I could see, but De Vigne refused all thanks, and the old man felt the kindness all the deeper for his disclaimer of it. 'You are a noble fellow,' he said heartily; 'you will find your reward some day.'

' My dear sir,' laughed De Vigne—when he felt things at all he generally turned them off in a jest—' I get many more rewards than I deserve, I fancy; my life's all prizes and no blanks, except, now and then, the blank of satiety. I am not one of those who "do good and blush to find it known;" for the simple reason that I never do any good at all, and have not blushed since I was seven, and fell in love with my mother's lady's-maid, a most divine Frenchwoman, with gold ear-rings, who eventually took up with the butler—bad taste, after me, was it not? You won't desert me for anybody I hope, Alma? You will see sublime Italians at Lorave?'

' They will not be as handsome as you are, Sir Folko,' responded Alma Tressillian, with frank admiration.

' Thank you, *cher enfant*; you will teach me to blush if you flatter me so much. Will you take me in, Alma, if I and my yacht call upon you any time?'

' Oh, do! do!' cried Alma, vehemently, ' and sail me on the sea, and I will show you the mermaids under the waves, with their necklets of seashells, and their fans of pink weed! You will see them, indeed you will, if you will only believe in them!'

'Most apt illustration of faith,' laughed De Vigne. 'People see tables turn, and violins dance with broomsticks, and hear Shakspeare talk through a loo-table, by sheer force of believing in them! When will that child ever learn to come down to the coarse realities of actual every day existence?'

' No,' said Tressillian, ' I am afraid I have hardly taken the best way of educating her for the real world. She should have gone to school, to learn the sober practicalities, and wise inanities of English schoolgirls. Her solitary life, with books and flowers, has encouraged the enthusiasm, and imagination, which come, I suppose, with her foreign blood; but then, I always thought she would be raised above heeding, or considering, the world! much more above ever working in it!'

A few days afterwards, Tressillian, with his grand-daughter and an English governess he had engaged for her, set off for Lorave. De Vigne and I saw them at the South-Eastern station, and little Alma cried as bitterly at parting with him as any of the women who loved him could have done; only the tears were not got up for effect, and washed off no rouge, like most of theirs! De Vigne consoled her with the promise of a yachting trip to Lorave, and came away from the station to drive the Trefusis down to dinner at the Star and Garter, where he was going to give an entertainment of unusual extravagance and splendour even for that dashing hotel, of which the Trefusis was undisputed Queen, and looked it too, drinking Badminton with much the same air as Juno must have worn drinking Ambrosia, and outshining all the women

in beauty, and figure, and toilette: for which
the women of course hated her, and respected
her in one breath: for, cordially as a lady de-
tests a handsome sister, it is notable that she
no less despises an ill-dressed or ugly one. To
be handsome a woman thinks an unpardonable
crime in her rival; but to be plain is a most
contemptible *faux pas*!

I can remember De Vigne now, sitting at the
head of the table, that bright June evening, at
Richmond. How happy he looked!—his forehead slightly flushed with pleasure and triumph,
his eyes flashing fire, or beaming softness and
tenderness, on the Trefusis, his musical voice
ringing out with a careless, happy harmony. Dear
old fellow! Life's best gifts seemed to lurk for
him in that goblet of Claret Cup, which he lifted
to his lips, with a fond pledge (by the eyes) to
the woman he loved. Yet, if he had known
his future, he would have filled the glass with
hemlock rather than have coupled the Bodmin-
ton with *her* name! Ah, well, mes freres! he is
not the only man for whom, the name that rang
so sweetly, breathed in the toast of love, has
chimed a bitter death-knell through all his after-
life!

The Trefusis did her best to lure him into

' definite action' that night, as he sat by her at
dinner; and leaned out of the window afterwards
beside her; the delicate perfume of her hair
mingling with the fragrance of roses and helio-
tropes from the garden below, the low jug-jug
of the nightingale joining with their own low
voices, and the summer starlight gleaming on both
their faces—his, impassioned, eager, earnest; hers,
fair indeed, but fair with the beauty of the rock-
crystal, which will melt neither for wintry frost
nor tropic sunshine. She did her best; and the
hour and the scene alike favoured her. She bent
forward, she looked up in his face, and the moon's
rays gave to her eyes a liquid sweetness never
their own : De Vigne began to lose control over
himself; the passion within him took the reins;
he who all his life through had denied himself
nothing; neither knew nor cared how to check
it. He bent towards the Trefusis, his fiery pulses
beating loud; while his moustaches touched her
low, smooth brow: Heaven knows what he might
have said, but I went up to them, ruthlessly:

' De Vigne, the horses are put to, and Miss
Trefusis wants to be in town by eleven, in time
for Mrs. Delany's ball; everybody's gone or
going.'

A fierce oath was muttered under De Vigne's

moustaches—he can be fiery enough if he's crossed. The Trefusis gave me a look—well! such as you, madame, will never give a man, if you are prudent, even though he be your lover's *fidus Achates,* and comes in just when he is not wanted. Then she rose, drawing on her gloves with a sweet, courteous smile :

' Oh ! thank you, Mr. Chevasney; how kind of you to come and tell us! I would not be late at dear Mrs. Delany's for the world; you know she is a very pet friend of mine.'

I had saved him that time, and, idiot-like, triumphed at my success. Might I not have known that no forty-horse power can keep a man from committing himself, if he is bent upon it? and might I not have known that if a fellow enters himself for any stakes with a woman, she will have cantered in and carried off the Cup before he has saved half the distance, let him pride himself upon his jockeyship never so highly?

I had saved De Vigne, and I don't think he bore me any good will for it, for he drove me and a couple of other men back in his phæton to Kensington, in gloomy silence. He could not go to Mrs. Delany's, for the best of all reasons—that he was not asked. Ladies never *do* invite with their pet friends the quarry their pet friends are trying the hardest to lure; not from envy, pretty little dears!—who would think of accusing them of *that?* Do they ever, by any chance, break the Tenth Commandment, and covet their neighbour's carriage, horses, or appointments, diamonds, point, flirtations, or anything that she has?

And the day after that the Trefusis went down to Brighton, to drive the Dragoons distracted, who should see her cantering over the South Downs, or waltz with her at their own balls, to drink in intoxication with the clang of the Express Galop; or meet her on the Esplanade, with that magnificent face shadowed by her little cobweb veil, swaying them all with her grand beauty, as if her carved ivory parasol-handle had been a sceptre, with a spell as potent as Venus's ceinture.

CHAPTER VIII.

THE FORGING OF THE FETTERS.

DE VIGNE and I consumed not a little cognac and
Cavendish, swearing over our durance vile, when
everybody was gone, and town was empty; and
after six weeks' consummation of anathemas, soda
water, and Latakia, sufficient to last a troop for a
twelvemonth, he and I were glad enough when
we were at last swinging down in the express to
Vigne on the 31st of August. I wondered in
my own mind he was not off to Kemp Town, but
I was too glad to find that the partridges out-
balanced the Trefusis to make any comment upon
it.

Vigne was about eighty miles from London; a
pretty picturesque village, of which nearly every
rood belonged to him; and his park was almost as
magnificent a sweep of land as Holcombe or Long-
leat. It was with something warmer than pride,
that he looked across, over his wide woodlands
glowing in the August sunset, the great elm-trees

throwing their wide cool shadows far over the rich pasture land beneath; the ferns, high as a man's elbow, waving in the breeze; the deer trooping away into the deep forest glades; and the length-ened avenues, stretching off in aisles of burnished green and gold, like one of Creswick's English landscapes. A mile and-a-half of one of those magnificent elm-avenues, brought us to the house, which was more like Hardwick Hall in exterior than any other place I know, standing grandly, too, something as Hardwick does; but in interior, though the hall and other parts of it, were mediæval enough, it was what Hardwick certainly is not— or was not, when last I saw it — luxurious and modern to the last degree, with every elegance and comfort which upholstery and science have taught the nineteenth century to look upon as absolute requirements.

De Vigne threw the ribbons of the drag to a groom, and sprang down, while the deep bay of the dogs in the kennels some way off, gave him a wel-come. In the hall he had another: as his mother, Lady Flora, a soft, delicate woman, with eyes and voice of great beauty and sweetness, came out from a morning-room to meet him, with both her hands outstretched, and a fond smile on her face. De Vigne loved his mother tenderly and reveren-

tially.   She had been a wise woman with him : as
a child, she had stimulated his energies instead of
repressing them, and, with strong self-command,
let him risk a broken limb, rather than teach him
his first idea of fear, a thing of which De Vigne
was as profoundly ignorant as little Nelson.   As a
boy, she had entered into all his sports and amuse-
ments, listening to his tales of rounders, ponies,
cricket, and boating, as if she really understood
them.   As a man she had never attempted to interfere with him.   She knew that she had trained him
in honour and truth, and was too skilled in human
nature to seek to pry into a young man's life.
The consequence was, that she kept all her son's
affection, trust, and confidence, and, when she did
speak, was always heard gently and respectfully ;
indeed, he would often tell her as naturally of his
errors and entanglements as he had, when a child,
told her of his faults to his servant or his Shetland.

The house was full, chiefly of men come down
for the shooting, with one or two girls of the
Ferrers family, Lady Flora's nieces, who would
have liked very well to have caught their cousin,
for their father, though he was a Marquis, was
as poor for a peer, as a curate with six daughters,
and no chance of preferment.   But their cousin

was not to be caught — by their trolling, at least.

'I am delighted to see you, Mr. Chevasney,' said Lady Flora, when I went down to the drawing-room after my bath, and hot coffee. 'You know you were always a favourite of mine, at first, *ne vous en déplaise*, because you were a friend of Granville's, and then for your own sake. There will be some people here to-morrow to amuse you, though you gentlemen never seem to me so happy as when you are without us. Shut you up in your smoking, or billiard, or card-room, and you want nothing more!'

'True enough!' laughed De Vigne. 'It is an ungallant admission, but it is a fact, nevertheless. See men at college wines, in the jollity and merriment of a camp, in the *sans géne* enjoyment of a man dinner! Deny it who will, we *can* be happy without ladies, but ladies cannot be happy without us!'

'How conceited you are, Granville!' cried Adelina Ferrers, a handsome blonde, who thought very well of herself. 'I am quite sure we can!'

'Can you, Lina?' said De Vigne, leaning against the mantelpiece, and watching his mother's diamond rings flash in and out, as she did some beadwork. 'Why do we never hear of ladies' parties, then? Why, when we come in after dinner, do we invariably find you all bored to the last extent, and half asleep, till you revive under our kindly influence? Why, if you are as happy without us, do we never see you establish Women Clubs to drink tea, or eau de Cologne, or sal volatile; to read new novels and talk over dress?'

'Because we are too kind. Our society improves you so much, that, through principle, we do not deprive you of it,' answered Lady Lina, with a long glance of her large azure eyes.

'That's a pity, dear,' smiled De Vigne, 'because, if we thought you were comfortably employed, we could go off to the partridges to-morrow with much greater pleasure; whereas to know, as we do, that you will all be victims of ennui till we come back again, naturally spoils sport to men like myself, of tender conscience and amiable disposition!'

'This is the fruit of Miss Trefusis's flattery, I suppose,' sneered Blanche Ferrers, the other cousin, who could not stand fun, and who had made hard running after De Vigne a season ago.

'Miss Trefusis never flatters,' said De Vigne, quietly.

'Indeed!' said Lady Blanche. 'I know nothing of her. I do not desire!'

The volumes expressed in those four last words

were such, as only women like Blanche Ferrers, could possibly compress in one little sneering sentence.   De Vigne felt all that was intended in it; his eyebrows contracted, his eyes flashed fire; he had too knightly a heart not to defend an absent woman, and a woman he loved; as dearly as he would his own honour.

'It would be to your advantage, Blanche, if you had that pleasure.   Miss Trefusis would make any one proud to know her; *even* the Ladies Ferrers, though the world does say they are fond of imagining the sun created solely that it may have the honour of shining on them.'

He spoke very quietly, but sarcastically.   His mother looked up at him hastily, then bent over her work; Blanche coloured with annoyance, and smiled another sneer.

'Positively, Granville, you are quite chivalrous in her defence!   I know it is the law at Vigne for nobody to disagree with you; nevertheless, I shall venture, for I must assure you, that far from esteeming it an honour to know Miss Trefusis, I should deem it rather a—*dis*honour!'

How like a lion fairly roused, and longing to spring, he looked!   He kept cool, however, but his teeth were set hard.

'Lady Blanche, it is rather dishonour to yourself, to dare to speak in that manner of a lady of whom you have never heard any evil, and who is *my* friend. Miss Trefusis is as worthy respect and admiration as yourself, and she shall never be mentioned in any other terms in my presence.'

Gallant he looked, with his steady eyes looking sternly down at her, and his firm mouth set into iron! A whole history of love and trust, honour and confidence, the chivalry which defended the absent, the strength which protected the woman dear to him, were written on his face. Was she, who was absent and slandered, worthy it?

Blanche laughed derisively, but a little timidly; it was not easy even for her to be rude to him.

'Respect and admiration! Really, Granville, one would believe report, and imagine you intended to give Lady Fantyre's—what?—niece, dependent, companion—which is it?—your name?'

'Perhaps I do. As it is, I exact the same courtesy for her, as my friend, that I shall do if ever she be—my wife!'

He spoke slowly and calmly, still leaning on the mantelpiece; but his face was white with passion, and his dark eyes glowed like fire. A dead silence followed on his words: the silence of breathless astonishment, of unutterable dismay:

Lady Flora turned as white as her bead-work, and she did not trust herself to look at her son, but in a moment or two she spoke, with gentle dignity.

'Blanche, you forget what you are saying. You can have no possible right to question your cousin's actions or opinions. Let this be the last I hear of such a discussion. Mr. Chevasney, if you wish to be useful, will you be kind enough to hold this skein of floss silk for me?'

Just at that moment some of the men came in and surrounded Adelina and Blanche; it was a relief to everybody: Lady Flora went on winding her silk, not daring to look up at her son, and he stayed where he was, leaning on the mantelpiece, playing with a setter's ears, till dinner was announced as served: then he gave his arm to the Marchioness, and was especially brilliant and agreeable all the evening.

That night, however, when most of us had gone off to the bachelor wing, De Vigne rapped at the door of his mother's dressing-room. She expected it, and admitted him at once. He sat by the fire for some moments, holding her hand in his own; De Vigne was very gentle with what he loved. His mother looked up at him, with a few words: 'Dearest, is it true?'

'Yes.' Where he meant much, he also generally said few words.

His mother was silent. Perhaps, until now, she had never realized how entirely she would lose her son to his wife; how entirely the new passion would sweep away and replace the old affection; how wholly, and how justly, his confidences, his ambitions, his griefs, his joys, would go to another instead of to herself. Perhaps she knew how unfit De Vigne was to be curbed and tied; how much his fiery nature would shrink from the burden of married life, and his fiery heart refuse to give the love exacted as a right: perhaps she knew, by knowledge of human nature, and experience of human life, how true it is that 'a young man married is a man that's marred.'

'Your wife!' she said, at last, tears in her voice and in her eyes. 'Granville, you little guess all those words sound to me; how much I have hoped, how much I have feared, how much I have prayed for, in—your wife! Forgive me, dear; I can hardly accustom myself to it yet.'

And she bent her head, and sobbed bitterly. May we believe with Madame de Girardin?—

> ' C'est en vain que l'on nomme erreur,
>   Cette secrète intelligence,
> Qui portant la lumière au fond,
>   Sur des maux ignorés nous fait gémir d'avance !'

De Vigne bent his head, and kissed her. It was very rarely he saw his mother's tears; and in proportion to their rarity they always touched him. They were both of them silent. The next question she asked, came with the resignation of a woman, to a man whose purpose she knew she could never alter, nor even sway, any more than she could stir the elm-trees in the avenues, from the beds that they had lain in for lengthened centuries.

'You really love her then?'

'More passionately than I have ever loved a woman yet!'

That sealed the sentence. Lady Flora knew, that never in love, as in sport, had De Vigne checked his fancy, or turned back from his quarry.

'God help you then!'

He started at the uncalled-for prayer; it was an involuntary utterance of the trembling tenderness, the undefined dread with which she regarded his future. He smiled down gaily at her. 'Why, mother, what is there so dreadful in love? One would fancy you thought shockingly of your sex, to view my first thought of marriage, through smoked glasses.'

She tried to smile. 'It is such a lottery!'

'Of course it is; but so are all games of chance; and, if one ventures nothing, one may go without play all one's life. As for happiness, *that* is at very uncertain odds at all times, and the only wise thing one can do is to enjoy the present. Does not La Bruyère tell us that no man ever married yet, who did not in twelve months' time wish he had never seen his wife? It is true enough for that matter; so that, whether one does it sooner or later, one is equally certain to repent.' He spoke with a light laugh and a fearless confidence in his own future which went to his mother's heart. She took both his hands in hers.

'Granville, you know I never seek to interfere with your opinions, plans, or actions. You are a man of the world, far fitter to judge for yourself than I am to judge for you; but no one can love you better than I?'

'Indeed no,' said De Vigne, tenderly, 'none so well.'

'And no one cares for your future life as I? Therefore, will you listen to me for a minute?'

'Sixty, if you like.'

'Then, tell me,' said his mother gently, 'do you really think yourself that you are fitted for married life, or married life fitted for you?'

'Don't put it in that way!' cried De Vigne,

impatiently. 'Married life? No! not if I were chained down into dull domesticity; but in our position marriage makes little or no difference in our way of life. We keep the same society, have the same diversions as before. We are not chained together like two galley-slaves, toiling away at one oar, without change of scene or of companion. She must be my wife, because, if she is not, I shall go mad; but she is no woman only fit "to suckle fools and chronicle small beer," and she would be the last to deprive me of that liberty, of which, you are quite right in thinking, I should chafe incessantly at the loss! But I am talking myself, not listening to you. What else were you going to say?'

'I was going to say—are you sure you will never love again?'

De Vigne grew impatient again. He threw back his head; these were not pleasant suggestions to him.

'Really, my dear mother, you are looking very far into futurity! How can I, or any man, by any possibility, answer such a question? We are not gods, to foresee what lies before us. I know that I love now—love more deeply than I have ever done yet, and that is enough for me!'

'That is not enough for me,' answered his mo-

ther, with a heavy sigh. 'I can foresee your
future, for I know your nature, your mind, your
heart. You will marry now, in the mad passion
of the hour; marry as a thousand men do, giving
up their birthright of free choice and liberty, and
an open future, for a mess of porridge of a few
hours' delight! I know nothing of Miss Trefusis,
nor do I wish to say anything against her; but
I know *you*. You marry her, no doubt, from
eye-love; for her magnificent beauty, which report says is unrivalled. After a time that beauty
will grow stale and tame to you; it will not be
your fault; men are born inconstant, and eye-love
expires, when the eye has dwelt long enough on it,
to grow tired and satiated. Have you not, times
out of number, admired and wearied before, Granville? Then there will come long years of regret,
impatience of the fetters once joyfully assumed,
perhaps; for you require sympathy and compre-
hension; miserable years of wrangling and re-
proaches, such as you are least fitted of all men to
endure. You will see that your earlier judgment
was crude, your younger taste at fault; *then*, with
your passions strengthened, your discernment
matured, you will love again—love with all the
tenderness, the depth of later years—love, to find
the crowning sorrow of your life, or to drag another

in to share the curse you already have brought upon yourself. Can you look steadily at such a future?'

A chill of ice passed through his veins as he heard her—the true foreshadowing of a most bitter doom! Then he threw the presentiment off, and his hot blood flowed on again in its wilful and fiery course; he answered her passionately and decidedly.

'Yes! I have no fear of any evil coming to me through my love. If she will, she shall be my wife, and whatever my future be, I accept it.'

The day after our arrival I found the reason for De Vigne's throwing over Brighton for his own home. The Trefusis and Lady Fantyre came down to stay at Follet, a place some three or four miles from Vigne, with some friends of the Fantyre, whose acquaintance she had made on the Continent; people whom De Vigne knew but slightly, but whom he now cultivated, more than he generally troubled himself to do, much more exclusive members of that invariably stiltified, stuck-up, and pitiably-toadied thing, the County.

The 1st of September came, gray, soft, still, as that delightful epoch of one's existence always should, and up with the dawn we swallowed beer and coffee, devils and omelettes, too hastily to appreciate them, and went out, a large party;

for Sabretasche had come there the night before,
with several other men, to knock the birds over,
in De Vigne's princely preserves. What magic
is there in sport to make us so mad after it?
What is the charm that lies hid in the whirr of
the covey up from the stubble, and makes dan-
dies contentedly wade through ploughed fields in
sloppy weather; carrying their gun through drip-
ping turnips; knee-deep in mud, or dead-beat, but
triumphant, from the knowledge of forty brace in
the bag on the pony's back? A strange charm
there *is*—a charm we enjoy too much to analyze ;
and De Vigne, whose head and heart were full of
different game, and Sabretasche, who hated dirty-
ing his hands, and shrank from most people and
most things as too coarse for his artistic taste, alike
swore to the truth of it, with the dogs and the beat-
ers round them in the open, or lying in the shade
of some great hedge-trees, discussing Bass and a
cold luncheon, with more appetite than they ever
had for the most delicious breakfast at the Maison
Dorée, or the daintiest *hors d'œuvre* at Tortoni's.

Though De Vigne did not allow a battue on his
lands, I think we had almost as many head of game
in the bags as if we had had one, when twilight
had put an end to the ever-longed-for First, and
we had returned to the bachelor's wing to dress for

dinner. Coming out of my room, I met De
Vigne, and he put his hand on my shoulder.

' Well, Arthur, hadn't we good sport to-day?
I say, send off any of that game you like anywhere; you know lots of people. Isn't it
beautiful to see Sabretasche knock down the
birds; such a lazy fellow as he is, too?'

' He's not a better shot than you?'

' Don't you think so? But then he's a disciple
of the dolce, and I always go hard at anything I
take in hand.'

' You don't sell your game?' I asked, knowing
I might just as well ask him if he sold hot pota-
toes!

' Sell it? No, thank you; I am not a
poulterer! I have sport, not trade; the fellows
who sell the game their friends help them to kill,
should write up over their lodge-gates, " Game
sold here, by men who would like to be thought
gentlemen, but find it a losing concern." I would
as soon send my trees up to London for building
purposes as my partridges to Leadenhall. The
fellows who do that sort of thing must have some
leaven of old Lombards, or Chepe goldsmiths in
them; and though they have an Escutcheon instead of a Sign now, can't get rid of the trader's
instinct!'

I loved to set De Vigne up on his aristocratic stilts, they were so deliciously contradictory to the radical opinions he was so fond of enunciating! The fact was, he was an aristocrat at his heart, a radical by his head, and the two Creeds sometimes had a tilt, and upset one another.

'Is anybody coming to dinner to-night?' I was half afraid somebody was, whom I detested to see near him at all.

'Yes,' he answered, curtly. 'There are the Levisons, Lady Fantyre and Miss Trefusis, Cavendish and Ashton.'

For my life I couldn't help a long whistle, I was so savage at that woman getting the better of us all so cleverly!

'The deuce! De Vigne, your mother and that nasty, gambling, story-telling old Fantyre will hardly run in couples?'

For a second his cheek flushed.

'It is *my* house, I invite whom I see fit. As for my mother, God bless her! she will hardly find a woman good or true enough to run in couples with her. She is *too* good and true to be prudish or censorious. I have always noticed that it is women who live in glass houses who learn quickest to throw stones, I suppose in the futile hope of inducing people to imagine that their dwellings are such as nobody could possibly assail.'

'Why the devil, De Vigne,' said I, 'are you so mad about that woman? What is it you admire in her?'

He answered with the reckless passion which was day by day getting more mastery over him.

'How should I define? I admire nothing—I admire everything! I only know that I will move heaven and earth to gain her, and that I would shoot any man dead who ventured to dispute her with me!'

'Is she worth all that?'

His eyes grew cold and annoyed; I had gone a step too far. He took his hand off my shoulder, and saying, with that hauteur which no man could assume more chillingly, 'My dear Chevasney, you may apply the lesson I gave Lady Blanche yesterday, to yourself; I never allow any remarks on my personal concerns,' passed down before me into the hall: where, just alighted from the Levisons' carriage, her cloak dropped off one shoulder, something shining and jewelled wreathed over her hair, the strong wax-light gleaming on her face, with its rich geranium-hue in the cheek, and its large, luminous eyes, and its short, curved, upper lip, stood in brilliant relief against the carved oak, dark armour, and deep-hued windows of the hall—the Trefusis. De Vigne went down the wide oak staircase and across the tesselated pavement to her side, to welcome her to Vigne; and she—she thought, I dare say, as she glanced round, that it would be a conquest worth making: the master and—the home.

Lady Flora looked earnestly at her as she entered. It was the first time she had seen her, for the Trefusis had been driving when, by her son's request, she had called on the Levisons, with whom she had not more acquaintance than an occasional dinner, or rencontre at some county gathering. Beautiful woman as the Trefusis looked—and that she was this her worst enemies could never deny—in that hard though superb profile, in those lips curved downwards while of such voluptuous beauty, in those eyes so relentless and defiant though of such perfect hue and shape, his mother found how little to hope, how much to fear!

Yet the Trefusis played her cards well. She was very gentle to Lady Flora. She did not seem to seek De Vigne, nor to try and monopolize him; and with the Ladies Ferrers she was so calm, so self-possessed, and yet had so little assumption, that, hard as Lina and Blanche were studying to pick her to pieces, they could not find where to begin, till she drew off her glove at dinner, when Blanche whispered to Sabretasche, who had taken her in, 'No sang pur *there*, but plenty of almond paste!' to which the Colonel, hating the Trefusis, but liking De Vigne too well to give the Ferrers a handle against their possible future cousin, replied, 'Well, Lady Blanche, perhaps so—but one is so sated with pretty hands and empty heads, that one is almost grateful for a change!'

Whereat Blanche, all her governesses, Paris schools, and finishing, not having succeeded in drilling much understanding into her brain, was bitterly wrathful, and, in consequence, smiled extra pleasantly.

The Trefusis acted her part admirably that night, and people of less skill in society and physiognomy than Lady Flora would have been blinded by it.

'What a master-spirit of intrigue that woman would be in a court!' said Sabretasche to me. 'No man—certainly no man in love with her —can stand against the strong will and skilful artifices of an ambitious and designing *intrigante*. Solomon tells you, you know, Arthur, that the worst enemy you young fellows have is Woman, and I tell you the same.'

' Yet, if report speak truly, Colonel, the sex
has no warmer votary than you ? '

' Whenever *did* report speak truly?   Perhaps
I may be only revenging myself; how should
you know ?   It is the fashion, to look on Pa-
mela as a fallen star, and on Lovelace as a horrid cruel wretch.   I don't see it always so, myself.   Stars that are dragged from heaven by the
very material magnets of guineas, cashmeres, love
of dress, avarice, or ambition for a St. John's
Wood villa, are not deeply to be pitied ; and men
who buy toys at such low prices are little to
be censured for not estimating their goods very
high.   The price of a virtuous woman is rarely
above rubies ; it has only this difference, that the
rubies set as a bracelet will suffice for Coralie, while
they must go round a coronet to win Lady Blanche !
A propos!—whatever other silly things you do,
Chevasney, never make an early marriage.'

' I never intend, I assure you,' I said, tartly.   I
thought he might have heard of Gwendolina, and
be poking fun at me; and Gwen, I knew, was not
for me, but for M. le Duc de Vieillecour, a poor,
wiry, effete old beau, who had been about
Charles X.

' Very well, so far ; but you need not look so
indignant, no man can tell into what he may be

drawn. No one is so secure; but that next year he may commit the sin, he utterly ridicules this. Look at De Vigne; six months past he would have laughed in your face if you had spoken to him of marriage. Now he would be tempted to knock you down if you attempted to dissuade him *from* marriage! What will he gain by it; what won't he lose? If she were a charming woman, he would lose his liberty, his pleasant bachelor life, his power of disposing of himself how and where he choses, without query or comment. With a woman like the Trefusis he will lose more; he will lose his peace, his self-respect, his belief in human nature; and it will be well if he lose not his honour! He will have always beside him a wife from whom his whole soul revolts, but to whom his hot-headed youth has fettered him, till one or the other shall lie in the grave. There is no knowing to what madness, what misery, his early marriage may not lead him, to what depths of hopelessness, or error, it may not drag him. Were he a weak man, he would collapse under her rein, and be henpecked, cheated, and cajoled; being a strong one, he will rebel, and, still acting and seeing for himself, he will find out in too short a time, that he has sacrificed himself, and life, and name, to—a Mistake.'

He spoke so earnestly for listless, careless, non-chalant, indolent Sabretasche, that I stared at him, for he was almost proverbially impassive; he caught my eye, and laughed.

'What do you think of my sermon, Arthur? Bear it in mind if you are in danger, that is all. Will you come out into the card-room, and have a game or two at écarté? You play wonderfully well for so young as you are; but then you say a Frenchman taught you? I hate to play with a man who cannot beat me tolerably often; there is no excitement without difficulty. The Trefusis knows that! Look at her flirting with Monckton in her stately style, while De Vigne stands by, looks superbly indifferent, and chafes all the time like a hound held in leash, while another is pulling down the stag!'

'She will not make you happy, Granville!' said his mother that night, when De Vigne bid her good night in her dressing-room, as was his invariable custom.

He answered her stiffly. 'It is unfortunate you are all so prejudiced against her.'

'I am not prejudiced,' she answered, with a bitter sigh. 'Heaven knows how willingly I would try to love anyone who loves you, but a woman's intuition sees farther sometimes than

a man's discernment can penetrate, and in Miss
Trefusis, beyond beauty of form and feature, I see
nothing that will satisfy you : there is no beauty
of mind, no beauty of heart ! The impression she
gives me is, that she is an able schemer, a clever
actress, quick to seize on the weak points of those
around her, and turn them to her own advantage ;
but that she is—forgive me !—illiterate, ambitious,
and heartless ! '

' You wrong her and you wrong yourself ! '
broke in De Vigne passionately. ' Your anxiety
for me warps alike your own penetration and
charity of feeling. I should have thought you
were above such injustice ! '

' I only wish I may do her injustice,' answered
his mother, gravely. ' But oh, Granville, I fear—
I fear ! Dearest, do not be angry, none will ever
love you more unselfishly than I ! If I tremble
for your future, it is only that I know your character so well. I know all that, as years go on,
your mind will require, your heart exact, from the
woman who is your wife. I know how quickly
the glamour fades in the test of constant intercourse. A commonplace, domestic woman would
drive you from her side to another's ; a hard,
tyrannous, beautiful woman will freeze you into
ice, like herself. I, who love you so dearly, how

can I look calmly on to see the shipwreck of
your life? My darling! my darling! I would
almost as soon hear that you had died on a
battle-field, as your father did before you, as hear
that you had given your fate into that woman's
hands !'

His mother's tenderness and grief touched De
Vigne deeply; he knew how well she loved him,
and that this was the first time she had sought to
cross his will, but—he stooped and kissed her with
fond words, and rose, of the same persuasion
still! It were as easy to turn the west wind from
its course, as it sweeps wild and free over the sea
and land, as by words or counsel, laws or warnings, to attempt to stem the self-willed, headlong
current of a man's mad passion.

Had any whispered warning to Acis of his fate,
would he have ever listened or cared when, in
the sunset glow, he saw the witching gleam of
Galatea's golden hair? When the son of Myrha
gazed up into the divine eyes, and felt his own
lips glow at the touch of ' lava kisses,' could he
foresee, or, had he foreseen, would he have ever
heeded, the dark hour when he should lie dying,
on those same Idalian shores?

The Trefusis played her cards ably. A few
days after she played her ace of trumps, and her

opponents were obliged to throw up] their hands.
De Vigne did not ask his mother to invite her
and Lady Fantyre there; infatuated though he
was, and wisely careless on such subjects generally, I think he felt that the old *ci-devant* orange-
girl, with her nasty stories, her dingy reputation,
and her clever tricks with the four honours, was
not a guest suitable to his high-born, high-bred
mother. But a day or two after was his birth-
day, a day which, contrary to his own taste, but
in accordance with old habit, had been celebrated,
whether he was present or not, with wonderful
éclat and magnificence. This year, as usual, ' the
County,' and parts of surrounding counties, too,
came to a dinner and ball at Vigne; and the
Levisons had been included in the invitations a
month before we went down, now, of course, the
Trefusis would accompany them.

As De Vigne had not even the slight admixture
of Roger de Coverley benevolence assumed by
some county men at the present time, as he had
not the slightest taste for oats or barley, did not
care two straws how his farms went or how his
lands were let, and hated toadying and flummery
as cordially as he hated bad wine, the proceedings
of the day very naturally bored him immensely;
and he threw himself down, after replying to his

tenants' speeches, on one of the couches of the smoking-room, with an anathema on the whole thing.

'What a happy fellow you are, Sabretasche!' said he to the Colonel, who had retired from the scene to one of the sofas with a pile of periodicals and a case of genuine Manillas. 'You have nothing on your hands but your town-house, that you can shut up, and your Highland lodge, where you can leave your dogs for ten months in the year; and have no yeomanry, tenants, and servants, to look to you yearly for sirloins and October, and a speech that is more trouble to make than fifty parliamentary ones!'

'Ah! my dear fellow,' yawned Sabretasche, 'I did stay in that tent pitying you beyond measure, till my feelings and my nerves couldn't stand seeing you martyrized, and scenting that very excellent beef, and hearing those edifying cheers any longer; so, as I couldn't help *you*, I took compassion on myself, shut myself up with the magazines, and thanked Heaven I was not born to that desideratum—"a fine landed property!"'

De Vigne laughed.

'Well, it's over now! I shouldn't mind it so much if they would't talk such bosh to one's face—praising me for my liberality and noble-

mindedness, and calling me public-spirited and
generous, and Heaven knows what. They're
a good-hearted set of fellows, though, I believe—'

'Possibly,' said Sabretasche; 'but what extent
of good-heartedness can make up for those dreadfully broad o's and a's, and those terrific " Sunday-
going suits," and those stubble-like heads of hair
plastered down with oil?'

'Not to you, you confounded refiner of refined
gold,' laughed De Vigne. 'By-the-by, Sabretasche, don't you sometimes paint lilies in your
studio? That *raffiné* operation would suit you to
a T. I suppose you never made love to a woman
who was not the ultra-essence of good breeding
and Grecian outline?'

Sebretasche gave a sort of shudder; at some
recollection, or at the simple suggestion.

'Well,' said De Vigne; 'Cupid has a vernacular
of his own which levels rank sometimes; a pretty
face, is a pretty face, whether it is under a Paris
bonnet, or a cottage straw. But what I hate so,
in this sort of affair, is the false light in which
it makes one stand. Here am I, who don't see
Vigne for nine months out of the year, sometimes
not at all, who delegate all the bother of it to
my steward, who neither know nor care when the

rents are paid, nor how the lands are divided,
cheered by these people as if I were a sort of god
and king over them—and, deuce take them! they
mean it, too! Their fathers' fathers worshipped my
father's fathers, and so they, in a more modern
fashion, cheer and toast me as if I were a combined
Cincinnatus and Titus! You know well enough I
am nothing of the kind! I don't think I have a
spark of benevolence in my composition. I could
no more get up an interest in model cottages, and
prize fruit, than I could in Cochin-Chinas or worsted
work, and the consequence is that I feel a humbug, and instead of returning thanks to-day to my
big farmers, and my small retainers, I should have
liked to have said to them, " My good fellows, you
are utterly mistaken in your man. I am glad you
are doing well, and I won't let any of you be
ground down if I know it; but otherwise I don't
care a jot about any of you, and this annual affair is
a very great bore to me, whatever it may be to you;
and I take this opportunity of assuring you that,
far from being a demigod, I am a very graceless
cavalry man, and instead of doing any good with
my twenty thousand a year, I only make ducks
and drakes of it as fast as I possibly can." If I
had said that to them, I should have relieved
myself, had no more toadying, and felt that the

Vigneites and I understood one another. What a horrid bother it is one can't tell truth in the world!'

'Most people find the bother lie, in having to tell the truth occasionally!' said the Colonel, with his enigmatical smile. '*You* might enjoy having, like Fénelon's happy islanders, only to open your eyes to let your thoughts be read, but I am afraid such an *exposé* would hardly suit most of us. You don't agree with Talleyrand, that language is given us to conceal our thoughts?'

De Vigne looked at him as he poked up his pipe.

'Devil take you, Sabretasche! Who is to know what you mean, or what you think, or what you are?'

'My dear fellow,' said the Colonel, cutting the *Westminster* slowly with one hand, and taking out his cigar with the other, 'nobody, I hope, for *I* agree with Talleyrand, if you don't.'

The County came—a few to dinner, many to the ball, presenting all the varied forms of that peculiar little oligarchy; a Duke, two Marquises, two Earls, four or five Barons, high-dried, grand old Dowagers, with fresh, pretty-looking daughters as ready for fun and flirtation as their maids; stiltified County Queens, with daughters long on hand, who had taken refuge in High-Churching their village, and starched themselves very stiff in

the operation. Pretty married women, who waltzed
in a nutshell, and had many more of us after them
than the girls. County beauties, accustomed to
carry all before them at race balls if not at Almack's, and to be Empresses at archery fêtes if
they were only units in Belgravia. Hunting
Baronets, who liked the music of the pack when
they threw up their heads, much better than the
music of D'Albert's waltzes. Members with the
down hardly on their cheeks; other Members,
whose mission seemed to lie much more in the
saddle than the benches. Rectors by the dozen,
who found a village dance on the green sinful, but
a ball at Vigne a very pardonable error; scores of
military men, who flirted more desperately and
meant less by it than any fellows in the room;
all the County, in fact, and among them little old
Fantyre, with her hooked nose, and her queer reputation, her dirty, priceless lace, and her jewels
got nobody knew how, and her daughter, niece,
or companion, the *intrigante*, the interloper, but
decidedly the belle of the rooms, the handsome
and haughty Trefusis. Superbly, in truth, she
looked in some dress, as light and brilliant as summer clouds, with the rose tint of sunset on them,
while her eyes, dark and lustrous as an East-
ern's, shot their dangerous languid glances. One

could hardly wonder that De Vigne offended past redemption the Ladies-in-their-own-right, all the great heiresses, all the County princesses royal, all the archery-party beauties; and—careless of rank, right, or comment, opened the ball with—the Trefusis. It was her crowning triumph, and she knew it. She knew that what he dared to begin, he would dare to follow out, and that the more censure he provoked, the more certainly would he persevere in his own will.

'We have lost the game!' said Sabretasche to me, as he passed me, waltzing with Adelina Ferrers.

It was true. De Vigne was then waltzing that same valse with her; whirling her round, the white lilies of her *bouquet de corsage* crushed against his breast; her forehead resting on his shoulder, his moustaches touching her hair as he whispered in her ear, his face glad, proud, eager, impassioned; while the County feminine sneered, and whispered behind their fans, 'what could De Vigne possibly see in that woman?' and the men swore what a deuced fine creature she was, and wondered what Trefusis she might be?

And—that waltz over—De Vigne gave her his

arm and led her out of the ball-room to take
some ice, and then strolled on with her into the
conservatories, which, thanks to Lady Flora, were
brilliant as the glories of the tropics, and odorous
as a rich Indian night, with their fragrance ex-
haling from citron and cypress groves, and their
heavy clusters of magnolias and mangoes. There,
in that atmosphere, that hour, so sure to banish
prudence and fan the fires of passion; there, to
the woman beside him, glorious as one of the
West Indian flowers above their heads, but chill
and unmoved at heart, as one of their brilliant
and waxen petals,—De Vigne poured out in terse
and glowing words the love that Beauty alone so
madly and strangely awakened, laying generously
and trustfully, as knight of old laid his spoils and
his life, at his queen's feet, his home, his name, his
honour before the woman he loved. And she sim-
ulated tenderness to perfection ; she threw it into
her lustrous eyes, she forced it into her blushing
cheek, it trembled in her softened voice, it
glanced upwards under her dark lashes. It was
all a Lie, but a lie marvellously acted :—and
while De Vigne bent over her, covering her
lips with passionate caresses, drinking in with
every breath a fresh draught of intoxication,
his heart beating loud and quick with the

triumph of success, was it a marvel that he forgot his past, his future, his own experience, others' warnings, anything and everything, save the Present, in its full and triumphant delirium?

CHAPTER IX.

THE BLOW THAT A WOMAN DEALT.

' I say, Arthur—she has outwitted us ! '

' The devil she has, Colonel ! '

' Who would have believed him so mad ? '

' Who would have believed her so artful ? '

' Chevasney, men are great fools ! '

' And women wonderful actresses, Colonel ! '

' Right ; but it is a cursed pity.'

' That De Vigne is taken in, or that women are embodied lies, sir—which ? '

' Both ! '

And with his equanimity most unusually ruffled, and his *nonchalant* impassiveness strangely disturbed, Sabretasche turned away out of the ballroom, which De Vigne and the Trefusis, after a prolonged absence, had just re-entered ; his face saying plainly enough, that his cause was won ; hers telling as clearly, that Vigne and its master were captured.

When the dawn was rising, and the great gates

had closed after the last carriage-wheels, De Vigne
went to his mother in her dressing-room. He
wished to tell, yet he shrank from paining her—
it came out with a jerk at last—'My mother,
wish me joy! I have won her, and *I* have no fear!'

And when his mother fully realized his words,
she burst into the most bitter tears that she had
ever shed for him; for whatever in his whole life
De Vigne's faults might be to others, in his conduct to his mother he had none. He let her
tears have their way; he hardly knew how to
console her; he only put his arm gently round
her as if to assure her that no wife should ever
come between herself and him. When she raised
her head she was deathly pale—pale, as if the
whole of his future hung a dead and hopeless
weight upon her. She said no more against it;
it was done, and she was both too wise, and loved
him too truly, to vex and chafe him with useless
opposition. But she threw her arms round him,
and kissed him, long and breathlessly, as she had
kissed him in his child's cot long ago, thinking of
his father lying dead on the Indian shore with
the colours for his shroud.

'My darling! my darling! God bless you!
God give you a happy future, and a wife who will
love you, as you can love—will love!'

That passionate broken prayer was all his
mother ever said to him of his marriage.

De Vigne received few congratulations; but
that sort of thing was quite contrary to his taste,
and on opposition, none of his relatives, not even
the overbearing, knock-me-down, Marchioness of
Marqueterie, who gave the law to everybody,
dared to venture. She only expressed her opinion
by ordering her own carriage for the hour, and the
day, at which the Trefusis came for the first time
to stay at Vigne. Lady Flora treated the Trefusis with a generous courtesy, which did its best
to grow into something warmer, and watched her
with a wistful anxiety which was very touching.
But it was evident to everyone that, though her
future daughter-in-law was most carefully attentive, reverential, and gentle to De Vigne's mother,
repressing everything in herself, or in Lady Fantyre, that could in the slightest degree shock or
wound her refined and highly - cultivated taste,
she and Lady Flora could never assimilate, or
even approach. This careful courtesy was all that
would ever link them together, and, in this in-
stance at least, the extremes did *not* touch.

However, for the three weeks longer, that I
remained there, on the surface all went on remarkably smooth. The Ferrers, of course, had left

with their mother. The Trefusis, as I have said, was irreproachable. Sabretasche was infinitely too polished a gentleman, to show disapproval of what he had no earthly business with; and limited himself to an occasional satiric remark on her, so veiled in subtle wit and courtesy, that, shrewd as she was, she felt the sting, but could not find the point of attack clearly enough to return it. De Vigne, of course, saw everything *couleur de rose*, and only chafed with impatience at the probation of an engagement which the Trefusis would not allow to end before Christmas (I think she rather enjoyed fretting and irritating him with denial and delay); and his mother resigned herself to the inevitable, and did her very best, poor lady! to find out some trace of that beauty of heart, thought, and mind, which her delicate feminine instinct had told her, was wanting in the magnificent personal gifts with which nature had enriched the woman who was to be his wife.

So all went harmoniously on at Vigne throughout that autumn; and the County talked themselves hoarse, speculating on his union with an unknown, *sans* rank, prestige, history, or anything to entitle her to such an honour, in whom, whether she were daughter or *protégée* of that disreputable old woman, Sarah Lady Fan-

tyre, Society could decide nothing for certain, nor
make out anything at all satisfactory. No wonder
the County were up at arms, and hardly knew
which to censure the most—De Vigne for daring
to make such a misalliance, or the Trefusis for
daring to accept it ! And the Colonel thought
with the County.

' If I ever took the trouble (which I don't,
because hate is an exhausting and silly thing) to
hate anybody, it would be that remarkably handsome and remarkably detestable Trefusis,' said
Sabretasche, as he wrapped a plaid round his
knees on the box of the drag, which was to con-
vey him and me to the station, to take the
train for Northamptonshire. To which county,
well-beloved of every Englishman for the mere
name of Pytchley, Sabretasche was going down
for the five weeks that still remained of his leave,
having invited me to accompany him; and where
I enjoyed myself uncommonly, hunting with
that slap-up Pack, and managing more than once
to be in at the finish, by dint of following that
best of mottoes, for which we are indebted to the
best Master of Hounds who ever went to cover,
' Throw your heart over, and your horse will
follow !'

Each day I spent with him I grew more at-

tached to the Colonel; the longer I saw him in his
own house, so perfect a gentleman, so perfect a
host; the longer I listened to his easy, playful
talk on men and things, his subtle and profound
satire on hypocrisies and follies. It was impossible not to get, as ladies say, fond of Sabretasche;
his courtly urbanity, his graceful generosity, his
ready wit, all made him so charming a companion;
though of the real man it was difficult, as De
Vigne said, to judge, through the nonchalance, indolence, and impassiveness, with which the Colonel
chose to veil all that he said or did. He might
have some secret or other in his past life, or his
present career, which no man ever knew; he
might be only, what he said he was, an idler, a
trifler, a dilettaute, a blasé and tired man of the
world, a nil admirari-ist. Nobody could tell.
Only this I could see, gay, careless, indolent
though he was, that in spite of the refined selfish-
ness, the exquisite epicureanism, the voluptuous
enjoyment of life which his friends and foes attributed to him, Vivian Sabretasche, like most of
the world's merry-makers, was sometimes sad
enough at heart.

'Friends? I don't believe in friends, my dear
boy,' said the Colonel, one night when we sat over
the fire, after a run with the Pytchley; a splendid

burst over the country up wind, fifteen minutes alone
with the hounds; and a kill in the open.   'There
are hundreds of good fellows who like Vivian
Sabretasche, and run after him because he amuses
them, and is a little of the fashion, and is held a
good judge of their wine, and their stud, and their
pictures.   But let Vivian Sabretasche come to
grief to-morrow, let his Lares go to the Jews, and
his Penates to the devil; let the Clubs, instead of
quoting, black-ball him, and the 'Court Circular,'
instead of putting him in the Fashionable Intelligence, cite him among the Criminal Cases, which
of his bosom friends will be so anxious then to
take his arm down St. James's Street?   Which of
them all will invite and flatter him then?   Will
Orestes send him haunches of venison?   Will
Iolaüs uncork his comet wine for him, and Pylades
stretch out his hand to him, and pick his fallen
pride out of the dirt of the gutter, and fight his
battle for him when he has crippled himself?
Pshaw! my dear Arthur, I take men at my
valuation, not at their own.   Don't you
know—

> " Si vous êtes dans la détresse,
>   O mes amis, cachez-le bien,
>   Car l'homme est bon et s'intéresse
>   A ceux qui n'ont besoin de rien ! " ' '

'It is a sad doctrine, Colonel,' said I, who was a boy, and wished to disbelieve him.

He laughed a little. 'Sad? Oh, I don't see that; nothing in life is worth calling sad. According to Heraclitus, everything is sad; according to Democritus, nothing is sad. The true secret is to take things as they come, and not trouble yourself sufficiently about anything to give it power to trouble you. Enjoy your youth. Take mine and your school-friend Ovid's counsel—

> " Utendum est ætate. Cito pede labitur ætas. . . .
> Hac mihi de spina grata corona data est." '

'But how's one to keep clear of the thorns?'

' By flying butterfly-like, from rose to rose, and handling it so delicately, as not to give it time to prick you! Love makes a poetic and unphilosophic man, like Dante or Petrarca, unhappy; but do you suppose that Lauzun, Grammont, the Duc de Richelieu, were ever made unhappy by love? No, the very idea makes one laugh; the poets took it *au sérieux*, and suffered in consequence; the courtiers only made it their pastime, and enjoyed it proportionately. It all depends on the way one lays hold of the roses of life; some men only enjoy the dew and fragrance of the flower, others mismanage it somehow, and get only the thorns.'

'You've the secret, then, Colonel,' said I, laughing, 'for you get a whole conservatory of the most delicious under the sun, and not a thorn, I'd bet, among them?'

'Or, at all events, my skin is hard enough not to be pricked,' smiled Sabretasche. 'I think many men begin life, like the sand on the top of a drum, which obeys every undulation of the air from the notes of a violin near; they are sensitive and susceptible, shrinking at wrong or injury, easily moved, quickly touched. As years go on, the same men are like the same sand when it has been pressed, and hardened, and burnt in fusion heat, and exposed to frosty air, and made into polished, impenetrable glass, on which you can make no impression, off whose icy surface everything glides away, and which it is impossible to cut with the hardest and keenest of knives. The sand is the same sand; it is the treatment it has met with that has changed it. How I do prose to you, Arthur!—and of all the ills, a man has least right to inflict on another, are his own theories or ideas! Fill your glass, my boy, and pass me those macaroons. How can those poor creatures live who don't know of the Marcobrunnen and Macaroons of existence? It is a good thing to have money, isn't it? It not only buys us friends,

but it buys us what is of infinitely more value—
all the pleasant little *agréments* of life. I would not
keep in the world at all if I did not lie on rose-
leaves!'

Wherewith the Colonel nestled himself more
comfortably into his arm-chair, laid his head on
the cushions, closed his eyes, and smoked away
at his perfumed hookah, the most fragrant and
delicate Narghille, that ever came out of Persia.

On the 31st of December, Sabretasche and De
Vigne, Curly and I (Curly had got his commission in the Coldstreams, and was the prettiest,
daintiest, most flattered, and most flirted with
young Guardsman of his time), went down by the
express, through the snow-whitened fields and
hedges, to Vigne, where, contrary to custom, its
master was to take his bride on the first morning
of the New Year. It was to be a very gay wedding. De Vigne, always liberal to excess, now
perfectly lavish in his gifts, had followed the
French fashion, he said, and given her a *corbeille*
fit for a princess of Blood Royal, which the Trefusis, having no delicacy of appropriation, accepted
as a right. There were to be twelve bridesmaids,
not the quite exclusive, and ultra high-bred, young
ladies who would have followed Adelina or Blanche
Ferrers, but still very stylish-*looking* girls, ac-

quaintances of the Trefusis. There were to be
such a breakfast and such rejoicings, as had never
before been seen, even at that proverbially magnificent place. Such a wedding was entirely contrary to De Vigne's taste and ideas, but the more
others had chosen to run down the Trefusis, the
more did he delight to honour her, and therefore
he had asked almost everybody he knew, and
almost everybody went; for all who knew him
wished him well, except his aunt and her daughters
the Ladies Ferrers. *They* went, because else, the
world might have said that they were disappointed
he had not married Blanche; but very far from
wishing him well, I think they fervently hoped
he might repent his hasty step, in sackcloth and
ashes, and their costly wedding presents were
much like Judas's kisses. Wedding presents sin-
gularly often are! As she writes the delicately
mauve-tinted congratulatory note, wishing dearest
Adeliza every joy that earth can give, and assuring her she is the very beau ideal of a perfect
wife, is not Madame ten to one saying to her
elder daughter, 'How strange it is that Fitz
should have been taken in—such a bold, flirty girl,
and nothing pretty in her, to my taste?' And
as we shake Fitz's hand at our Club, telling him
he is the luckiest dog going to have such a pretty

girl, and such a lot of money by one *coup*, are we not fifty to one thinking, 'Poor wretch! he's glad of the tin, I suppose, to keep him out of the Queen's Bench? But, by George; though I *am* hard up, I wouldn't take one of those confounded Peyton women if I knew it! Won't she just check him nicely, with her cheque-book and her consols!'

One could hardly wonder that if the Trefusis had been proved a perfect Messalina or Frédégonde, no man in love with her would have given her up as she sat that last evening of the Old Year on one of the low couches beside the drawing-room fire at Vigne, looking with the ruddy glow of the fire-gleams upon her like one of Rubens', or Guido's, dark, glowing, voluptuous goddesses or sybils. De Vigne was leaning over her with eyes for none but her. His mother sat opposite them both, delicate, graceful, fragile, with her diaphanous hands, and fair pure profile, and rich, soft, black lace falling in folds around her, her eyes yearningly fixed upon her son; while just behind her, playing *écarté* with Curly, who was devotedly fond of that little dangerous French game, was old Lady Fantyre, with her keen, wicked eye, and her rouged, withered cheek, and her fan and feathers, flowers and jewels, and her dress—*décolletée* at seventy-six !

'Look at De Vigne !' said Sabretasche to me. 'His desires on the eve of fulfilment, he imagines his happiness will be also. How he bends over that chair, and looks down into her eyes, as if all his heaven hung there ! Twelve months hence he will wish to God he had never looked upon her face.'

'Good Heavens, Colonel !' I cried involuntarily, ' what evil, or horror, do you know of her ? '

'None of her, personally,' said Sabretasche, with a surprised smile. 'But is she not a woman ; and is not De Vigne, poor fellow, marrying too early ? With such premises my prophecy requires no diviner's art to make it a very safe one. As great a contrast as that rouged, atrociously-dressed, abominable old orange-woman is to his own charming and graceful mother, will be De Vigne's real future to his imaginary one. However, he is probably in Socrates' predicament, whether he take a wife or not, either way he will repent; and he must be satisfied ; he will have the handsomest woman in England ! Few men have as much as that ! '

'Ladies ought to hate you, sir,' said I, 'instead of loving you as idolatrously as they do ; for you certainly are their bitterest enemy ? '

'Not I,' laughed Sabretasche. 'I am very fond of them, except when they try and hook my favourite friends, and then I would say to them, as Thales said to his mother, that in their youth men are too young to be fettered, and after their youth they are too old. I am sorry for De Vigne—very sorry; he is doing what in a little time, and for all his life through, he will long to undo. But he must have his own way; and perhaps, after all, as Emerson says, marriage may be an open question, as it is alleged from the beginning of the world, that such as are in the institution want to get out, and such as are out want to get in! Marriage is like a mirage: all the beauty it possesses lies in keeping at a distance from it.'

He moved away with that light laugh which always perplexed you as to whether he meant what he said in mockery or earnest, and began to arrange the pieces for a game at chess with one of the ladies. He was very right. His wife would be the woman of all others, from whom, in maturer years, De Vigne would be most certain to revolt. A man's later loves, are sure to be widely distinct in style from his earlier. In his youth, he only asks for what charms his eyes and senses; in manhood —if he be a man of intellect at all—he will go further, and require interest for his mind, and response for his heart.

The last hour of the Old Year chimed at once from the bell-tower of Vigne, the belfry of the old village-church, and the countless clocks throughout the house ; as a little gold Bayadère on the mantel-piece struck the twelve strokes slowly and musically on her tambourine. Lady Flora, in her own boudoir, heard it with passionate tears, and on her knees, prayed for her son's new future which this New Year heralded. De Vigne, alone in the library with his betrothed, heard it, and pressed his lips to hers, with words of rapturous delight, to welcome this New Year coming to them both. Sabretasche heard it as he leant over the chair of a lovely married woman, flirting à outrance, and bent backward to me as I passed him : 'There goes the death-knell! The last day of De Vigne's freedom is over. Go and put on sackcloth and ashes, Arthur.'

The Colonel's words weighed curiously upon me as I rose and dressed on the morning of New Year's-day. I, aj young fellow, who looked on life and all its chances as gaily as on a game at cricket, who should have come to this wedding as I had gone to a dozen others, only to enjoy myself, drink the Aï and Sillery, and flirt with all the bridesmaids, dressed with almost as dead a chill upon me, I could not have told why, as if I had come to De Vigne's funeral rather than to his marriage. There seemed little reason for regret, however, as I met him that morning coming out of his room, and held out his hand with his sunny smile. I wished him joy in very few words—I wished it him *too* well to be able to get up an eloquent or studied speech.

'Thank you, dear Arthur,' he answered, turning his door-handle with a joyous, light-hearted laugh; 'I am sure all the fairies would come and bless my marriage if you'd anything to do with the ordering of them. Come in, old fellow, and have a cigar —my last bachelor smoke—it will keep me quiet till she is out of her maid's hands. Faugh! how I hate the folly of wedding ceremonial! The idea of dressing up Love in white favours, and giving him bride-cake! It was not *so* Cupid and Psyche were wed. I think Eros would have turned his back on the whole affair if they had subjected him to a bishop's drawl, and an attorney's prosaic busi- ness, eh? Try those Manillas, Arthur.'

He smoked because, my dear young ladies, men accustomed to the horrid weed, can't do without it, even on their wedding-day; but quiet he was not: he had at all times more of the tornado in

him, than anything like the Colonel's equable calm;
and he was restless and excitable, and happy as
only a man in the same cloudless and eager youth,
with the same fearless and vehement passion, can
ever be. He soon threw down his cigar, for a
servant came to tell him that his mother would
like to see him in her own room ; and De Vigne,
who had been ceaselessly darting glances at the
clock, which, I dare say, seemed to him to crawl
on its way, went out, joyous as Romeo's,

> ' Come what sorrow may
> It cannot countervail this interchange of joy.'

He never thought of Friar Laurence's prophetic
reply :

> ' These violent delights have violent ends,
> And in their triumph die ; like fire and powder,
> Which as they kiss consume ! '

By noon we were all ready. In the dining-hall,
with its bronzes and its deer-heads, and the regi-
mental colours of his father's Corps looped up
between the two end windows, with his helmet,
sabre, and gloves above them, the breakfast, sump-
tuous enough to have done for St. James's or the
Tuileries, was set out, with its gold plate, its hothouse flowers, and its thousand delicacies ; and in
the private Chapel the wedding party was assembled, with the sun streaming brightly in, through

the coloured light of the stained windows. It was a very brilliant gathering. There' were the Marchioness of Malachite and the Ladies Ferrers, looking bored to the last extreme, and appearing to consider it too great an honour for the mosaic pavement to have the glory of bearing their footsteps. There were other dainty ladies of rank, friends of Lady Flora's. There were the dozen bridesmaids in their gauzy dresses and their wreaths of holly or of forget-me-not; there were hosts of men, chiefly military, whose morning mufti threw in just enough shade among the bright dresses, as brilliant by themselves as a bouquet of exotics. There were, strangely enough, close together, bizarre, quick-eyed, queer old Lady Fantyre, and soft, fragile Lady Flora; and, there was De Vigne, standing near his mother, chatting and laughing with Sabretasche, but all his senses alive, to catch the first sound which should tell him, of the advent of his bride.

How well I can see him now, as if it were but yesterday, standing on the altar-steps—where his ancestors, through long ages past, had wedded noble gentlewomen and fair patrician girls from the best and bravest Houses in the land—I can see him now, standing erect, his head up, one hand in the breast of his waistcoat, his eyes, dark as night, brilliant and luminous with eagerness; a flush of excitement and anticipation on his face; not a shade, not a fear, seeming to rest upon him! His mother's eyes were riveted on him, with a mournful tenderness, she could not, or did not care to, conceal; her lips quivered; she looked at me, and shook her head. That wedding party was very brilliant, but there was a strange, dull gloom over it which everyone felt, yet none could explain; and little of the joyous light-heartedness which make "marriage-bells" proverbial for mirth and gaiety.

There was a very low but an irrepressible murmur of applause, as his bride swept silently up · the aisle. Never had we seen her look so handsome. Her voluptuous form was shrouded in the shower of lace that fell around her, and about her, from her head, till it trailed behind her on the ground. The glowing damask-rose hue of her cheeks, not one whit the paler this morning, and the splendid brilliance of her eyes, were enhanced, not hidden, by the filmy floating veil. A wreath of orange-flowers, of course was woven in her hair, and a ceinture of diamonds, worthy an imperial trousseau—one of the gifts of her lavish and bewitched lover—were jewels fitted to her. She was matchless as a dream of Rubens'; but I looked in vain, as her eyes rested on De

Vigne's, for one saving shadow of love, joy,
natural emotion, tremulous feeling, to denote that
he was not utterly thrown away; and only wedded
to a priceless statue of responseless marble!

She passed up to the altar with her retinue of
bridesmaids, in their snowy dresses and bright
wreaths, into the light streaming from the painted
windows. She stood beside him; and the service
began; one of the Ferrers family, the Bishop of
Southdown, read the few words which linked them
for life with the iron fetters of the Church. Everyone who caught the glad, firm, eager tone of De
Vigne's '*I will,*' remembers it to this day—remembers with what trusting love, what unhesi-
tating promptitude he took that vow for 'better
or worse!' Prophetic words! which say, whatever
ill may come of that rash oath sworn, there will
be no remedy for it; no help, no repentance that
will be of any avail; no furnace strong enough, to
unsolder the chains they forge for ever!

De Vigne passed the ring over her finger; they
knelt down, and the priest stretched his hands
over them, and forbade those whom God had
joined together any Man to put asunder. And
they rose—husband and wife.

They came down the altar steps, De Vigne's
face radiant, in its frank joy, its noble pride,

looking down upon her with his brilliant eyes,
now soft and gleaming; while she — looked
straight before her, her lips slightly parted with
a smile, probably of triumph and of exultation,
that she, unknown and unsupported, called by all
an interloper, by many an adventuress, was now
the wife of the last of a haughty House, whose
pride throughout lengthened centuries had ever
been that all its men were brave and all its women
chaste; that not a taint rested on its name, not a
stain upon its blood, not a spot upon its shield.

We passed down the chapel into the vestry,
De Vigne gazing down on her with all the
eagerness of passion. But he had no an-
swering glance of love. The day of acting, because the need for acting, was over now. The
register was open; he took the quill, and
dashed down hastily his old ancestral name; passing it into her hand with fondly whispered words.
She took it, threw back her veil, and wrote—

"LUCY TREFUSIS—OR —— DAVIS."

De Vigne was bending fondly over her, his lips
touching her hair, with its virginal crown, as she
wrote. With one great cry he suddenly sprang
up, as men will do upon a battle-field when struck
with their death-wound. Seizing her hands in

his, he held her away from him, reading her face
line by line, feature by feature, with the dim
horror of a man in some vague dream of hideous
agony. And she smiled up in his face; the smile
of a fiend.

'Granville de Vigne, do you know me *now?*'

Aye! he knew her now. He still held her at
arms' length, staring down upon her, the truth in
all its vile horror, its abhorred shame, eating
gradually into his very life; seeming as it were to
turn his warm blood to ice, and chill his very
heart to stone. She laughed—a mocking derisive
laugh, which broke strangely, coarsely, brutally,
on the dead silence round them.

'Yes! Granville, yes! my young lover, I am
your Wife, of your own act, your own will. Do
you remember the poor mistress you mocked at?
Do you remember the summer day when you
laughed at my vengeance? Do you remember, *my
husband?* Before all your titled crowd, I take
my revenge, that it may be the more complete.
I would not wait for it, nor spare you one iota
of your shame, nor let you keep it secret hidden
in your heart! I renounce my own ambitions to
humble you lower still. They are hearing us!
All your haughty relatives, your fastidious friends,
who have tried so long to stop you in your mad

passion. They listen to me! They see you dis-
honoured for ever in your eyes and theirs! They
will go and tell the world, what *you* would never have
told it, that the last of his Line has given his home,
his honour, his mother's place, his father's name—
that proud name which only yesterday you told me
no disgrace had ever touched, no bad blood ever
borne !—to the despised love of his boyhood, his
own cast-off low-born toy ; a beggar's child ; a—'

'PEACE!'

At that single word, hoarse as a death-cry in
its unutterable agony, she was silenced perforce.
The blood had left his lips, and cheeks, a blue and
ghastly hue ; and settled on his forehead in a dark
crimson stain—like the stain on his own honour.
His eyes were set and fixed, as in some mortal torture, wide-open and vacant in their pain ; his teeth
were clenched as men clench them in their last
struggle ; and his hand was pressed upon his heart,
as he gasped for breath, like one suffocated by
a deadly grip that throttles him. In the horror
of the moment, all round him were dumb and
paralyzed; even she, in her rancorous hate, paused,
awe-stricken at the ruin she had wrought, silent
before the anguish, shame, and loathing that con-
vulsed his face, as he flung her from him with a
wild shrill laugh.

'Peace! woman—devil! or I shall have your life!' ....

But his mother threw herself before him. 'Oh, God! he is mad! Stay, for *my* sake, stay!'

He strained her to his heart with convulsive force:

'Let me go—let me go!'

None could attempt to arrest him. He pushed his way through the crowd, hurling them aside, like a madman, and we heard the rapid rush of carriage-wheels as they rolled away—God knows where.

CHAPTER X.

ON THE FIRST DAY OF A NEW YEAR.

ON another New Year's Day, ten years from that fatal marriage in the church at Vigne, the tropic sun streamed down on parched sand, and tangled jungle, where, in the sultry stillness of the noon, a contest for life and death was raging. Far away on the blue hills slept the golden day; the great palm-leaves drooped languidly; the jaguars, and the tigers, lay couched in the grasses; the florikens, and parrots, closed their soft, brilliant-hued wings to sleep; all nature in the vast solitudes was at peace; even the broad sheet of the river was calm as a tideless lake, pausing in its rapid rush, from its mountain cradle, to its ocean grave. All nature was hushed and still, but the passions of man were warring; when do they ever rest? It was a skirmish of English cavalry and Beloochee infantry, in a small plain between large woods or hunting grounds, and the red sun shone with an arid glare on the glittering sabres, and white linen helmets of the Europeans, and the gorgeous turbans, and dark shields of the mountaineers, who were darkening the air with their clashing swords, and breaking the holy hush of wood and hills with long rolling shouts, loud and terrible as thunder. The mountaineers doubled the English force; they had surprised them, moreover, as, not thinking of attack, they trotted onwards from one garrison to another, and the struggle was sharp and fierce. The English were but a handful of Hussars, under command of their Major, and the odds were great against them. But at their head was one to whom fear was a word in an unknown tongue, in whose blood was fire, and whose heart was bronze. Sitting down in his saddle as calmly as at a meet, his eyes steady and quick as an eagle's, hewing right and left like a common trooper, the English Major fought his way. The Beloochee swords gleamed round him without harm, while, crashing through their bright-hued turbans, every stroke of his sabre told. They surged around him, they climbed, they wrestled, they tore, they panted for his blood, they caught his charger's bridle, they opposed before him one dense and bristling forest of swords; still, he bore a charmed life, alike in single combat hand to hand, or in the broken charge of his scattered troop. In the fierce noontide glow; in

the pitiless vertical sun-rays ; while the wild shouts
of the natives rang up to the heavens, and the
ceaseless clang and clash of the sabres and shields
startled the birds from their rest, and the tigers
from their lair ; the English Major fought like grim
death. as these blows glanced harmless off him, as
from Achilles of old ; fought till the native warriors,
savage heroes though they were, fled from his path,
awe-stricken at his fierce valour, at his matchless
strength, at his god-like charm from danger.   He
pursued them at the head of his Cavalry, after
the skirmish was over, far away across the plain ;
then, as he drew bridle, and put his reeking sword
back into its sheath, another man near him, looked
at him in amazement: 'On my life, De Vigne,
what an odd fellow you are ! You look like the
very devil in the midst of the fight ; and yet when
it's over, after sharper work than any even we
have seen, deuce take you if you're not as cool as
if you'd walked out of a barrack-yard !'

*   *   *   *   *

The same 1st of January, while they were enjoying this Cavalry skirmish in Scinde, we were
bored to death by a review at Woolwich. The
day was soft and bright, no snow or frost, as Sabre
tasche, with his Italianized constitution, remarked

with a thanksgiving. There was Royalty to inspect us; there were pretty women in their carriages in the inner circle; and there was as superb a luncheon as any military man could ask, in the finest mess-room in England; and we, ungrateful, I suppose, for the goods the gods gave us, swore away at it all, as the greatest curse imaginable. It is a pretty scene enough, I dare say, to those who have only to look on; the bright uniforms and the white plumes, the greys and the bays, the chesnuts and the roans, the dashing staff and the cannon's peaceful roar, the marching and the counter-marching, the storming and the sortie, the rush and the charge! I dare say it may be all very amusing to lookers-on, but to us, heated and bothered and tired, obliged to go into harness, which we hated as cordially as we loved it the first day we sported in our Cornethood, it was a nuisance inexpressible, and we should have far preferred fatiguing ourselves for some better purpose under the jungle-trees in Scinde.

We were profoundly thankful when it was all over and done with, when H.R.H. F.M. had departed to Windsor without luncheon, and we were free to go up and chat with the women in the inner circle, and take them into the mess-room. There were very few we knew, yet up in town;

but Parliament was about to meet, unusually early that year, and there were several from jointure houses, or little villas at Richmond, or Twickenham, or Kew, with whom we were well acquainted.

'There is Lady Molyneux,' said Sabretasche, who was now Lieut.-Colonel of Ours. 'I dare say that is her daughter with her. I remember she came out last season, and was very much admired, but I missed her by going that Ionian Isle trip with Brabazon. Shall we go and be introduced, Arthur? She does not look bad style, though to be sure these English winter days, are as destructive to a woman's beauty, as anything well can be!'

The Colonel wheeled his horse round up to the Molyneux barouche, and I followed him. Ten years had not altered Sabretasche in one iota; he had led the same lounging, indolent, fashionable, artistic kind of life; his face was as handsome, his wit as light, his conquests as various and far-famed as ever. He was still soldier, artist, sculptor, dilettante, man of fashion, all in one, the universal criterion of taste, the critic of all beauties, pictures, singers, or horses, popular with all men, adored by all women, and really chained by none. Therefore Vivian Sabretasche, whose word at White's or the U. S. could do more to damage, or increase, her daughter's reputation as a belle, than any other man's, had a very pleasant bow and smile in the distance, from Lady Molyneux; and a very delicate lavender kid glove belonging to that peeress, put between his fingers, when he and I rode up to her carriage.

'Ah!' cried the Viscountess, a pretty, super-cilious-looking woman, who was *passée*, but would not by any means allow it, 'I am delighted to see you both. We only came to town yesterday; Lord Molyneux has taken a house in Lowndes Square, and there is positively scarcely a soul that we know here as yet! Rushbrooke persuaded us to come to this review to-day, and Violet wished it. Allow me to introduce my daughter to you. Violet, my love, Colonel Sabretasche, Mr. Chevasney, Miss Molyneux.'

Violet Molyneux looked up in the Colonel's face as he bowed to her; and probably thought—at least she looked as if she did—that she had never seen any man so attractive, as he returned her gaze with his soft, mournful eyes, and that exquisite gentleness of manner, to which he owed half his reputation in the tender secrets of the boudoir and flirting-room; and leaning his hand on the door of the carriage, bent down from his saddle, studying the new beauty, while he laughed and chatted with her and her mother. We used to say Sabretasche kept a list of the new beauties entered for the year,—as 'Bell's Life' has a list of the young fillies entered for the Oaks; made a cross against those worth noticing, and checked off those already flirted with and slain; for the Colonel was indisputably as dangerous to the *beau sexe* as Lauzun.

Violet Molyneux was certainly worthy of being entered in this mythical book if it existed; her complexion white as Parian, with a wild-rose colour in her cheeks, her eyes large, brilliant, and wonderfully expressive, generally flashing with the sweetest laughter; her hair of a soft, bright, chesnut hue; her figure slight but perfect in symmetry; on her delicate features the stamp of quick intelligence, heightened by the greatest culture; and in her whole air and manner the grace of high rank, and fashionable dress. Gifted with the gayest spirits, the cleverest brain, and the sweetest temper possible, one could not wonder that she was talked over at Clubs; engaged by more than her tablets could record at every ball, and followed by a perfect cavalcade when she cantered down the Ride. Sabretasche soon took her off to the mess-room, a Lieutenant-General

escorting her mother, and I found myself sitting
on her left at the luncheon: an occasion I did not
improve as much as I otherwise should have done,
from the fact of his being on the other side, and
persuading the young lady to give all her attention to him; for, though he was scarcely ever
really interested in any woman, he liked to flirt
with them all, and always made himself charming.
The Hon. Violet seemed to find him charming
too; and chatted with him gaily and frankly, as if
she had known him for ages.

'How I enjoyed the review to day!' she began.
'If there are three sights greater favourites of
mine than another, they are a review, a race, and
a meet, because of the dear horses.'

'Or—their masters?' said Sabretasche, quietly.
Violet Molyneux laughed.

'Oh! their masters are very pleasant too, though
they are certainly never so handsome, or so tract-
able, or so honest as their quadrupeds! Most of
my friends abuse gentlemen. I don't; they are
always kind to me, and unless they are very young
or stupid, generally speaking amusing.'

'Miss Molyneux, what a treat!' smiled Sabretasche, who could say impudent things so gracefully,
that every one liked them from his lips. 'You
have the candour to *say* what every other young

lady *thinks*. We know you all like us very much, but none of you will ever admit it! You say you enjoyed the review? I thought no belle, after her first season, ever condescended to "enjoy" anything.'

'Don't they?' laughed Violet; 'how I pity them! I am an exception, then, for I enjoy an immense number of things; everything, indeed, except my presentation, where I was ironed quite flat, and very nearly crushed to death, and, finally, came before her Majesty in a state of collapse, like a maimed india-rubber ball. Not enjoy things! Why, I enjoy my morning gallop on Bonbon; I enjoy my flowers, and birds, and dogs. I delight in the opera, I adore waltzing, I perfectly idolize music, and the day when a really good book comes out, or a really good painting is exhibited, I am in a seventh heaven. Not enjoy things! Oh, Colonel Sabretasche, when I cease to enjoy life, I hope I shall cease to live!'

'You will die very early, then!' said Sabretasche, with something of that deepened melancholy which occasionally stole over him, but which he was always careful to conceal in society.

She started, and turned her bright eyes upon him, surprised and stilled:

'Colonel Sabretasche! Why?'

He smiled; his usual gay, courteous smile:

'Because the gods will grudge earth so fair a flower, and men so true a vision, of what angels *ought* to be ; but—thanks to preachers, poets, and painters—never *are.*'

She shook her head with a pretty impatience :

'Ah! pray do not waste compliments upon me ; I detest them.'

'Vraiment ?' murmured the Colonel, with a little, quiet, incredulous glance.

'Yes, I do indeed. You don't believe me, I dare say ? Because I have so many of them, Captain Chevasney ? Perhaps it is. I have many more than are really complimentary, either to my taste or my intellect.'

'Ladies like compliments as children like bonbons,' said Sabretasche, in his low *traînante* voice. 'They will take them till they can take no more ; but if they see ever so insignificant a one going to another, how they long for it, how they grudge it, how they burn to add it to their store ! This is œil de perdrix, will you try it ?

'No, thank you,' answered the Hon. Violet, with a ringing laugh. The sarcasms on her sex did not seem to touch or disturb her ; she rather enjoyed them than otherwise. 'What is the news to-day ?'

'Nothing remarkable,' answered Sabretasche.

'Births, deaths, and marriages all put together, to remind men, like Philip of Macedon's valet, that they come into the world, to suffer in it, and go out again! Much like all other news, Miss Molyneux, except that your name is down as among those arrived in town, and my friend De Vigne is mentioned for the Bath.'

'Ah! that Major de Vigne!' cried Violet. 'Where is he?—who is he?—what has he really been doing? I heard Lord Hilton talking about him last night, saying that he had been a most wonderful fellow in India, and that the natives called him—what was it?—" the Charmed Life," I think. Is he your friend?'

'My best,' said Sabretasche. 'Not Jonathan to my David, you know, nor Iolaüs to my Orestes; we don't do that sort of thing in these days. We like each other, but as for dying for each other, that would be far too much trouble; and, besides, it would be bad ton—too demonstrative. But I like him; he is as true steel as any man I know, and I shall be delighted to have a cigar with him again, provided it is not too strong a one. Dying for one's Patroclus would be preferable to enduring his bad tobacco.'

Violet looked at him with her radiant glance:

'Well, Colonel Sabretasche, if your cigar be not

kindled warmer than your friendship, it will very soon go out again, that's all!'

'*Soit!* there are plenty more in the case,' smiled Sabretasche, 'and one Havannah is as good as another, for anything I see. But about De Vigne you have heard quite truly; he has been fighting in Scinde like all the Knights of the Round Table merged in one. He is Major of the —th Hussars, and he has done more with his handful than a general of division might have done with a whole squadron. His Colonel was put *hors de combat* with a ball in his hip, and De Vigne, of course, had the command for some time. The natives call him the Charmed Life, because, despite the risks he runs, and the carelessness with which he has exposed his life, he has not had a single scratch; and both the Sepoys he fights with, and the Beloochees he fights against, stand in a sort of awe of him. The —th is ordered home, so we are looking out to see him soon. I shall be heartily glad, poor old fellow!'

'Provided, I suppose, he brings cheroots with him good enough to allow him admittance?' said Violet.

'*Sous entendu,*' said the Colonel. 'I would infinitely prefer losing a friend to incurring a disagreeable sensation. Would not you?'

'Oh! of course,' answered the young lady, with a rapid flash of her mischievous eyes. 'Frederick's feelings, when he saw Katte beheaded, must have been trifling child's play, to what the Sybarite suffered from the doubled rose-leaves!'

'Undoubtedly,' said Sabretasche, tranquilly. 'I am glad you agree with me! If we do not take care and undouble the rose-leaves for ourselves, we may depend on it we shall find no one who will take so much trouble for us. To *Aide-toi et Dieu t'aidera*, they should add *Aide-toi et le monde t'aidera*, for I have always noticed that Providence and the world generally befriend those who can do without their help.'

'Perhaps there is a deeper meaning in that,' answered Violet, 'and more justice than first seems? After all, those who do aid themselves may deserve it the most, and those whose heads and hands are silent and idle, hardly have a right to have the bonbons of existence picked out and given to them.'

'I don't know whether we have a right to them, but we find them pleasant, and that is all I look at; and besides, Miss Molyneux, when you have lived a little longer in the world, you will invariably find that it is to those who have much, that much is given, and *vice versâ*. Guineas pour into the gold plate held by that "decidedly pious person," Lord Savinggrace, but pence will do for the parish poor-box. Turtle and tokay are given to an heir-apparent, but a cutlet and new port will suffice for a younger son. Establish yourself on a pedestal, the world will worship you, even though the pedestal be of very poor brick and mortar ; lie modestly down on a moorland, though it be, like James Fergusson, for genius to study science, why, you may lie there for ever if you wait for anybody to pick you up ! The world has a trick of serving, like the Swiss Guard and the secret police, whichever side is uppermost and pays them best. However, thank Heaven I want nothing of it, and it is very civil to me.'

'*Because* you want nothing of it?'

'Precisely.'

CHAPTER XI.

THE 'CHARMED LIFE' COMES BACK AMONG US.

'THANK God I have found a girl who has some notion of conversation. I believe, with the Persians, that ten measures of talk were sent down from Heaven, and the ladies took nine; but of conversation, argument, repartee—the real use of that most most facile, dexterous, sharp-pointed weapon, the tongue—what woman has a notion? They employ a thousand superlatives in describing a dress, they exhaust a million expletives in damning their bosom friend, their boudoirs hear more twaddle than the Commons—*si c'est possible!*—and they rail harder over their coffee-cups, at their sisters' short-comings, than a popular preacher over his sounding-board, at the vices he pets sub rosâ. But as for conversation, they have not a notion of it; if you begin an argument, they either get into a passion or subside into monosyllables! A woman who has good conversation is as rare as one who does not care for scandal. I have met them in Paris salons, and we have found one to-day.'

So spoke Sabretasche at mess that night à propos of Violet Molyneux, who was under discussion in common with our ox-tail and our wine.

'Then you allow her your approval, Colonel,' said Montressor, of Ours.

'Certainly I do,' said Sabretasche. 'This soup is not good, it is too thin. She is exquisitely pretty, even through my eye-glass, which has a sad knack of finding the lilies cosmetique and the eyebrows tinting; and, what is much better, she is actually natural and fresh, and can talk as if Nature had given her brains, and reading had cultivated them. I dare say they count on her making a good marriage.'

'No doubt they do. Jockey Jack has hardly a rap,' replied another man. 'They can't keep up their Irish place, so they hang out in town three parts of the year, and take a shooting-box, or visit about for the rest. Confound it, I wouldn't be one of the Upper House, without a good pot of money to keep up my dignity, for anything I could see! Violet came out last season, you know?'

'Yes, I know; I remember hearing she made a great sensation,' answered the Colonel. 'Ormsby

told me she was the best thing of the season—the
first, by-the-by, I was ever out of London. Lady
Molyneux must try to run down Regalia, or
Cavendish Grey, or one of the great matrimonal
coups. My lady knows how to manœuvre, too ;
I wonder she should have a daughter so frank and
unaffected.'

'They've seen nothing of one another,' answered
Pigott, who always knew everything about everybody, from the price Lord Goodwood gave for his
thorough-bred roan fillies, to the private thoughts
that Lady Honoria Bandoline wrote each night in
her violet-velvet diary. 'My lady's always running out somewhere ; if you were to call at eight
in the morning you'd find her gone off to early
Matins ; if you were to call at twelve, she'd be
off to the Sanctified and Born-again Clear-
starchers' jubilee with Lord Savinggrace ; at two,
she'd be closeted and lunching with her spiritual
master—whoever he chance to be—who gives
her confession and eats her *croquis ;* at three,
she'd be having a snug boudoir flirtation ; at
four, she'd be in the Park, of course, or at a
morning concert ; at six, she'd be dressing for
dinner ; at ten, she'd be off to three or four balls
and crushes ; and so between the two she certainly
carries out that delightful work, " How to Make

the Best of Both Worlds," which my Low Church
sister sent me the other day!'

'With the idea that you were doing your very
utmost to make the worst of 'em, Charlie?'
laughed Sabretasche. 'I don't know the volume
—Heaven forfend!—but the title sounds to me
sneaky, as if it wanted to get the sweets out of
both, yet compromise itself with neither. Your
sketch of Lady Molyneux is as true to life as one
of Leech's; but certainly her child is about as unlike her as could possibly be imagined.'

'Oh, by George! yes,' assented Montressor,
heartily; 'Mis Vy hasn't one bit of nonsense
about her.'

'And she's a divine waltzer—turn her round
in a nutshell.'

'And can't she ride, just!'

'And her voice smashes Alboni's to pieces, her
shake's perfection.'

'And—she can talk!' added Sabretasche, in his
quiet voice. 'I will call in Lowndes Square to-
morrow. So the —th is ordered home? We
shall see De Vigne again.'

'Unless he exchange to a regiment still on
active service,' said Pigott.

'He won't do that,' I answered. 'I heard from
him last Marseilles mail, and he said he intended

to return overland. Poor fellow? what ages it is since we've seen him !'

'It is ten years, isn't it?' said Sabretasche, setting down his champagne-glass with half a sigh. 'He has had some sharp work out there. I hope it has done him good. I never wish to see a man look as he looked last time I saw him.'

'Where's his rascally wife?' asked Montressor.

'The Trefusis? For Heaven's sake don't call her his wife,' said I, impatiently. '*I*'ll never give her his name, though the law may. She is at Paris, cut by all his set of course, living with the Fantyre, in a dashing hotel in the Champs Elysées, keeping a green and gold Chasseur six feet high, and giving *suivies soirées* to a certain class of untitled English and titled French, who don't care a fig for her story, and care a good deal for her suppers.'

'Which she buys with De Vigne's tin, hang her! She calls herself Mrs. De Vigne, I think!'

'She *is* Mrs. De Vigne,' said Sabretasche, with that bitter sneer which occasionally passed over his features. 'You forget the sanctity, solemnity, and beauty of the marriage tie, my dear Montressor. You know it is too "holy" to be severed, either by reason, justice, or common sense!'

'Holy fiddlesticks, Colonel,' retorted Montressor, contemptuously; 'the best law for that confounded woman would have been Lynch law; and if I'd had my way, I would have taken her out of church that morning and shot her straight away out of hand.'

'Too handsome to be shot, Fred.'

'She will not be so handsome in a few years; she will soon grow coarse,' said the Colonel, that most fastidious of female critics. 'She is the full-blown dashing style to strike youngsters, but there is not a single charm that will *last.*'

'Are there in any of them? None last long with you, Colonel, I fancy?'

Sabretasche laughed gaily.

'To be sure not!

> "Therefore is love said to be a child,
> Because in choice he is so oft beguiled."

Don't you admit the truth of that?'

'I should hope I do. Well, after all, his marriage won't matter to De Vigne, except the loss of the three thousand a year he allows her; to be sure, there's the blow to his pride, and he is a terribly proud fellow.'

Sabretasche looked up. 'Some men's honour is sensitive, Pigott; others—like their understandings—somewhat dull.'

Pigott did not relish the hit.

' Well, why did he do it ? He needn't have been such a fool! ' he said, sulkily.

Sabretasche's eyes lit angrily.

' If you are never more of a fool, Pigott, than De Vigne, you may thank Heaven ! His passions led him into error; but if every man I know were as worthy respect as he, the world would be a better one. *I*, at least, will never sit by to hear him ridiculed.'

Those were very strong words from our careless, impassive, indolent Colonel, and they had their effect accordingly. He spoke very quietly—not raising his voice; but Pigott cared not to provoke him further. He drank down his sherry with rather a nervous laugh :

' Oh ! we know he's a brick ; all I hope is, that he won't come home and tumble into love with Violet Molyneux, or some other young filly.'

Sabretasche laughed ; he hated dissensions, and was always ready to restore harmony to any table.

' I hope not, too. That young Irish beauty is exceedingly love-provoking. She has done a good deal of damage, hasn't she ? '

Six weeks or so after this, I was dining with Sabretasche at his own house—one of those charming, exclusive little dinner parties which were his *spécialité.* The other men had just left; and the Colonel and I were sitting before the inner drawing-room fire, with the Cid stretched on the rug between us; Sabretasche lying full length on a sofa inhaling perfume from his hookah, and I in a low chair smoking, talking of De Vigne, for the —th had been ordered home, and he coming *viâ* Marseilles, was expected in a few days at furthest.

'What a sin it is that such a union should be valid,' said Sabretasche. 'I think I hear that wretched woman tell me, with her cold, triumphant smile, "Colonel Sabretasche, my father's name was Trefusis, my mother's name was Davis —one was a gentleman, the other a beggar-girl. I have as much, or as little, right to one as to the other. Let your friend sue for a divorce, the law will not give it him."'

'Too true; the law will not. Our divorce law is—'

'An inefficient, insufficient, cruel farce!' said Sabretasche, more energetically than I had ever heard him say anything in his life. 'In an infatuated hour a man saddles himself with a she-devil like the Trefusis—a liar, a drunkard, a mad woman; what redress is there for him? None. All his life through he must drag on the same clog;

fettering all his energies, crushing out all his
hopes, chaining down his very life, festering at
his very heart-strings. There, at his hearth,
must sit the embodied curse—there, in his home,
it must dwell—there, at his side, it must be, till
God release him from it! '

I looked up at him in surprise, it was very unusual to see him so warm about anything. He
took up his hookah again ; yawned, and pointed
to a marble statuette of his own chipping, on
which the firelight was gleaming.

' Look at that little Venus Anadyomene, Arthur,
with the fire-light shining on her; quite Rem-
brandtesque, isn't it ? I'll paint it so to-morrow.'

' Do, and give the picture to Violet Molyneux.
But if you divorce for insanity, every husband sick
of his wife can get a certificate of lunacy against
her? If for drunkenness, what woman will be safe
from having drams innumerable sworn to her? If
for incompatibility of temper, after every little
temporary quarrel, scores would fly to the divorce
courts, and be heartily sorry for it after? Come,
how would you redress it ?'

' My dear fellow,' said Sabretasche, languidly,
' I'm not in parliament, thank Heaven for it; for,
if I were, my conscience would be always pricking
me to try and introduce a little common sense

among that body, and, as the operation would be of an Augean-stable character, I'm much too idle a man for it to be to my taste. You talk like a sage. *I* only feel—for poor De Vigne, I mean.'

'You don't feel more for him than I, Colonel— the Jezebel of a woman! That such an union should be legal, is a disgrace. At the same time, divorce seems to me, of all the niceties of legislature, the most ticklish and unsatisfactory to adjust. If you were to shut the door on divorce, there is an evil unbearable; if you open it too wide, almost as much harm may accrue?'

'My dear Chevasney, you talk like a paterfamilias, a Solon of seventy, a moral machine without blood, or bones, or feelings,' said Sabretashe, impatiently. 'I don't care a straw for theories; I look at facts. Put yourself in the position, Arthur, and then sit in judgment. I take it if every man had to do that, the laws would be at once wiser and more lenient; whereas now, on the contrary, it is your man who has the stolen pieces in his pocket, who cries out the most vehemently for the thief to be hanged, hoping to throw off suspicion! Put yourself in the position! Now you are young and easily swayed, you fall in love —as you phrase it—with some fine figure or pretty face. Down you go headlong, never stopping to

consider whether her mind is attuned to yours, her
tastes in common with yours, her character such as
will go well with yours, in the long intercourse
that takes so much to make it harmony, so little
to make it discord. You marry her; the honeymoon is barely out, before the bandage is off your
eyes. We will suppose you see your wife in her
true colours—coarse, perhaps low-bred, with not
a fibre of her moral nature that is attuned to yours,
not a chord in heart or mind that is in harmony
with yours. She revolts all your better tastes,
she checks all your warmer feelings, she debases
all your higher instincts; union with her, humbles
you in your own eyes; contact and association
with her, lower your tone of thought, and imper-
ceptibly draw you down to her own level. Your
home is one ceaseless scene of pitiful jangle, or of
coarser violence. She makes your house a hell,
she peoples your hearth with fiends; she and her
children—hideous likenesses of herself—bear your
own name, and make you loathe it. Perhaps you
meet one the utter contrast of her, the fond ideal in
your youth of what your wife was to be; one in
whom you realize all you might have been, all you
might have done! You look on Heaven, and
devils hold you back. You thirst for a purer life,
and fiends mock at you and will not let you reach

it. What escape is there for you? None but the grave! Realize this—*realize* it—and you will feel how as a prisoner lies dying for the scent of the fresh air, while the free man sits contentedly within; so a man, happily married, or not married at all, looks on the question of divorce, in a very different light to a man fettered thus, with the torments of both Prometheus and Tantalus, the vulture gnawing at his vitals, the lost joys mocking him out of reach!'

His indolence was gone, his impassiveness changed to vivid earnestness; his melancholy eyes darkened and dilated:—I shuddered involuntarily.

'You draw a terrible picture, Colonel, and a true enough one, no doubt, as many men would witness if one could see into their homes and hearts. But what I want to know is, how to redress it? What judge could dive into the hidden mysteries of human life, the unuttered secrets of mutual love or mutual hate? What judge could say where the blame lay; or, seeing only the surface, and hearing only the outside, weigh the just points of fitness or unfitness? Who can decide between man and woman? Who, seeing the little of the inner existence that is ever revealed in a law court, could judge between them? We know how mischievously absurd the divorce

mania was in Germany? How Dorothea Veit
broke with the best of husbands, on the plea of
"want of sympathy," and went over to Frederick
Schlegel ; and how the Sensitive doctrine of
which Schleiermacher was inaugurator, made it
only necessary to be tied, to feel the want of being
"sympathetically matched," and being untied
again. Men would marry then as carelessly as
they flirt now, and would, as soon as a pretty face
had grown stale to their eye, find out that she
was a vixen, a virago, addicted to gin, or anything
that suited their purpose, though she might really
have every virtue under heaven. Don't you think
that it is impossible, as long as human nature is
so changeable, and short-sighted, or marriage num-
bered among our social institutions at all, to trim
between too much liberty in it and too little?'

'Hush, hush, my good Arthur!' cried the
Colonel, with a gesture of deprecation; '*pray
keep all that for the benches of St. Stephen's
some twenty years hence, it is far too chill, sage,
and rational for me to appreciate it. I prefer
feeling to reasoning—always have done. Possibly,
the evils might accrue that you prophesy; but
that does not at all disprove what I say, that the
marriage fetters are at times the heaviest handcuffs
men can wear; heavier than those which chain

the galley-slave to his oar, for *he* has committed crime to justify his punishment, whereas a man tricked into marriage by an artful intrigante, or hurried into it by a mad fancy, has done no harm to any one—except himself! If you have such a taste for reason, listen to what John Milton— that grave, calm Puritan and philosophic Republican, the last man in the universe to let his passions run away with him—says on the score.' He stretched out his hand to a stand of books near him, and took out a Tetrachordon, bound, as all his books were, in cream-coloured vellum. 'Hear what John Milton says:—"Him I hold more in the way to perfection who foregoes an impious, ungodly, and discordant wedlock, to live according to peace, and love, and God's institution, in a fitter choice; than he who debars himself the happy experience of all godly, which is peaceful conversation in his family, to live a contentious and unchristian life not to be avoided; in temptations not to be lived in; only for the false keeping of a most unreal nullity, a marriage that hath no affinity with God's intentions, a daring phantasm, a mere toy of terror; awing weak senses, to the lamentable superstition of ruining themselves: the remedy whereof God in his law vouchsafes us; which, not to dare use, he warranting, is not our perfection, but is our infirmity, our little faith, our timorous and low conceit of charity; and in them, who force us to it, is their masking pride, and vanity, to seem holier and more circumspect than God." What do you say now? Can you deny the justice, the wisdom, the wide charity and reason of his arguments? It is true he was unhappy with his wife, but he was a man to speak, not from passion, but from conviction. Milton was made of that stern stuff that would have you cut off your right hand if it offended you. In Rome he would have been a Virginius, a Cincinnatus; in the early Christians' days, he would have died with Stephen, endured with Paul. He is not a man like myself, who do no earthly good that I know of, who am swayed by impulse, imagination, passion—a hundred thousand things, who have never checked a wish or denied a desire. Milton is one of your saints and heroes, yet even he has the compassionate wisdom to see that divorce would save many a man, whom an unfit union drives headlong to his ruin. He knows that it is cowardice and hypocrisy, and, as he says, a wish to seem holier and more circumspect than God, which makes your precisians forbid what nature and reason alike demand, and to which, if the Church and the Law forbade freedom ever so, men would find some means to pioneer their own way. You may cage an eagle out of the sunlight, but the bird will find some road to life, and light, and liberty; or die beating his wings in hopeless effort.—Look there! Good Heavens!'

I sprang up; he rose very quickly for his usual indolent movements. In the doorway stood De Vigne, and we grasped his hands silently, none of us speaking. The memory of that last scene in the chapel at his fatal Marriage Altar, was strong upon us all.

Then Sabretasche put his hand on his shoulder, pushed him gently into an arm-chair before the fire, and said, softly, as a man speaks to a woman,

'Dear old fellow! there is no need for us to say welcome home?'

De Vigne looked up with something of his old smile, though it faded instantly.

'No need, indeed: and *don't* say it. I know you are both glad to see me, and let us forget that we have ever been separated. Arthur, old boy, if it wouldn't sound an insult, I should tell you you were *grown*; and as for you, Sabretasche, you are not a whit altered; it is my belief you wouldn't change if you lived as long as Sue's Wandering Jew! They told me at the barracks, Arthur was dining with you, and so I came on straight. My luggage is still in the *Pera*, but I brought up some cheroots. Try them, both of you.'

We saw that he wished to sweep away the past, and avoid all allusion to his own fate; and we fell in with his humour. Smoking round the fire, we tried to ignore every painful subject; but as I looked at him, I found it hard not to utter aloud my curse on the woman who had sent him out into exile.

Ten long years had not passed without leaving their stamp upon him. His face had lost the glow, the bright eagerness the rounded outline of his earlier youth. Pale he had always been but now the pallor was that of marble, as if the hot young blood surging through his veins had been suddenly frozen ; as when the first breath of winter checks, the free, warm, vehement waters in their course, and chills them into ice. It was still the face of a man of wayward will, and strong passions. but of waywardness which had cost him dear, and of passions that were chained down perhaps for ever.

,You have seen good service out there, De Vigne,' begun Sabretasche, to lighten the gloom which was stealing upon us. 'On my word we feel quite proud of you! What a lion you have been, old fellow.'

De Vigne smiled.

'I looked a lion because I was among puppy dogs! Yes, I saw good service, not so much, though, as I should have liked. Some of it was pretty sharp work, but we dawdled a whole year away at that miserable Calcutta court; if it had not been for pig-sticking I should never have borne it at all, but I got no end of spears. Then we went up to a hill station, where there was nobody but an old judge, and a missionary or two, who had been bankrupt shoemakers, and taken to dispensing Grace, as a means of getting a few shillings from those discerning Christians who sent them out, firmly crediting their assurances that they felt "specially called." There the hill deer, and the ortolans, and a tiger or two, kept us going; and then we were ordered off to have a shy at the mountain rebels. They fought magnificently, I must say. Ah! by Jove!' cried De Vigne, his eyes lighting up, 'there at last I really *lived*. The constant danger, the ceaseless vigilance, the free life, the sharp service, roused me up, and gave me a zest for existence which I thought I had lost for ever.'

'Nonsense, nonsense!' cried the Colonel. 'You will have zest enough in it again by-and-by. No man on the sunny side of forty has lost what he may not regain.'

'Except where one false step has murdered pride and ruined honour!' said De Vigne, between his teeth. 'Well, Sabretasche, what have *you* been doing all these years? Flirting, buying pictures and painting them, setting the fashion, and criticizing new singers, as usual, I suppose.'

'Don't talk of the years!' cried Sabretasche, lifting his eyebrows. 'If I see to-morrow I shall be forty-five. It is disagreeable to grow old; one begins to doubt one's attractions!'

'You are young enough!—and yet, I don't know; it is a popular fallacy that time counts by years. One is old according to the style of one's life, not the length of it.'

'I heard Violet Molyneux tell you last night, Colonel, that you were in your second youth, and the first prime of manhood. So take comfort,' said I.

He smiled. 'Poor little fool!' he muttered, under his moustaches.

'Violet Molyneux—who is she?' asked De Vigne. 'That's a new name to me. Is she a daughter of Jockey Jack, as we used to call him?'

'Yes,' I answered; 'and a lovely creature. She's a fresh beauty, and a new love for Sabretasche, who worships him most devoutly especially since she came to his studio this morning and saw his last painting of Esmeralda and Djali.'

' Don't crack me up, Arthur,' said Sabretasche, rather impatiently. ' Jockey Jack has a daughter who knows how to talk, and sings well enough to please *me* (two especial miracles, as you can fancy, my dear De Vigne); but, certainly, both her tongue and her thorax, do their business unusually well, and she is very lovely to boot. What have I been doing, did you say? Leading just the same life I have led for the last twenty years. Making love to scores of women, wasting my time over marble and canvas, heading a Hyde Park campaign, or directing a Richmond fête! Caramba! one gets tired of it.'

' Why lead it, then?'

'Because none are any better. Do my scientific friends, who absorb their energies in classifying a fossil encrinite; my parliamentary friends, who concentrate their energies in bribing the Unwashed; my philanthropic friends, who hoax the public, and get hoaxed themselves, by every text-quoting thief who has the knack, and the tact, to touch up their weak points; my literary friends, who write to line portmanteaus; my celebrated friends, who toil to get heart-disease, and three damning lines in history,—do these, any of them,

enjoy themselves one wit the more ; or fail to say
with Solomon, "Vanity of vanities—all is vanity"?
Tell me so—show me so, and I will begin their
life to-morrow. *Our* vocation is to amuse ourselves, and slay our fellow-creatures by way of in-
termediate pastime; and it is as good a one, for
all I can see, as any other.'

'To slay our fellow-creatures!' cried De Vigne.
' Come, come, put it a little more gracefully. Tn
fight like Britons—to die for our colours. Something a little more poetic and patriotic!'

'Same thing, my dear De Vigne; only the
wording different!'

'You like the same life as the Cid, Colonel,'
said I, smiling. ' To eat daintily, sleep warmly,
lie on cushions without anybody to trouble you,
and kill your game when the spirit moves you.'

'And love most truly, and do my duty, as far
as I see it, most faithfully? No, no, Arthur,
that doesn't do for me at all; it's not in my
rôle.'

'You'll write on the Cid's grave,' said De
Vigne, ' as Byron wrote on Boatswain's,

" In life the firmest friend,
The first to welcome, foremost to defend." '

' Yes, indeed ; and like him

" I never had but one, and here he lies."

The Cid,' said Sabretasche, drawing the dog's ears through his hands—'the Cid is the only thing that cares for me.'

' For *you*, the adored of all women, the *cher ami* of all beauties, the "good fellow" of every man worth knowing in town ! What do you mean by only having a dog to care for you? The world would never believe you.'

'I mean what I say. *Bon Dieu!* how much does the world know of any of us?'

' Little enough,' said De Vigne, 'but it is always of those of whom it knows least, that it will affect to know most; and the stranger you sit next at a dinner-party, is ten to one far better acquainted with your business than you are yourself. We shall hear you are to marry—what is her name?—Violet Molyneux soon?'

' Not I,' said Sabretasche; 'at least you may *hear* it, but I shall live, and die, as I am now—alone ! Who would care for reports? I can as soon imagine a man taking heed of every tuft of dandelion that passes him in the air, or every insect that crawls beneath his feet, as taking note of the reports that buzz round his career.'

' By Jove, yes !' cried De Vigne. 'Out campaigning, one is free from all that trash. Before the can-

non's mouth men cannot stop to split straws; and
with one's own life on a thread, one cannot stop to
ruin another's character. I do not know how it
is,—I have read pretty widely, but philosophers
never preached endurance to me as well as Nature. A few months ago I was camping out to
net ortolans. Round us was the dense stretch of
the forests and jungles; no wind, no sound, except the cry of the hill deer; nothing stirring,
except now and then an antelope flitting like a
ghost across the clearing, and, over it all, the
southern stars. On my life, as I lay there by our
watch-fire alone, with my pipe, it struck me that,
if we would let her, Nature would be a truer
teacher than creeds or homilies. Human life
seems so small beside the vast life of great forests.
The calm grand silence rebukes our own feverish-
ness. We who fancy that the eyes of all the universe are on us, that we are the sole love and
charge of its Creator, feel what ephemera we are
in the giant scale of existence; what countless
myriads of such as we, have been swept from their
place out of sight, and not a law of the spheres
around been stirred, not a moment's pause been
caused, in the silent march of creation! Under
men's tutelage, I grow impatient and irritated.
What gage have I that they know better than I?

They rouse me into questioning their dogmas, into penetrating their mysteries, into searching out, and proving, the nullity of the truths they assume for granted; but under the teaching of Nature I am silent. I recognize my own inferiority. I grow ashamed of my own pride.'

'Aye!' answered Sabretasche. 'A wayside flower, a sunny savannah, even a little bit of lichen on a stone in the Campagna, has taught one truer lessons than are taught in the forum or the pulpit. Man sees so little of his fellow-man; he is so ready to condemn, so slow to sympathize with him, that, if he attempt to teach, he is far more apt to irritate than aid; but, to the voices of Nature, the bluntest sense can hardly fail to listen, and they speak in a tongue, translatable alike to the Indian in his woods, and the savant in his study.'

'But one is apt to lose sight of Nature in the hurry and conflict of actual every-day social life? Standing alone among the Alps, a man learns his own insignificance; but once back in the world, the first line of a favourable review, the first hurrah of an admiring constituency, the first applause that feeds his ear in the world he lives in, will give him back his self-appreciation, and he will find it hard not to fancy himself of the im-

portance to the universe that he is to his clique.
That is partly why I was unwilling to leave campaigning. There the jungle and the stars took me
in hand, and there, by my camp-fire, I would listen
to them, though God knows whether I be the
better for it. Here, on the contrary, men will be
prating at me, and I shall chafe at them, and it
will be a wonder if I do not kick out at some of
them. My guerilla life suits me better than my
fashionable one.'

' You are too good for it all the same,' said
Sabretasche ; ' and if you should put the kicking
process into execution, it will be a little whole-
some chastisement for them, and a little sanitary
exertion for you ! Jungles and planets are grander
and truer, *sans doute*, but Johannisberger and Society are equally good for men in their way, and,
besides—they are very pleasant !'

' Your acme of praise, Sabretasche,' laughed De
Vigne. ' I agree with you that human nature is,
after all, the best book we can learn, only the
study is irritating, and one sees so much *en noir*
there, that if we look too long we are apt to fling
away our lexicon, with a curse.'

'The best way, after all,' said the Colonel, with
a cross between a yawn and a sigh, ' is to take
nothing seriously ! Men and women are mario-

nettes; learn the tricks of their wires and strings, and make them perform, at your will, tragedy, comedy, farce, whatever pleases your mood. Human life is a kaleidoscope, with which the wise man amuses himself; it has pretty pictures for the eye, if you know how to shake them up, and as for analyzing it, pulling it to pieces, for being only bits of cork and burnt glass, and quarrelling with it for being trumpery instead of *bonâ fide* brilliants — *cui bono?* — you won't make it any better.'

'Possibly; but I shall not be taken in by it.'

'My dear fellow, I think the time when we *are* taken in by it is the happiest part of our lives.'

'Maybe. His drum is no pleasure to a boy after he has broken it, and found the music is empty wind, with no mystery about it whatever! I say, what is your clock? Am I not keeping you from some engagemeut or other?'

'None at all,' answered Sabretasche, 'and you will just sit where you are for the next four hours. Give me another cheroot, and take some more brandy. Is it likely we shall let you off early?'

We did not let him off early; and all the small hours had chimed before we had done talking, with the fire burning brightly, and the Cid lying full length between us, with his muzzle between his fore-pads, while De Vigne told us tales of his Indian campaign that roused even listless Sabretasche, and fired my blood like the war-note of the Long Roll, or the trumpet call of Boot and Saddle!

CHAPTER XII.

SABRETASCHE, HAVING MOWED DOWN MANY
FLOWERS, DETERMINES TO SPARE ONE VIOLET.

FROM the hour he had left her in the vestry
at Vigne church, De Vigne had never seen the
woman who, by law, stood branded on him as his
wife. His passion changed to loathing, and the
hate wherewith he hated her was far greater than
the love wherewith he had loved her. Could it
be otherwise? Could any man feel anything but
deadliest hate towards the woman who had outwitted and entrapped him, outraged his honour,
shivered his pride to the dust, and shaped her vengeance in a form which must press upon him with
a dead and ice-cold weight, strike from his path
all the natural joys that bloom so brightly for a
man so young; and stretch over his whole existence a shadow all the blacker that its giant upas-
tree sprang from the forgotten seed of a boyish
sin. He left her in the madness of his agony;
and swore never to touch even her hand again.

Passion changed to abhorrence, and what had
charmed and intoxicated him with the sensual
beauties of form, now filled him only with abhorrence and disgust. He saw her bearing his own
name, holding his own honour; coarse, cruel, ill-
born, ill-bred, the pollution of her past life vainly
covered with the varnish of society; and seeing
her thus, knew that till one or other was in the
grave this woman was his WIFE. Remorse, too,
was added to his curse. His mother had died of
that fatal blow which had struck at the root of
her son's peace and honour. She had been for
some years aware, though she had never allowed
De Vigne to be told of the frail tenure on which
she held her life, that any sudden emotion or
excitement might at any time be her death-blow :
a secret she had kept with that silent heroism of
which here and there women are found capable.
As De Vigne left the chapel, Sabretasche had
lifted her up in what he believed to be a faint-
ing fit : it was a swoon, from which she never
awoke, and her son was left to bear his curse
alone.

I have seen men writhing in their death agony,
I have seen women stretched across the lifeless
body of their lover on the battle-field; I have
seen the torture of human souls cooped up by

shoals in hospital sick-wards; I have seen mortal
suffering in almost all its phases—and they are
varied and pitiful enough, God knows!—but I never
saw any so silent and yet so awful as De Vigne's,
when we hurried after him up to town. When we
found him, the Trefusis's revenge had done its
work upon him; lengthened years would not
have quenched life, and light, and youth, as the
remorse, the humiliation, the conflicting passions
at war within him, had already done. The
tidings we brought crowned the anguish that had
entered into his life. Gently as Sabretasche
broke it to him, I thought it would have killed
him. His lips turned grey as stone, he staggered
like a drunken man, and threw up his arms in his
blind agony.

'My God! and *I* have murdered her!'—That
was all he said. Under what throes his iron
pride was bowed in his night watches beside the
lifeless form of the mother whose love for him had
slain her, no one knew. He was alone in his
doom, and I could only guess by my knowledge of
him how madly he cursed the passions that had
wrought his ruin, how long and silently the vulture of remorse gnawed his heart away, with the
haunting memory of his folly and its fruit.

As rapidly as possible he exchanged into the

—th Hussars, and sailed for Scinde. He saw none of his old companions and acquaintance, save the Colonel and myself; he shunned all who had been witnesses of his marriage, all who knew of the stain upon his name. It is easy to bear the contempt and censure of the world when defiance of its laws brings fame and rapture; but its sneer may be hard even to a brave man to bear, when the world has cause to call him Fool, when it can triumph in vaunting its own superior penetration, in recalling its own wise prophecies of his fall, and in compelling him to make the most difficult of all confessions to a proud heart— *'I was wrong !'*

He commissioned Sabretasche to make arrangements with his wife, but all that the Colonel, consummate man of the world though he was, could do, was to exact that she should receive an allowance of three thousand a year, on condition that she never came to England. The Trefusis accepted it, possibly because she knew the law would not give her so much, and went to Paris and the Bads, leading a pleasant life enough, I doubt not, but careful to make it far too proper a one—outwardly, at the least—to give him any chance of a divorce. Separated from him at the altar, she was still legally his wife and bore his name. By what miracle of metamorphosis, by what agency, assistance, or self-education, she had been enabled to change and exalt herself, we knew not then, nor till long afterwards. That De Vigne had not recognized her was scarce astonishing. In those long years the unformed girl of seventeen had changed into the mature beauty of five-and-twenty; she had grown taller, her form had developed, fashion, dress, and taste lent her beauty a thousand aids unknown to her in her earlier days. It was not wonderful that, having forgotten Lucy Davis, and almost all connected with her, he should fail to recognize her in so utterly different a sphere, so entirely altered as she was in feature, manner, station, and appearance; though how she had so metamorphosed herself I used to think over many and many a time, never able to find a solution.

At length, after ten years' absence, De Vigne returned home to resume the social life he had so suddenly snapped asunder. To careless eyes he was much the same, but *I* felt that the whole man was changed. Reserved, sceptical of all truth and of all worth, his generous trust changed to chill suspicion, his fiery impetuosity chained down under a semblance of icy cynicism, his strong passions held down under an iron curb, the treachery of which he had been the victim seemed to have wholly altered his once frank, warm, and cordial nature.

'The fact is,' said Curly to me, as we were riding down Piccadilly to the Park, 'De Vigne, poor fellow! is as frozen by this miserable *mésalliance* as the ships in the Arctic Seas. It would do him a world of good to fall in love again, but he won't. Ah, by Jove, here he is! Beautiful creature, that mare, of his is—three parts thorough-bred; and just look at her wild eye. How are you, De Vigne? My dear fellow, I'm deucedly glad you're come back!'

'Very kind of you, Curly,' laughed De Vigne, 'but I'm not sure I re-echo you. A gallop in the cool night through the jungle is preferable to pacing up and down the Ride yonder.'

'Wait till the Ride is full,' replied Curly, 'with all the gouty wits, and the dandy politicians, and the amazoned belles, and the intensely got-up stock-brokers, and the immensely showy livery-stable hacks, who would go so delightfully if they weren't, *par hasard*, broken-winded, or knocked-kneed by way of diversity! Wait till the season, my good fellow—till you drink Seltzer as thirstily as a tired hound drinks water, till you spend the summer nights crushed up on the staircases, till you waste a couple of hundred giving a dinner to men and women who, having eaten your *croustades*, drive away to demolish your character,—wait till the season, and *then* you'll admit the superiority of enjoyment to be found in Town! There's nobody in it yet, except, indeed, Violet Molyneux.'

' Whom I have not seen,' said De Vigne; ' but I will call, for I used to know her mother very well; an eminently religious flirt! I have a curiosity to see this young beauty, because she has Sabretasche's good word.'

' A good word, by-the-by, that's apt to do them as much damage in one way as his condemnation does in another. She little knows what a desperate Lothario he is. I wonder if he'll ever marry?'

' I wonder if you'll ever hang yourself, Curly?' said De Vigne, dryly. ' I say, shall we go and call on the Molyneux now? May as well.'

' Do! I like calling,' responded Curly. ' You kill the hour, you learn all the news, you enjoy the luxury of hearing one best friend scandalize and cut up another dear acquaintance; and you can win Lady A.'s love for life by revealing to her the strictly private secret Mrs. B. has just confided to you, under a solemn seal of silence, relative to Miss C.! Society wouldn't half go on; there wouldn't be a tithe of the *on dits* sown that are necessary to our welfare if it weren't for that blessed institution, " morning calls." '

Lady Molyneux was at home, a rare thing for that restless mosaic of religion and fashion, of decided '*ton*' and pronounced 'piety;' and we found her, chatting with one of her beloved spiritual brothers, the Bishop of Campanile, a most pleasant *bon viveur*, by no means a Saint Anthony on the score of earthly temptations, while in a low chair sat Violet Molyneux talking to Sabretasche, who was listening to her with an air of half-indolent amusement, and magnetizing her with the soft lustrous gaze of his mournful eyes, that had wound their way into so many women's love.

Lady Molyneux welcomed us all charmingly. She was made of milk of roses, that dear woman; while there was a shadow of impatience in her daughter's tell-tales eyes at having her talk interrupted : of course she was too much of a lady to show it, and the Colonel, who had a knack of monopolizing a woman quietly, did not give up his seat, and soon resumed his discussion with her, which it seemed was on the poets of the present day.

' What do you think of the " Ideals of the Lotus and the Lily ? " ' asked Violet of De Vigne, re-

ferring to the book they were discussing, the last
mystical nonsense that had issued from the imagination of the pet rhymer of the day.

'I cannot say I think much,' smiled De Vigne.
'To read that man's works one wants a dictionary
of all his unintelligible jargon, his "double-bar-
relled adjectives," his purposely-obscured meanings!
I suppose he fancies *chiar'oscuro* the best tone for
paintings, that he draws his word-pictures in such
densely dark style.'

'All that is treason here, De Vigne,' said
Sabretasche, with a smile. 'Miss Molyneux is
the patron and champion of everything visionary,
high wrought, and unintelligible to ordinary mortals. These raving individuals, "sad only for
wantonness," strangely please dreamy young ladies
and gentlemen ignorant of the true meaning, sorrows, and burdens of this "work-a-day world."'

Violet made him a graceful *révérence*.

'Thank you. Is that a hit at me? It does not
strike home, if it is, because my worst enemies
could never say I was dreamy, though they may
call me—what is it, high wrought? But you forget, that feeling—romance, as you are pleased to
call it—has been the germ and nurse of all great
writers. The swan must suffer before it sings.
Did not his child-love inspire Dante? Would

Petrarch have been all he is but for the "*amore veementissimo ma unico ed onesto?*" Did not his passion for Mary Chaworth have its influence for life upon the writings of Byron? And was not Leonora d'Este to Tasso what Diana's kiss was to Endymion?'

'And was not the domestic misery of Milton's married life the inspiration of that glorious tirade upon women in Adam's magnificent speech?' asked Sabretasche quietly; 'and but for Anne Hathaway, might we have ever had that fiery oration of Posthumus:

> " Even to vice
> They are not constant ; but are changing still
> One vice, but of a minute old, for one
> Not half so old as that?" '

'Some better woman taught him, then,' cried Violet, 'that from women's eyes

> " Sparkles still the right Promethean fire.
> They are the books, the arts, the academes
> That show, contain, and nourish all the world !" '

Sabretasche bowed his head in acknowledgment of defeat.

' You have conquered me, as Rosaline conquered Biron !'

He said the words as he had said such things to scores of other women as lovely as Violet Moly-

neux; from anybody else she would have taken
them at their value; at the Colonel's glance her
colour deepened.

'But don't you think, Miss Molyneux,' suggested
De Vigne, 'that when Tasso languished in Fer-
rara dungeons, he must have wished he had never
seen the Este family? Don't you fancy that
Gemma Donati must have rather cancelled Dante's
good opinion of the *beau sexe*, and that his "wife
of savage temper" may have been a bitter tonic,
rather than sweet balm to his genius? And as
for Byron—well! Miss Milbanks was rather a
thorn in his side, wasn't she? And with all the
romance in the world, I think, when he called on
Mrs. Musters, he must have thought he had been
rather a fool. What do you say?'

'I say, Major De Vigne,' responded Violet,
'that you have not a trace, not a particle, not an
infinitesimal germ of romance!'

'Thank Heaven—no!' said De Vigne, with a
laugh.

I doubt, though, if the laugh was heartfelt. I
dare say he thought of the time when romance
was hot and strong in him, and trust and faith
strong too!

'I pity you, then! Where I think you sceptical
men err so much,' said Violet, turning her bril-

liant eyes on Sabretasche, 'is in confounding false and true, good and bad, feeling with sentiment, genius with pretension. Why at one sweep condemn the expression of unusual feeling as sentiment, simply because it *is* unusual? Deep feeling is rare;.but it does not follow that it is unreal. You tread on a thousand ordinary flowers —daisies, buttercups, cowslips, anemones—in an every-day walk; they are all fair, all full of life; but out of all the Flora, there is only one Sensitive Plant that shrinks and trembles at your touch. Yet, though the Sensitive Plant is organized so far more tenderly, it is no artificial offspring of mechanism, but as fresh and real, and living a thing as any of the others!'

De Vigne and Curly were now chatting with Lady Molyneux, whose bishop had taken his *congé*. Sabretasche still sat by Violet a little apart.

'I believe you,' he said, gently; 'there *are* sensitive plants, so fresh and fair, that it is a sin they should ever have to shiver in rude hands, and learn to bend with the world's breath. But live as long as we have, and you will know that the deep feeling of which you are thinking is never found in unison with the poetic and drivelling sentiment we ridicule. Boys' sorrows vent themselves in words—men's griefs are voiceless. If ever you feel—pray God you never may—vital suffering, you will find that it will never seek solace in confidences, never *lament itself*, but rather hug its torture closer, as the Spartan child hugged the fierce wolf-fangs. You will find the difference between the fictitious sorrows which run abroad proclaiming their own wrongs; and the grief which lies next the heart night and day, and, like the iron cross of the Romish priest, eats it slowly, but none the less surely, away.'

They were strange words to come from Vivian Sabretasche! Violet looked at him in surprise, and her laughing eyes grew sad and dimmed. He had forgotten for the moment where he was; at her earnest gaze he roused himself with the faintest tinge of colour on his face.

'I am going to ask you to do me a most intense kindness; would you mind singing me Hullah's "Three Fishers?" I declare to you it has haunted me ever since I heard you sing it on Tuesday night; and it is so seldom I hear any music that is not a screech—rarely, indeed, anything that *satisfies* me as your songs do.'

She sprang up joyously. 'Oh yes, if you will sing *me* those glorious Italian songs of yours. 'Major de Vigne, if you have no romance, I am

quite sure you cannot care for music, so I give
you full leave to talk to mamma as loudly as ever
you like, I am going to sing only to Colonel
Sabretasche.'

Sabretasche looked half-pleased, half-amused at
the distinction accorded to him, and followed her
to the back drawing-room, where he leaned on the
piano looking down upon her, while Violet sang
with one of the best gifts of nature a clear, bell-
like, melodious voice, highly tutored, and as flexible
and free as the song of a mavis in spring-time. I
am not sure whether her mother was best pleased
or not at that musical *tête-à-tête*, for Sabretasche
had an universal reputation as a most unscrupulous
flirt, and Lady Molyneux knew his character too
well to think he was likely to be doing any more
than playing with Violet, as the most attractive
beauty in town. But then, again, his word was
almost law in all matters of taste. He could
injure Violet irretrievably by a depreciating criti-
cism, and could make her of tenfold more market-
able value by an approving word, for there were
numbers of men at the Clubs who moulded themselves by his dictum. So Lady Molyneux let
them alone.

I don't suppose, however, that she noticed
Violet drawing out a large bunch of her floral

namesakes from a Bohemian glass, and lifting them up for Sabretasche to scent.

'Are they not delicious? They remind me of dear old Corallyne, when I used to gather them out of the fresh damp moss. Do you know Kerry, Colonel Sabretasche? No? Oh, you should go there; it is so beautiful, with its blue lakes, and its wild mountains, and its green, fragrant woodlands.'

'I should like it, I dare say,' said Sabretasche, smiling, 'with you for my guide. I want some added charm now to give "greenness to the grass and glory to the flower." Once I enjoyed them for themselves, as you do; but as one gets on in life there is too silent a rebuke in nature for us to enjoy it unrestrainedly. Is Lord Molyneux's estate in Kerry?'

'Don't call it an estate,' laughed Violet; 'it always amuses me so when I see it put down in the peerage. It is only miles and miles of moorland, with nothing growing on it but tangled wood and glorious wild-flowers. There are one or two cabins with inhabitants like kelpies. The house has been, perhaps, very grand when all we Irish were kings, and you Sassenachs, Roman slaves; but at the present moment, having lost three-quarters of its roof and nine-tenths of its

timbers, having rats, and owls, and ghosts innumerable, no windows, and no furniture, you would
probably think it more picturesque than comfortable, and feel more inclined to paint it than to
live in it.'

'But *you* lived in it?'

'Ah! when I was a child; but it was a little
better then. There was a comfortable room or
two in it, and I was very happy there with my favourite governess and my little rough pony, when
papa and mamma were up here or in Paris, and
left us to ourselves in Corallyne. I wonder if I
shall ever be as happy as I was there?'

'You are very happy here?' said Sabretasche,
with a sort of pity for the joyous heart to which
sorrow was yet but a name.

'Happy? Oh, yes; I enjoy myself, and I am
always light-hearted; but I have things to annoy
me here; the artifices and frivolity of society
worry me. I want to say always what I think,
and nobody seems to do it in the world.'

'The world would be in hot water if they did.
But pray speak it to me.'

'I always do! Yes, I enjoy London life. I like
the whirl, the excitement, the intellectual discussion, the vivid, *real* life men lead here. I
should enjoy it entirely if I did not see too many

hard, cruel, worn faces under the fair smiling masks.'

'*Pauvre enfant!*' murmured Sabretasche. 'Do you suppose there are any light hearts under the dominoes?'

'*Yours* is not a light one?'

'Mine!' echoed the Colonel, with a strangely melancholy intonation; then he laughed his gay soft laugh. 'If it is not, mademoiselle, you are the first who had penetration enough to find it out. I am *quêteur* of amusement in general to all my friends! There is De Vigne going, and so must I. I shall not thank you for your songs.'

'No! I am so tired of meaningless thanks and vapid compliments,' she said laughingly. 'You would not have asked me to sing if you had not wished to hear me, for I know that on principle you never bore yourself.'

'Never,' replied Sabretasche, in his usual indolent tone. 'No one is worth such a self-sacrifice.'

'Not even I?' asked Violet, raising her eyebrows.

'To suppose such a case, I must first imagine you boring me, which just at present is an hypothesis *not* to be imagined by any stretch of poetic fancy,' laughed Sabretasche, as he held out his hand to bid her good morning.

She held the violets up to him.

'You have forgotten the flowers?'

'May I have them?' he asked, softly, with one of those glances, in which his lengthened experience in that mysterious book, a woman's heart, had perfected him.

She gave them to him with a bright flush and smile. He slipped them hastily into the breast of his waistcoat, and came forward to Lady Molyneux.

'Violet, my love,' began her mother, as the door closed on us, 'Colonel Sabretasche comes here a great deal; I wish you would not be quite so— quite so—expansive with him.'

'Expansive!' repeated Violet, in sheer astonishment. 'What do you mean?'

'I mean what I say, my dear Violet,' repeated the Viscountess, the milk of roses turning a little sour. 'You treat him quite as familiarly as if he were your father or your lover. You need not colour, I don't say he *is* the last; God forbid he should be, with his principles. I know he makes himself agreeable to you, but so, as every one will tell you, he has done for the last twenty years to any pretty woman that came across his path; and your speech to his friend De Vigne, about " singing *only* to Colonel Sabretasche," was not alone unmaidenly, it was absurd.'

'How so? I only cared for him to hear it and like it.'

'It was all very well for him to hear it and like it,' replied my lady, irritably—prominent piety has a queer knack of souring the temper—'his extreme fastidiousness makes his good word well worth having; the best way to make your opinion of value in society is to admire nothing, as he does! But, at the same time, it is a dear way of gaining his applause to keep all other men in the background while you are flirting with him. Before you saw him you liked Regalia, and Killury, and plenty of others, well enough ; now you really attend to no one else.'

'Because I see their inferiority to him,' interrupted Violet, vehemently. 'All they can do is to ride, and waltz, and smoke ; he has the genius of an artist. They think they please me by vapid flattery; he knows better. They are one's subjects, he is one's master!'

Lady Molyneux was seriously appalled by such an outburst. She raised her eyebrows sarcastically :

'You admire Vivian Sabretasche very much,

Violet? I should not advise you to say so, my dear.'

'Why not? it is the truth.'

'Few truths can be spoken,' replied the eminently religious, fashionable lady, coldly. 'Why you had better not proclaim your very Quixotic admiration for Sabretasche, because he bears as bad a character for morality as he bears a good one for talent and fashion. What his life has been every one knows; he is a most unprincipled libertine. No one ever dreams of expecting anything serious of him; he is the last man in the universe to marry, but a flirtation with him may very greatly injure your prospects—'

'Oh, mamma, pray don't!' said Violet, with a dash of contemptuous hauteur. 'I am so sick of those words; they are so lowering, so pitiful, so conventional, making a market of oneself! I cannot bear to hear you speak so. As to his being —to his meaning—anything "serious," I would rather die than learn to look upon him as a speculation, or class him with all those men who try to buy me with their settlements. As to his life, he has led the same life as most men, probably; but you need only look in his eyes to see whether anything base or cruel can attach itself to him.'

Her mother sighed, and sneered, and smiled unpleasantly.

'My love, the way you talk is too absurd. You forget yourself strangely. How is it possible for you to judge of the character of a man over forty, a *blasé* man of the world, who was one of the greatest *roués* about town while you were a little child in the nursery; it is too ridiculous! But go and dress for dinner. The dear bishop, and Cavendish Grey, and Killury will dine here.'

'Poor sensitive plant, it would be a pity my hands should touch it and wither its freshness and fairness,' thought the Colonel, as he turned his tilbury from the door. 'Vivian Sabretasche, I say, are you growing a fool? Don't you know that the golden gates won't open for you? You barred them yourself; you have no right to complain. Have you not been going to the bad all the days of your life? Have you not persuaded the world, ever since you lived in it, that you are a reckless, devil-may-care Don Juan, a smasher of the entire Decalogue? Why should you now, just because you have looked into that girl's bright eyes, be trying to trick yourself and her into the idea that you possess such affairs as heart, and feeling, and regrets, because she, fresh to life, is innocent enough to have a taste for such nonsense? All

folly—all folly! Back to your animate friends,
horses and men, and your inanimate loves, chisel
and palate, or you may grow a fool in your older
years, as many wise men have done before. You've
pulled up many fair flowers in your day, you can
surely leave that one Violet in peace.'

'Oh, mamma, she is such a pretty girl, and
Ashton is so abominably stupid; he must have
knocked them down on purpose. Open the door,
Colonel Sabretasche, and let me out. It is of no
use telling me not—I will!'

With which enunciation of her own self-will
the Hon. Violet Molyneux sprang to the ground
in the middle of St. James's Street, just opposite
the bay-window, to the unspeakable horror of her
mother, and the excessive amusement of De Vigne
and Sabretasche, who were driving in the Molyneux barouche. One of the powdered, white-
wanded, six-feet-high plushes that swayed to and
fro at the back of the carriage, having dismounted
at some order of his mistress's, had happened to
push, as those noble and stately creatures are
given to pushing every plebeian peripatetic, against
a young girl passing on the pavement. The girl
had with her a portfolio of pictures, which the
abrupt rencontre with Ashton sent out of her

grasp, scattering its contents to the four winds of heaven, and to apologize was the work of a second with that perfectly courteous, but, according to her mamma and her female friends, much too impulsive and unconventional young beauty, the Hon. Violet, whose fatal lessons, learnt on the wild moorlands and among the fragrant woods of her beloved Corallyne, the aristocratic experiences of her single season had been sadly unable to unteach her.

'Ashton, how can you be so careless? Pick those drawings up immediately and very carefully,' said the young beauty, as, turning to the young girl, she apologized with polished courtesy for the accident her servant had caused, while Ashton, in disgusting violence to his own feelings, was compelled to bend his stately form, and even to so far fall from his pedestal of powdered propriety and flunkeyism grandeur, as to run—yes,. absolutely run—after one of the sketches, which, wafted by a little breeze that must have been that mischievous imp Puck himself, ambled gently and tantalizingly down the street. The young girl thanked her with as bright a smile as Violet's, and votes were divided in the club windows as to which of the two was the most charming, though the one was a fashionable belle, with every adjunct

of taste and dress, and the other an unprotected little thing walking with a woman-servant
in St. James's Street; an artist probably, or a
governess. She took her portfolio (by this time
men in the clubs were all looking on, heartily
amused, and Sabretasche and De Vigne were
picking up the pictures, on the back of which
they had time to observe the initials "A. T., St.
Crucis-on-the-hill, Richmond Park," with much
more diligence than the grandiose Ashton;)
thanked Violet with a low graceful bow, and was
passing on, when she looked up at De Vigne.
Her lips parted, her eyes darkened, her face
brightened; she stood still a minute, then she
came back: 'Sir Folko!' But he neither saw nor
heard her, his foot was on the step of the barouche; Ashton shut the door with a clang,
swung himself up on the footboard, and the
carriage rolled away into Pall Mall.

'Violet, Violet! how you forget yorself, my
love?' whispered Lady Molyneux, scandalized and
horror-stricken. 'I wish you would not be quite
so impulsive. All the gentlemen in White's were
staring at you.'

'Let them stare, mamma, dear,' laughed Violet,
merrily. 'It is a very innocent amusement, it
gives them a great deal of pleasure and does me

no harm. What glorious blue eyes that girl had, and such lovely hair. You should laud me for my magnanimity in praising another woman so pretty.'

'For magnanimity in that line is not a virtue of your sex,' said De Vigne.

'You cynical man! I don't see why it should not be.'

'Don't you? Did you, on your honour, then, fair lady, ever speak well of a rival.'

'I never had one.'

'You never could,' whispered Sabretasche, bending forward to tuck the tiger-skin over her.

'But supposing you had?' persisted De Vigne.

'I hope I should be above maligning her; but I am afraid to think how I should hate her.'

She spoke with such unnecessary vehemence, that her mother and De Vigne stared. Violet's eyes met the Colonel's; her colour rose, and he, incongruously enough, turned his head away.

'If Miss Molyneux treats the visionary things of life so earnestly, what will she do when she comes to the realities?' laughed De Vigne.

Lady Molyneux sighed; on occasions she would play at tender maternity, but it did not sit well upon her.

'Ah! Major de Vigne, if we did not find some armour besides our own strength in our life pilgrimage, few of us women would be able to endure to the end of the Via Dolorosa.'

'True! Britomart soon finds a buckler studded with the diamonds of a good dower, or stiffened with the parchment-skins of handsome settlements; and, tender and gentle as she looks, manages to go through the skirmish very unscathed by dint of the vizor she keeps down so wisely, and the sharp lance of the tongue she keeps always in rest against friend and foe!'

'What thrusts of the spear you deserve, Major de Vigne; you are worse than your friend, and he is bad enough!' cried Violet, looking rather lovingly, however, on the Colonel, despite his errors. 'I am sure if women take to lance and vizor, it is only in self-defence, for you would pierce us with your arrows if you could find a hole in our armour.'

'But here and there is a woman who unhorses us at once, and on whom it is a shame to draw our swords. Agnes Hotots are very rare, but when we do find them, Ringsdale is safe to go down before them,' said Sabretasche, with his eloquent glance.

'I should think you have both of you been conquered or imprisoned some time or other by some Cynisca, or Maria de Jesu, whom you cannot forgive, and who makes you so bitter upon us all !' laughed Violet.

She said it in the gay innocence of her heart! Both were silent: and Violet instinctively felt that she had trodden on dangerous ground—then De Vigne laughed, though a curse would have been better in unison with his thoughts.

'Miss Molyneux, with all due deference to your sex, there are few men I fear, who, if they told you the truth, would not have to confess having found, that those warm and charming feelings with which you young ladies start fresh in life, have a knack of disappearing in the atmosphere of society, as gold disappears melted and swallowed up in aqua regia.'

'Will you let your pure gold be lost in De Vigne's metaphorical aqua regia?' whispered the Colonel, half smiling, half sadly, as he handed her out, at her own house.

'Oh! never!'

'You mean it now, but—Well, we shall see!' And Sabretasche led her up the steps with his low, careless laugh. 'When you are Madame la Princesse d'Hautecour, or her Grace of Regalia, perhaps you will not smile so kindly on your old friends!'

She turned pale; her large eyes filled with unshed tears. She thought of the violets she had given him a few days before.

'You are unkind and unjust, Colonel Sabretasche,' she said haughtily. 'I thought you more kind, more true—'

'I am neither,' said Sabretasche, abruptly for that ultra suave and tender squire of dames. 'Ask your mamma for my character, and believe what she will tell you. I would rather you erred in thinking too ill—though that people would say is impossible—than too well of me.'

'I could never think ill of you—'

'You would be wrong, then,' said Sabretasche, gravely.

Just then her mother and De Vigne entered, and the Colonel, with his light laugh, turned round to them with some jest. Violet could not rally quite so quickly.

That night, at a loo party at Sabretasche's house, De Vigne and I told the other fellows of Violet's impulsive action in St. James's Street; while the Colonel went on with his game in silence.

'She's a great deal too impulsive; it's horrid bad ton,' yawned little Lord Killtime, an utterly blasé gentleman of nineteen.

'I like it,' said Curly. 'It's a wonderful treat now-a-days to see a girl natural.'

'She is very lovely, there is no doubt about that,' said De Vigne. 'I dare say they mean to set her up high in the market. Her mother is trying hard for Regalia.'

'He's a lost man, then,' said Wyndham, who had cut the Lower House and Red Tape for the lighter loves of Pam and Miss. 'I never knew the Molyneux, senior, make hard running after any fellow but what she finished him (she's retreated into the bosom of the Church now, and puts up with portly bishops and handsome popular preachers: women often do when they get *passées*; the Church is not so difficile as the laity, I presume!)'; but ten or less years ago I vow it was dangerous to come within the signal of her fan, she'd such a clever way of setting at you.'

'Jockey Jack didn't care,' laughed St. Lys, of the Eleventh. 'Well, her daughter's no manœuvrer; and, by George, it's worth a guinea a turn to waltz with her.'

'She's not bad looking,' sneered Vane Castleton, the youngest son of his Grace of Tiara, the worst of all those by no means incorruptible, and very far from stainless pillars of the state, the 'Castleton family.' 'But, by George, I never came across so bold, off-hand, spirited a young filly.'

Sabretasche looked up, anger in his languid, tired eyes.

'Permit me to differ from you, Castleton. Your remark, I must say, is as much signalized by knowledge of character as it is by elegance of phraseology! Young fellows like Killtime *may* make such mistakes of judgment; we who know the world should be wiser.'

De Vigne, sitting next him, looked up and raised his eyebrows at the Colonel's unusual interference and warmth.

'*Et tu, Brute?*'

Sabretasche understood, and gave him an admonitory kick under the table.

'Whose portrait is that, Sabretasche?' asked De Vigne, to stop Vane Castleton's tongue, pointing to a portrait over the mantelpiece in the inner drawing-room, where we were playing; the portrait of a very pretty woman.

'My mother, when she was twenty. Didn't you know it? It was taken just before she married. I believe it was an exact likeness, but I don't remember her.'

'It reminds me of somebody—I cannot think of whom. I beg your pardon, I take "miss."'

'Why will you talk through the game?' said
I. 'Don't you think the picture is like that
girl who occasioned Violet's championship this
morning? That's whom you are thinking of, I
dare say.'

'Who's talking now, I wonder?' said De Vigne.
'Heart's trumps? I did not notice that girl; I
was too amused to see Miss Molyneux. No, it is
somebody else, but who, I cannot think, for the
life of me.'

'Nor can I help you,' said Sabretasche, 'for
there is not a creature related to my mother living.
But now Arthur mentions it, that little girl was
not unlike her; at least, I fancy she had the same
coloured hair. *A propos* of likenesses, there will
be a very pretty picture of Lady Geraldine Ormsby
in the Exhibition this year. I saw it, half finished,
at Maclise's yesterday.'

'Why don't you exhibit, Sabretasche?' said
Wyndham. 'You paint a deuced deal better than
half those Fellows and Associates!'

'*Bien obligé!*' cried the Colonel. 'I should be
particularly sorry to hang up my pets off my easel
to be put level with people's boots, or high above
their possible vision, or—if honoured with the
" second row "—be flanked by shocking red-
haired pre-Raphaelite angels and staring por-

traits of gentlemen in militia uniform; and criti-
cized by a crowd of would-be cognoscente and dilettante cockneys, with a catalogue in their hand
and Ruskin rules in their mind, who go into
ecstasies over cottage scenes with all Teniers'
vulgarities, and none of Teniers' redeeming talent.
Exhibit my pictures? The fates forefend! Wyndham, help yourself to that Chablis, and, De Vigne,
there is some of our pet Madeira. How sorry I
am Madeira now grows graves instead of grapes!
Nonsense! Don't any of you think of going
yet. Let us sit down again for a few more
rounds.'

We did, and we played till the raw February
dawn was growing gray in the streets, while we
laughed and talked over Sabretasche's wine—
laughs that might have jarred on Violet's ear,
and talk that might have made her young
heart heavy, coming from her hero's lips. But
when we were gone, and the fire was burning
low, the Colonel sat before the dying embers
with his dog's head upon his knee, and
thought:

'What a fool I am! Women, wine, cards, art,
play—are they all losing their enchantment? Are
my rose-leaves beginning to lose their scent, and
crumple under me? That girl—child she is to

me—has been the only one who has had penetration enough to see that the bal masqué has
ceased its charm. She reads me truer than all of
them. She will believe no ill of me. She almost
makes me wish there were no ill for her to believe ! Shall she be the first woman to whom I
have shown mercy, the first for whom I have renounced *self?* Cid, old boy ! is your master wholly
dead to generosity and honour because the world
happens to say he is?'

That night De Vigne and I smoked our pipes
together over his fire in Wilton Crescent, where
he had taken a furnished house. Vigne had been
shut up since his mother's death, and he rarely
alluded even distantly to the scene of his folly and
his wrongs; I do not think he could have endured
to revisit, far less to live in it.

' Is Sabretasche really getting touched by that
bewitching Irish girl ?' said I to him, as we sat
smoking.

' God knows! He was rather touchy about
her, wasn't he? But that might only be for the
pleasure of setting down Castleton, a temptation I
don't think I could forego myself. According to
his own showing, he's never in love with any
woman, but he makes love to almost all he comes
across.'

'Oh, he's a deuced fellow for women!—but he might be really caught at last, you know.'

'Certainly,' assented De Vigne; 'none are so wise that they may not become fools! Socrates, when he was old, sage that he was, did not read in the same book with a woman without falling in love with her.'

'You are complimentary to love? Is it invariably a folly?'

'I think so. At least, all *I* wish for is to keep clear of it all the rest of my life.'

'Why?'

'Good God! need you ask? From my boyhood I was the fool of my passions. To love a woman was to win her. I stopped for no consideration, no duty, no obstacle; I let nothing come between me and my will. I was as obstinate to those who tried ever to stop me in any pursuit, as I was weak and mad in yielding up my birthright at any price, if I could but buy the mess of porridge on which I had for the time being set my fancy. Scores of times I did that—scores of times some worthless idol became the thing on which I staked my soul. Once I did it too often! It is such eternal misery that that woman, so lowborn, so low-bred, shameless, degraded, all that I *know* her to be, should bear my name, should proclaim abroad all the folly into which my reckless passions led me. Thank God I knew it when I did—thank God I left her as I did—thank God that no devils like herself were born to perpetuate my shame, and make me loathe my name because they bore it! *Then* you ask me if I am steeled to love! It has changed my whole nature—the misery of that loathsome connection! It is not the tie I care for—it is the shame, Arthur—the bitter, burning, shame! It is the odium of knowing that she bears my name, the humiliation that twice in my life have I been fooled by her beauty; it is the agony that my mother, the only pure, the only true friend whom fate ever gave me, was murdered by my reckless passions!'

His hands clenched on the arms of his chair, and the black veins swelled upon his face; it looked as though cast in chill, grey stone. It was my first glimpse of those ghastly dark hours, which, exorcised or invisible, in society and ordinary life, fastened relentlessly upon him in his hours of solitude; of that sleepless and merciless Remorse which dogged his steps by day, and made night horrible.

At that same hour, in a little bed whose curtains

and linen were white and pure as lilies, a young girl slept, like a rosebud lying on new-fallen snow; her golden hair fell over her shoulders, her blue eyes were closed under their black, silky lashes, a bright, happy smile was on her lips, and as she turned in her dreams, she spoke unconsciously in her sleep two words—'Sir Folko!'

CHAPTER XIII.

THE QUEEN OF THE FAIRIES IS FOUND IN RICHMOND.

NOT content with his house in Park Lane, Sabre-tasche had lately bought, beside it, a place at Richmond that had belonged to a rich old Indian millionnaire. It had been originally built and laid out by people of good taste, and the merchant had not lived long enough in it to spoil it : he had only christened it the ' Dilcoosha,' which title, being out of the common, Sabretasche retained. It was very charming, with its gardens, sloping down to the Thames, and was a pet with the Colonel; a sort of Strawberry Hill, save that his taste was much more symmetrical and grace-ful than Horace's; and he spent plenty of both time and money, touching it up and perfecting it till it was beautiful in its way as Luciennes. De Vigne and I drove down there one morning, towards the end of February, to see the paces tried, on a level bit of grass-land outside the

grounds, of a chesnut Sabretasche had entered for
Ascot. Stable slang and the delights of 'ossy
men' were not refined enough for the Colonel's
taste, but he liked to keep a good racing stud;
and he wished to have De Vigne's opinion on
Coronet, who had won the Champagne Stakes the
autumn before at Doncaster, and run a good
second at the Cesarewitch; for De Vigne, who
was very well known in the Ring and the Rooms,
was one of the surest prophets of success or failure
that ever talked over a coming Derby on a Sunday
afternoon at Tattersall's.

'What trick do you think my man Harris
served me yesterday?' said De Vigne, as we
came near Richmond.

'Harris—that good-natured fellow? What
has he done?'

'Cut and run with a dozen of my shirts, three
morning, two dress-coats; in fact, a complete
wardrobe; and twenty pounds or so—I really
forget how much exactly—that I had left on the
dressing-table when I went to mess last night.
And that man I took out of actual starvation at
Bombay!—have forgiven him fifty peccadilloes,
let him off when I found him taking a case of
my sherry, because he blubbered and said it was
for his mother, found up the poor old woman, who

wasn't a myth, and wrote to Stevens at Vigne to give her an almshouse; and then this fellow walks off with my goods! And you talk to me of people's gratitude! Bah! How can you have the face, Arthur, to ask me to admire human nature?'

'I don't ask you to admire it—Heaven fore-fend!—I don't like it well enough myself. What a rascal! 'Pon my life there seems a fate in your seeing the dark side of humanity.'

'The *dark* side? Where's any other? I never found any gratitude yet, and I don't expect any. People court you while you're of use to them; when you are not, you may go hang. Indeed, they will help to swing you off the stage, to lessen their own sense of obligation. By Jove! we're half-an-hour too early for the Colonel.'

'Too early?' said I. 'Then let's go and see that pretty little artist of St. James's Street. I always meant to look her up; and you said she lived somewhere near here.'

'I think she did; St. Crucis something or other. What a naughty fellow you are, Arthur,' laughed De Vigne. 'We'll try and find her out, if you like; though I don't think it's worth while. Hallo! my good man; is there a place called St. Crucis anywhere in Richmond?'

'St. Crucis-on-the-Hill be you meaning, sir? a little farm?' said the hedge-cutter he asked, who was sitting in the sun eating his dinner. 'Take the road to your left, then the turning to the right, and a mile straight on will see you there.' De Vigne tossed him half-a-crown, tooled the greys in the direction told him, and we soon arrived in the quiet lane where the little farm-house stood; turned in at the gate—it was as much as the dashing mail-phæton could do to pass it—and into a small paved court on one side of which stood the house, long, low, thatched, and picturesque, more like Hampshire than Middlesex; with a garden, an orchard, and a paddock adjoining; all now black and bare in the chill February morning.

'Does a young lady, an artist, reside here?' De Vigne inquired at the door; scarcely had he spoken than the young girl herself, looking temptingly pretty in-doors, came out of an inner room and ran up to him. 'Ah! it is you? how glad I am! Do come in, pray do?'

'What a strange little thing!' whispered De Vigne to me, as we followed her through the house to a room at the west end, a long, low chamber with an easel standing in its bay-window, and water-colours, etchings, pastels, études, pictures of all kinds, hung about its walls; while some books, and casts, and flowers, gave a refinement to its plain simplicity, often wanting in many a gilt and gorgeous drawing-room I have entered.

'So you recognized me? How kind of you to come!' said the girl, looking up in De Vigne's face.

De Vigne was wholly surprised; he looked at her for some moments.

'Recognize you? I am ashamed to say I do not.'

'Ah! and yet you have called on me. I do not understand?' said the little artist, with a sunny smile, but very marked bewilderment in her eyes and words. 'I have never forgotten *you*, Sir Folko. I knew you the other day, when that young lady's servant knocked down my portfolio. Have you quite forgotten little Alma? I am so glad to see you—you cannot think how much!'

And Alma Tressillian held out both her hands to him, with a bright, joyous welcome on her upraised face.

'Little Alma!' repeated De Vigne. 'Yes, yes! I remember you now. Where could my mind have gone not to recognize you at once? You are not the least altered since you were a child. But how can you have come from Lorave to London? Come, tell me everything? My dear

child, you are not more pleased to see me than I
am to see you ! '

Alma was little altered since her childhood:
now, as then, her golden hair and eloquent dark-
blue eyes, with the constant change, and play, and
animation of all her features, made her greatest
beauty.   They were not regularly beautiful as
Violet Molyneux's, their mobility and extreme in-
tellectuality of expression was their chief charm,
after all.   She was not so tall as Violet, nor had
she that exquisite and perfect form which made
the belle of the season compared with Pauline
Bonaparte ; but she had something graceful and
fairy-esque about her, and both her face and figure
were instinct with a life, an intelligence, a radi-
ance of expression which promised you a rare
combination of· sweet temper and hot passions,
intense susceptibility, and highly-cultivated intellect.   You might not have called her pretty: you
must have called her much more—irresistibly
winning and attractive.

'Come, tell me everything about yourself,'
repeated De Vigne, as he pushed a low chair for
her, and threw himself down on an arm-chair
near.   'You must remember Captain Chevasney
as well as you do me.   We shall both of us
be anxious to hear all you have to tell; though,

I am ashamed to say that in taking the liberty to
call on the fair artist whose pictures I picked up,
I had no idea I should meet my little friend the
Queen of the Fairies!'

'Indeed! Then I wonder you came, though I
am very glad to see you? Why should you call
on a stranger! Yes, I recollect Captain Chevasney,' smiled Alma, with a pretty bend of her
head (she did not add 'as well'). 'I was so
sorry when you did not see me that day in Pall
Mall; I thought I might never come across you
again.'

'But where is your grandpapa?—is he in
town?'

She looked down, and her lips quivered:

'Grandpapa has been dead three years.'

'Dead! My dear child, how careless of me!
I am grieved, indeed!' exclaimed De Vigne, involuntarily.

'You could not tell,' answered Alma, looking
up at him, great tears in her blue eyes. 'He
died more than three years ago, but it is as fresh
to *me* as if it were but yesterday. Nobody will
ever love me as he did. He was so kind, so
gentle, so good. In losing him I lost everything;
I prayed day and night that I might die with
him; he was my only friend!'

'Poor little Alma!' said De Vigne, touched out of that haughty reserve now habitual to him. 'I am grieved to hear it, both for the loss to you of your only protector, and the loss to the world of as true-hearted a man as ever breathed. If I had been in England he would have seen me at Lorave, as I promised, but I have been in India since we parted. I wish I had written to him; I ought to have done so; but one never knows things till too late.'

'He left a letter for you, in case I should ever meet you. You were the only person kind to us after the loss of his fortune,' said Alma, as she sprang across the room—all her movements were rapid and foreign—knelt down before a desk, and brought an unsealed envelope to De Vigne, directed to him by a hand now powerless for ever.

'This for me? I wish I had seen him,' said De Vigne, as he put it away in the breast of his coat. 'I ought to have written to him; but my own affairs engrossed me, and—we are all profound egotists, you know, to whatever unselfishness we may pretend. What was the cause of his death? Will it pain you to tell me?'

'Paralysis. He had a paralytic stroke six months before, which ended in congestion of the brain. But how gentle, how good, how patient he was through it all!'

She stopped again; the tears rolled off her lashes. She was quite unaccustomed to conceal what she felt, and she did not know that feeling is bad *ton* !

'And you have been in England ever since?' asked De Vigne, to divert her thoughts.

'Oh no!' she answered, brushing the tears off her lashes. 'You know the governess grandpapa took for me to Lorave? She has been extremely kind. She was with me at his death. I was fifteen then, and for a year afterwards she stayed with me in Lorave; I loved the place so dearly, dearer still after his grave was there, and I could not bear to leave it. But Miss Russell had no money, and no home. She works for her living, and she could not waste her time on me. She was obliged to look for another situation, and when she came over to it—it is in a rector's family near Staines— I came with her, and she placed me here. My old nurse has this farm; grandpapa bought it for her many years ago, when she left us and married. Her husband is dead, but she still keeps the farm, and makes bread to send into town. It was the only place we knew of, and nurse was so delighted to let me have the rooms, that I have been here ever since.'

' Poor little thing, what a life!' cried De Vigne, involuntarily. 'How dull you must be, Alma.'

She raised her eyebrows and shrugged her shoulders. Gesticulation was natural to her, and she had caught it from the Italians at Lorave.

' Buried alive! Sylvo to talk to, and the flowers to talk to me ; that is my society. But wherever I might have been, I should have missed *him* equally, and I can never be alone while I have my easel and my books.'

' Have you painted these?' I exclaimed, in surprise, for there were masterly strokes in the sketches on the walls that would have shamed more than one ' Associate.'

' Yes. An Italian artist, spending the summer at Lorave, saw me drawing one day, something as Cimabue saw little Giotto, and had me to his studio, and gave me a regular course of instruction. He told me I might equal Elizabetta Sirani. I shall never do that, I am afraid, but I find a very good sale for my sketches; they take them at Ackermann's and Rowney's, and I work hard. I sketch every day out of doors, to catch the winter and summer tints. But I hate winter; it is so unkind, so cheerless! I always paint Summer in my pictures ; not your poor pale English season, but summer golden and glorious, with the boughs hanging to the ground with the weight of their own beauty, and the vineyards and corn-fields glowing with their rich promise!'

'Enthusiastic as ever?' laughed De Vigne. 'How are our friends the fairies, Alma?'

'Do you suppose I shall give news of them to a disbeliever?' said Alma, with a toss of her head. 'I have not forgotten your want of faith. Are you as great a sceptic now?'

'Ten times more—not only of fairy lore, but of pretty well everything else. Fairies are as well worth credence as all the other faiths of the day; I would as soon credit Queen Mab as a "doctrinal point!" What do *you* think of the fairies now?'

'Look? Do you not think I sketched that from sight!' said Alma, turning her easel to him, where she had drawn a true Titania, such as 'on pressed flowers does sleep,' for whom 'the cowslips tall her pensioners be:'

> 'Where oxlips and the nodding violets grow,
> Quite over-canopied with lush woodbine,
> With sweet musk-roses, and with eglantine,
> Lulled in those flowers with dances and delight;'

the veritable fairy queen of those dainty offsprings of romance, who used to meet

> 'in grove or green,
> By fountain clear or spangled starlight sheen.'

' How splendidly you draw, Alma ! ' exclaimed
De Vigne. ' If you exhibited at the Water-Colour
Society, you would excite as much wonder as Rosa
Bonheur.   And do these pay you well ? '

' Yes ; at least, what seems so to me.'

' *Pauvre enfant !* ' smiled De Vigne ; her ideas
of wealth and his were strikingly different. ' A
friend of mine is a great connoisseur of these
things.   I must show them to him some day ; but
I cannot stay now, for I have an engagement at
two, and it is now striking.'

' But you will come and see me again,' interrupted Alma, beseechingly. ' Pray do. You cannot think how lonely I am.   I have no friends,
you know.'

' Oh yes, I will come,' answered De Vigne.   ' I
have much more to hear about you and your pur-
suits.   How could you know us, Alma, after so
long ? '

' I did not know Captain Chevasney,' said the
little lady, with uncomplimentary frankness, ' but
I knew you perfectly.   The first picture I could
sketch was one of you for Sir Folko.   You know
I always thought you like him !   Besides, grandpapa talked of you so constantly, and I was so
expecting you to come to Lorave with your yacht,
as you had promised, that it was impossible for me

to forget you. I was so grieved when you did not notice me in Pall Mall. I called you, but you did not hear. You were thinking of that young lady. How lovely she was! Who is she?'

'Lord Molyneux's daughter, I was not thinking of her, though, but that the pair of horses in her carriage were not worth half what I heard they gave for them,' said De Vigne, laughing, as he offered her his hand; 'and now, good-by. I am very pleased to have found you out, and you must pardon us our impertinence in calling on one whom we thought a stranger, since it has led us to one whom we may fairly claim as an old friend!'

Alma looked gratefully in his face, and bid him, with a radiant smile, not defer his visit to St. Crucis, as he had done his yachting to Lorave. She guessed little enough *what* had prevented that yachting to Lorave.

'Strange we should have lighted on that child! That's your doing, Arthur, going after the beaux yeux!' said he, as we drove to the Dilcoosha. 'She is the same frank, impulsive, enthusiastic little thing as when we first saw her. She was the heiress of Wieve Hurst then; now she has to work for her bread. Who can prophesy the ups and downs of life? Boughton Tressillian was game to the backbone. Perhaps she inherits some of his

pluck—it is to be hoped so—she will want it.   A
woman, young, unprotected, and attractive as she
looks, is pretty sure to come to grief some way or
other.   Her very virtues will be her ruin !   She
is not one of your sensible, prudent, cold, commonplace women, who go through the world scathless ;
too wise to err, too selfish to sacrifice themselves !
Alma will come to grief, I am afraid.   Here, take
the reins, Arthur, and I will see what her grandfather says.'

He tore open the letter, and gave a long
whistle.

' What's the matter ? ' said I.

' She isn't his grandchild after all.'

' Not?   His daughter, I suppose ? '

' No ; no relation at all.   The letter is broken
off unfinished ; probably where his hand failed
him, poor old man.   He says my name recurred
to him as the only person who had not heeded his
decline of fortune, and the only man of honour whom
he could trust.   Out of his income as consul he con-
trived to save her a few hundreds—*voilà tout!*
He must leave her, of course, to struggle for herself ; and this is what weighs so heavily upon him,
because, it seems, he adopted this child when she
was two years old, believing he would make her
an heiress ; and, according to his view of the case,

he considers he has done her a great wrong. Who she is he does not tell me, except that she was a little Italian girl. He was going, no doubt, to add more, as he began the letter by saying he wished her secret to be known to some one, and having heard much of my mother, appealed to her, through me, to aid and serve Alma if she would; but here the sentence breaks off unfinished.'

'Do you think Alma knows it; she calls him her grandfather still?'

'Can't say—yet of course she does,' said De Vigne, with a cynical smile. 'No woman's curiosity ever allowed her to keep an unsealed letter three years and never look into it! Here we are. It will be as well not to tell Sabretasche of his neighbour, eh? He is such a deuced fellow for women, and she would be certain to go down before his thousand-and-one accomplishments! Not that it would matter much, perhaps; she will be somebody's prey, no doubt, and she might as well be the Colonel's, save that he is a little quicker fickle than most, knowing better than most, the value of his toys.'

With which concluding sarcasm De Vigne threw the reins to his groom, who met him at the door, and entered that abode of perfect taste and epicurean luxury, known as the Dilcoosha, where Sabretasche and luncheon were waiting for us. And where, after due discussion of Strasbourg pâtés, Comet Hock, Bass, and the news of the day, we inspected the chesnut's paces, pronounced him pretty certain, unless something unforeseen in the way of twitch and opium-ball occurred, to win the Queen's Cup, and drove back to town together, De Vigne to go to billiards at Pratt's, Sabretasche to accompany the Molyneux to a morning concert, and I to call on a certain lady who had well-nigh broken my heart, when it was young and break-able, who had exchanged rings with me under the Kensington Garden trees, when she was fresh, fair, Gwen Brandling, and who was now staying in town as Madame la Duchesse de la Vieillecour, black velvet and point replacing the muslin and ribbons, dignity in the stead of girlish grace, and a *fin sourire* of skilled coquetry in lieu of that heart-felt smile, Gwen's whilom charm. I take it doves are sold by the dozen on the altar-steps of St. George's? but—it is true that the doves have a strange passion for the gold coins that buy them, and would not fly away if they could?

N'importe! Madame de la Vieillecour and I met as became people living in good society; if less fresh she was perhaps more fascinating, and though one begins life tender and transparent as Sèvres, one is stone-china, luckily, long before the finish, warranted never to break at any blows whatever.

CHAPTER XIV.

HOW A WIFE TALKED OF HER HUSBAND.

In a very gay and gaudy drawing-room in the
Champs Elysées, in an arm-chair, with her feet on a
chaufferette, in a rich cashmere and laces, looking
a very imposing and richly-coloured picture, sat
De Vigne's wife, none the less handsome for the
wear of Paris life, intermixed with visits to the
Bads, where she was almost as great an attraction
as the green.tables, and the sound of her name as
great a charm as the irresistible " *Faites votre jeu,
messieurs !* " A little fuller about the cheek and
chin, a trifle more Juno-esque in form, a little
higher tinted in the carnation hue of her roses,
but otherwise none the worse for the ten years
that had passed since she wore the orange-blos-
soms and the diamond ceinture on her marriage
morning.

She had an English paper in her hand, and was
running her eye over the fashionable intelligence.

Opposite to her was old Fantyre, her nose a little more hooked, her eye sharper, her rouge higher, a little more dirty, witty, and detestable, than of yore; taking what she called a *demie-tasse*, but which looked uncommonly like cognac uncontaminated by Mocha. And these two led a very pleasant life in Paris; with the old lady's quick wits, questionable introductions, and imperturbable impudence, and the younger one's beauty, riches, and excessive freedom !

'What's the matter, my dear?' asked Lady Fantyre; 'you don't look best pleased.'

'I am *not* pleased,' said the Trefusis (such I must call her), her brow dark, and her full underlip protruded. 'De Vigne is back.'

'Dear, dear! how tiresome !' cried the Fantyre ; 'and just when you'd begun to hope he'd been killed in India. Well, that *is* annoying. It's a nice property to be kept out of, ain't it? But you see, my dear, strong men of his age are not good ones to be heir to, even with all the chances of war. So he's come back, is he? What for, I wonder?'

'Here it is, among the arrivals: "Claridge's Hotel: Major de Vigne." He is come back because he is tired of Scinde, probably. I wonder if he will come to Paris? I should like to meet him.' And the Trefusis laughed, showing her white teeth.

'Why, my dear? To give him a dose of aconite? No, you're too prudent to do anything of that sort. Whatever other commandments you break, my dear, it won't be the Sixth, because there's a capital punishment for it,' said the old lady, chuckling at the idea. 'You'd like to meet him, you say—I shouldn't. I don't forget his face in the vestry. Lord! how he did look! his face as white as a corpse, and as fierce as the devil's.'

'Did you ever see the devil?' sneered the Trefusis.

'Yes, my dear—in a scarlet cashmere; and very well he looks in women's clothes, too,' said the Fantyre, with a diabolical grin.

The Trefusis laughed too.

'*He* has found me dangerous, at any rate.'

'Well, yes; everybody has, I think, that has the pleasure of your acquaintance,' chuckled Lady Fantyre. 'But I don't think so much of your revenge, myself. Very poor! What's three thousand a year out of his property? And as for not letting him marry, I think that's oftener kindness than cruelty to a man. Don't you think it would have been better to have queened it at Vigne, and had an establishment in Eaton Square, and spent his twenty thousand a year for him, and made yourself a London leader of fashion, and ridden over the necks of those haughty Ferrers people, and all his stiff-necked friends—that beautiful creature, Vivian Sabretasche, among 'em. What do you think, eh?'

'It might have been better for me, but it would have spoilt my revenge. He would have left me sooner or later, and as he is infinitely too proud and reserved a man to have told any living soul the secret of his disgrace, I should have lost the one grand sting in my vengeance—his humiliation before the world.'

' Pooh, pooh, my dear, a man of fortune is never humiliated; the world's too fond of him! The sins of the fathers are only visited on the children where the children are going down in the world.' (The Fantyre might be a nasty old woman, but she spoke greater truths than most good people.) 'So, you sacrificed your aggrandisement to your revenge? Not over sensible, that.'

' You can't accuse me of often yielding to any weakness,' said the Trefusis, with a look in her eye like a vicious mare's. 'However, my revenge is not finished yet.'

'Eh? Not? What's the next act? On my word, you're a clever woman, Lucy. You do my heart good.'

The first time, by the way, that Lady Fantyre ever acknowledged to a heart, or the Trefusis received such a compliment!

'This. I know his nature—you do not. Some day or other De Vigne will love again, and passionately. *Then* he will want to be free; then, indeed, he shall realize the force of the fetters by which I hold him.'

The old lady chuckled over the amusing prospect.

'Very likely, my dear. It's just what they can't do, that they always want to do. Tell a man wine's good for him, and forbid him water, he'd forswear his cellar, and run to the pump immediately! And if you heard that he'd fallen in love, what would you do?'

'Go to England, and put myself between her and him, as his deserted, injured, much enduring, and loving wife.'

Old Fantyre drank up her coffee, and nodded approvingly.

'That's right, my dear! Play your game. Play it out; only take care to keep the honours in your own hand, and never trump your partner's card.'

'Not much fear of my doing that,' said the Trefusis, with a smile.

There was not, indeed; she marked her cards too cleverly, for she was keen enough to be Queen of the Paris Greeks.

END OF VOL. I.

LONDON : PRINTED BY W. CLOWES AND SONS, STAMFORD STREET
AND CHARING CROSS.